last train
to
babylon

last train *to* babylon

CHARLEE FAM

wm

WILLIAM MORROW
An Imprint of HarperCollins*Publishers*

P.S.™ is a trademark of HarperCollins Publishers.

LAST TRAIN TO BABYLON. Copyright © 2014 by Charlee Fam. All rights reserved. Printed in the United States of America. No part of this book may be used or reproduced in any manner whatsoever without written permission except in the case of brief quotations embodied in critical articles and reviews. For information address HarperCollins Publishers, 195 Broadway, New York, NY 10007.

HarperCollins books may be purchased for educational, business, or sales promotional use. For information please e-mail the Special Markets Department at SPsales@harpercollins.com.

FIRST EDITION

Designed by Diahann Sturge

Library of Congress Cataloging-in-Publication Data has been applied for.

ISBN 978-0-06-232807-6

14 15 16 17 18 OV/RRD 10 9 8 7 6 5 4 3 2

For Marv

Prologue

THE RAIN ASSAULTS my car in the far corner of the empty train station lot, and the wipers dance to a furious beat, so awkwardly out of sync with everything else.

Smoke streams off the end of the lit cigarette. It's balanced against the car's ashtray—masking the scent of three-year-old air freshener—vanilla and sandalwood. I don't smoke it, but I crave the thick mist spreading beneath my ribs, filling my lungs—filling the space where you hollowed me gutless.

I look up at the brick building and think of jumping. I imagine myself standing tall, arms outstretched, feet perched against the edge.

And a voice comes through the station speakers: "The last train to Babylon is operating on time."

The train rumbles overhead, and the wipers dance to a furious beat.

My knees are pinned between my chest and the oversized steering wheel.

And smoke streams off the end of the cigarette.

I have this memory of summer camp when I was six, maybe seven. There are other kids, but I can never place faces. We're all clad in these baggy tie-dyed T-shirts that say LAKE WALTER ROCKIN' SUMMER '95, *or something equally lame.*

We are seated at a picnic table under a rusted tin roof. Construction paper is scattered carelessly—red, yellow, black. Blue, green, orange. It's impossible to find a whole piece. They're all cut up and butchered with those awful, awkward left-handed scissors—safety scissors.

A little boy spills a tube of blue glitter. I may have gotten some in my eye.

I am making a house out of Popsicle sticks. I think I used too much glue.

I always use too much glue.

My knees press against the vibrating steering wheel. And the wipers dance to a furious beat. And the smoke streams. The car sits in park—a stagnant machine —shaking and rumbling.

"The one fifty-three to Babylon is operating on time."

Rain pelts beneath the bright lights—tall giraffelike lights. No one sees me. And the windshield wipers dance. And the smoke. And I feel you still, the rough pads of your fingers, your Cheshire grin, as you devour me. Piece. By. Piece. And your hair is like soft down, and I think you must condition and this surprises me. Something your mother must have taught you. And then I remember that your mother is dead. And I feel sorry. I feel sorry for your dead mother. And the windshield wipers dance and the smoke streams and the engine screams and I am building a house out of Popsicle sticks and you devour me and maybe it's the weed but I think I'm about to split and you tell me to relax and you tell me to shut up and your friend is trying to sleep and I tell you to stop to stop to stop and I wonder if your friend can hear and I wonder what your dead mother thinks now and you tell me to shut up and the wipers dance and the smoke streams and your hand muffles my silent screams and I realize there is not much more I can do here but wait it out and you devour me. Piece. By. Piece. And the windshield wipers and the smoke and your friend clears his throat and I try to fill the space where you hollowed me gutless and I try to ignore this world we've created, and your power to destroy, our power to create, and the wipers dance to a furious beat and the smoke streams off the end of a lit cigarette and your friend clears his throat and I'm building a house out of Popsicle sticks.

Part One

Chapter 1

Friday, October 10, 2014. 3:53 A.M.

IT FEELS LIKE someone scraped out my sinuses and poured Clorox up my nose. Everything is damp and warm, and my temples pound against the empty, sterile feeling inside my head. The window is open, and I can hear the rain clicking against the metal screen. I can smell it, too—rain, antiseptic, and latex. I guess this is what it smells like when you wake up in a hospital.

My eyes open for just a second then fall back shut. I blink twice and I can't tell if my contacts are still in. Everything is blurry except for the white walls and a metal bedpan hovering next to my face.

A woman clears her throat near the door.

"Hi there." The voice hits me, and it's like everything inside my head aches again. "How are you feeling, Aubrey?"

The sound bounces off the hollow walls of my skull, and I

have to squint across the room to see her. She offers a small wave and stands up.

"My name is Laura." Her voice is slow, and she enunciates every word. She steps toward my bedside, like she expects me to shake her hand, but there's an IV shooting clear, cold fluid through my veins, so I couldn't move even if I did feel the need to be polite.

"Hi?" I say. My voice cracks. She wears a pale green sweater and jeans. Her hair falls into blond ringlets around her face, and bounces off her shoulders as she moves toward me. Maybe it's just the hair, but she has this spring in her step that makes her seem inappropriately chipper. I already don't like her.

At first I think she's not much older than I am, maybe late twenties, very early thirties—but when she speaks, her voice has this slow, sensible tone, the kind that only comes when you're hovering somewhere around forty.

"You're at the hospital, Aubrey," she says. I don't like how she keeps saying my name, like it's supposed to make me feel more at ease. "I work here. I'm a social worker—or a therapist." There's a brief moment of silence, and she takes another step toward me. "But I like 'therapist' better. Sounds less official." I think she smiles, but I still can't see very well.

"I know where I am," I say. She sits back down in a metal chair by the door. "But why am I here?"

"Do you remember what happened last night?" She's holding a clipboard on her lap.

I want to tell her no. I want to say, *No, Laura. I obviously don't remember what happened tonight or else I wouldn't be asking, would I?* But instead, I stay quiet, squeeze my eyes shut and try to force out some sliver of memory. I take a breath and close my eyes again. It's not much, but pieces of the night start to come back to me like shards of glass—a snapshot, a sound, a smell. Broken pieces, but nothing I can really hold on to.

I remember O'Reilly's—walking in, and then I see Eric Robbins in his mint-green tie, spinning his bottle of Bud on the bar. I think I see Adam coming at me, and the air feels thick and opaque, coming down around me, but then it's just rain. It's just rain, smoke, windshield wipers, and hot whiskey breath splattered over my bare lap.

But I don't tell Laura any of this.

"Nothing," I say. "I don't remember anything. I'm sorry."

"That's okay," she says. "Don't be sorry." She scoots a few feet closer. The metal chair screeches against the tile floor. I wince.

I still can't figure out how the hell I ended up here, so I play dumb and wait for her to fill me in. I wonder for a second if maybe I've killed someone, crashed my car, run over a small child. But I think I'd be handcuffed to the bed if that were the case. At least that's what happens on *Law & Order*.

And then panic sweeps through me, and I think maybe I did something desperate. Maybe I threw myself down over the railroad tracks, or something awful and cliché like that. But I dismiss the thought almost as swiftly as it comes, and the panic quiets inside me. I'm way too practical to inconvenience a trainful of people, most of whom I'm probably acquainted with in one way or another.

That's the thing about Long Island. You can't even jump in front of a train without knowing at least ten people on board.

I want to know why I'm here. Well, part of me does. Part of me just wants to bury my face into the starchy pillow and forget I ever came back to this twisted shit hole of a town. But Laura just smiles, all smug, like she's waiting for me to ask—like it's all part of the process.

"Are my parents here?" I ask. I'm dreading having to face Karen, but half expecting her to be out in the hallway as we speak, pressing her ear up against the thick wooden door, waiting for her cue. It's also possible that no one called her. I'm twenty-three and I think there's got to be some sort of patient confidentiality law, something that says I'm allowed to fuck up once and no one will call my mother. But I'm not really sure how this whole hospital thing works. Despite my questionable choices over the past five years, this is a first.

"Your mother was here, but she went home for the night," Laura says. "She thought it would be best that we have a chance to speak in private before she sees you."

Of course she would think that. I reach up and rub the bridge of my nose with my thumb and forefinger. Karen is a school shrink herself—technically a guidance counselor, but whatever, same thing. She knows how it works; whether you're an eighth-grade wrist cutter, all torn up over cyberbullying and bulimia, or you're like me—a seemingly well-adjusted twenty-something in the midst of a bender/a breakdown/whatever-is-happening-but-I'm-too-afraid-to-ask. I'm sorry, but nobody, thirteen or twenty-three, wants to divulge her deepest, darkest secrets to her mother. Mothers only complicate things with their messy emotions.

Karen also happens to be a middle-school cheerleading

coach, and her attempts at emotional guidance are always accompanied by way too much pep and hurrah! for my taste.

But Karen is smarter than I give her credit for. She knows I'll never talk to her, really talk to her. I've never been the type to open up and cry on her shoulder. Not like my brothers. They were always the weepy, whiny, cuddly type. Real mama's boys. But the gene for basic human compassion seems to have been lost on me—or at least that's what Karen quips when I pull away from a hug or avert eye contact during a serious conversation. She knows I'm way more likely to confide in some random therapist lurking in my hospital room—strictly business.

My head feels fuzzy, and my eyes start to cloud over again. "I was wearing contacts," I say, too low, as I start to think that maybe they've rolled to the back of my head or dissolved, just dissolved into my eyes. She stares at me, totally unconcerned. There's an arrogant silence between us, so I start to speak again, even though I can feel her judging, assessing, taking mental notes on my mental state. "I'm not supposed to sleep with my contacts . . ." I say. My voice trails off, and there's a sort of tingling in my chest—tingling but heavy. Like my body could either float off or sink like a stone at any moment. She's still watching me, and the tingling starts to spread up through my throat. I don't know what this feeling is but I don't like it. For a second I think it's whatever drug they're pumping into me, maybe even a bad hangover. I'm trying to find words; I'm trying to think of anything to say—anything that makes me sound less like a patient and more like normal-calm-casual Aubrey.

I start to rub at my eyes and sit up in the bed, tugging at the IV. "How long have I been here?"

Laura smiles, like her facial expressions have any impact on my level of calmness right now. "Don't worry about your contacts," she says. But I am worried, and the fact that she's telling me how to feel loses her some serious points.

The rain pounds harder against the metal screen.

For the first time, I catch a glimpse of my reflection in the window. My hair is a mess—a complete shit show—tangled and frizzed out in every direction. My lips are swollen and cracked, and all I can think is that I've got a little bit of a *Girl, Interrupted* thing going on. I can't quite pull off hot and crazy like Angelina, but I'm close. Pretty fucking close.

A slow, impish grin starts to slide across my face.

"What's so funny?" Laura says, with a confused smile, an attempt, I think, to mirror my amusement, like she's waiting for the punch line.

"Nothing," I say. "I just—I just look the part is all."

"What part?" She gets all serious again. She's a tough crowd, this one. I'm trying to read her. And I know she thinks she's reading me. I'm ninety percent sure I know what she's thinking and I'm seventy-five percent sure that she's wrong.

"I'm not crazy," I say. I don't mean to say it out loud. But it sort of just slides off my tongue.

"No one's saying that you are."

"Then why am I here?" I can feel my voice start to shake, so I stop with the questions and start to twist the bed sheet in my hands.

"You had a lot of alcohol in your system," she says, resting her clipboard on her lap again.

I wait for her to continue—to get into the details. To tell me how bad I fucked up. But she just stares at me. Like this should be enough to take in. And it still doesn't answer any questions. Of course I had *a lot of alcohol* in my system. I usually have *a lot of alcohol* in my system, but that's never been enough to land me in a hospital with a social worker camped out at the foot of my bed.

"Do you remember what upset you tonight, Aubrey?"

I shrug, and I hate that she says my name at the end of the question, like I'm not the only other person in the room.

Why so cryptic, Laura? I want to say. *Why can't you just say it?*

"Were you upset about Rachel? Losing a friend can be extremely traumatic. Your mom told me the funeral was today."

And here it is. I should have known this was coming. Of course my mother would share this key piece of information. I should have planned for it. *Well played, Laura. Well played.*

"She wasn't my friend. We haven't spoken in years." I lie. It's all I can say. I think it's enough. I think she even believes it—at least for now. Laura just smiles and leans back in her chair.

For some reason, I think of Adam again, but push the thought down almost as quickly as it comes. I've learned to compartmentalize, over the years. Rachel or Adam, I don't have the energy or space in my head right now to handle Rachel *and* Adam, so I slouch back down into the bed and close my eyes.

"What's upsetting you, Aubrey?" She says my name again, and I want to say, *I don't know, Laura. I don't know what's upsetting me, Laura, but it's not Adam, and it's definitely not Rachel*, but I don't say that. Because if I claim to know what's not upsetting me, then I must know what is, and I'm just not ready to go there yet. I don't even know this woman, so I'll spare her all the gory details.

She offers a sympathetic shrug and says, "Maybe that's enough for tonight."

Chapter 2

Five days earlier. Sunday, October 5, 2014.

I'M STILL IN my gym clothes when I get the call from Karen. Danny had left ten minutes before to get coffee and bagels.

"Aubrey?" My mother's voice is shaky and slow with sympathy that I cannot be bothered to emulate.

"Yeah," I say, standing in front of the bathroom mirror. It's where I take most of my calls. It's the only private room in the apartment.

"Are you all right?"

"Yup."

"You haven't said anything."

"What's there to say?"

"She was your best friend."

"She was not my best friend."

We both breathe on the line. I hear my mother's brain churning, desperate to evoke some sort of emotion from me.

"Well, I hope you decide to come home. It's the right thing," she says. I take a deep breath and blow hard into the phone. It is the right thing. I know that. It's obviously the right thing. But since when has the right thing been a thing with Rachel? I can practically hear my mother shaking her head on the other side of the line, wondering, pleading where she went wrong with her cold, hard little girl.

"Aubrey," she starts again, and I take another obnoxiously loud breath so that she knows I'm reaching my limit. "Fine," she says. "But let me know what you decide. I've been using your room as an office."

I know she never sees students outside of school property, and she's most likely just using my room as some sort of filing cabinet—a safe space to sort through her notes and referrals; but I still have this disturbing vision of pimply thirteen-year-old boys parading in and out of my childhood bedroom before going home and jerking off to the memory of my unmade bed and white wicker furniture.

"We'll see," I say.

"Okay. I love you." She holds her breath, no doubt waiting for a response, even though I haven't said it back in years. I hang up the phone and place it down on the edge of the sink. I try to push Rachel out of my mind, but I can feel my curiosity bubbling up. Did she really want to die? Did she leave a note?

I consider my own collection of suicide notes. I've compiled them over the years: five different drafts, which comes out to roughly one a year. I won't get all pathetic about it. I promised myself a long time ago—well, five years ago—that I'd never be *that* girl. Five years, five finished suicide notes. Five also happens to be my favorite number—but that's unrelated. And after five years of my crafting the perfect good-bye letter, Rachel is the one to go and do it. I guess it's sort of funny, but that's only if you care enough to analyze it, really mull it over, and I don't have that kind of time.

Sometimes, when I'm alone, I'll write one out—a thoughtful and methodical process that requires my best handwriting, the kind saved for birthday cards and job applications. I write out the whole tired story—at least what I want people to take from it. Then, realizing I forgot some crucial detail or some subtle, accusatory remark, I crumple the paper into a ball, tear off a fresh page from my monogrammed stationery, and start over.

I keep them all in a neat little folder, tucked away in my top desk drawer, just in case.

I pull my hair out of its bun, run my fingers through, and stare at myself in the mirror. My hair is still damp and knotty from the gym, but I don't feel like showering yet. I rub the soft side of my fist over a white spot on the glass. I should probably Windex; I can barely see my face through the murky streaks of toothpaste and hair spray. I make a mental note to pick up a bottle at Duane Reade this afternoon. I add it to the list: *Windex, paper towels, toilet paper.* It's my job to restock the paper goods and cleaning supplies, and I always mean to do it, but sometimes I just forget; and it doesn't cross my mind until I get a passive-aggressive Snap Chat from Danny of the empty roll while he's taking a shit.

But now I remember to get to the store. And I realize it's not exactly the time for shopping lists, considering I just found out my best friend—ex-best friend—is dead, but I can't think of anything else I could be doing right now.

I widen my eyes, lean in close, and blink three times, just to be sure. Nothing. I'm completely dry. I figured as much. I can't even remember the last time I cried anyway.

Typical. What a typical way for Rachel to go. I hold my thumb under the leaky faucet, letting the droplets catch in the corner of my fingernail and notice that the dark red nail polish has started to chip.

I try to imagine her doing it, counting out the pills. She probably only took six or seven, just enough to make it seem legit, but not quite enough to kill her right away. That would be such a Rachel thing to do, too—threaten suicide, and then revel in the attention. *Poor Rachel. Fragile Rachel. How can we all be there for Rachel?*

Too bad no one cared enough to stop her.

My BlackBerry balances on the edge of the sink, and I can see the voice-mail alert still blinking up at me.

Rachel had called late Friday, the night before she did it. I was out with college friends at some hipster bar in Williamsburg. I don't do Brooklyn—I rarely leave the Upper East Side—so I was already in a pissy mood, and the thought of speaking to Rachel was an even bigger buzzkill. I didn't answer. I haven't since that day at the diner, but nobody knows about that. This was the only time she'd left a message. Now the tiny envelope on the screen taunts me: *Do it. Do it, girl. Press me. Hold me to your ear. Let me tell you a secret.*

My phone still teeters on the sink's ceramic ledge, and I think about plugging the drain, turning on the faucet, and casually nudging it into a pool of hot water. I close my eyes and start to count to three, imagining the BlackBerry sinking, drowning the last remains of Rachel Burns.

One. I breathe in through my nose.

It's not like I could have known she'd actually do it.

Two.

It's not like I could have really done anything about it.

Three.

It's not my problem anymore.

I try to remember the name of the nail polish as the water rolls off my fingertips and pools above the drain.

She'd always been weaker than me. She was bossy, definitely bossy. But she was weak. I know that for sure now.

I rub my fist over the mirror again. It squeaks against the glass, which fogs up even more. I'm trying to ignore the throbbing pain on my left hipbone. My tattoo burns, like a fresh wound, beneath my gym pants, but I know the pain isn't really there. I know it's in my head. It's all just in my head. So I focus on trying to wipe the streaks off the mirror instead.

I think they call them phantom pains.

We got them together, matching. Rachel had just turned eighteen, and I'd used my fake ID. I let her choose the design, but I'm sure I wouldn't have had a say in it anyway. She called it a *heartigram*, but I never knew if that was the actual term or just something she made up on the spot. She was always doing that sort of thing, making shit up and then calling me out on not keeping up with her lingo: *God, Aub. You're such a dumb ass. Everyone knows what a heartigram is.*

I can feel where she branded me. The letters *R* and *A* are tangled and twisted together into a black heart. It pulsates beneath my stretchy pants. It *has* to be in my head. I've thought about getting it removed. I hide it as best I can, but there have still been too many times, too many guys, and just enough skin for me to have to explain the meaning behind the mysterious *heartigram* etched into my left hipbone. This had been especially true in college—and early on, before Danny. I stopped explaining the heartigram, and it always played out the exact same way.

It would start with a make-out session against the walls of some musty basement bar with a random frat boy on a Friday night. I was careful at this point. I'd had my fair share of hookups, but I was always in control. At last call, we'd fumble outside, usually into the sleet, snow, or rain; I'd have no clue where my friends went, but never really cared. I'd learned not to rely on people in these situations.

So we'd hop in a cab—the guy would always be way drunker than me, drooling over my tits all the way back to the dorms—and we'd go back to my room, always my bed. Never his. My shirt would come off, and then he'd spy the sharp black ink peeking out from my unbuttoned jeans.

Him: Cool tat.

Me: Thanks.

Him: What's it mean?

Me: Nothing.

Him: Who's R.A.? Hope it's not another dude!

And then thinking he was totally original, a real romancer in the sack, he'd prop himself up on his elbow, get all coy and smiley, lean in, and kiss me real slow.

They'd be gone before anything else could happen. I'd usually just fake a sudden bout of the spins, jump up, and run to the bathroom. I'd retch over the bowl, flush a few times to make it believable, and then politely ask them to leave. Worked every time.

The ink has faded over the past five years, but I'm still reminded every time I go to the bathroom, every time I undress, every time I stand naked in front of a fucking mirror. And now Rachel is dead, and all I'm left with is a *heartigram*.

I can't decide if I'm jealous. No, "jealous" is not the word. But a part of me resents the fact that she beat me to it. Suicide is no longer an option for me. It would just come off as tacky and melodramatic. I can hear everyone back home now: *She just couldn't live with the guilt; maybe she couldn't go on without her; I heard it was a pact.*

I'd rather not be eternally associated with Rachel if I can help it.

I leave the bathroom and plop down on the couch to wait for Danny. I sit cross-legged and stare at my fingernails some more. It's all I can do to stay in the moment.

I've been seeing him for three years—a tall Irish boy from somewhere outside of Albany—and I have never mentioned Rachel to him, or what she did to me. I've never mentioned much before my college years—especially from those last few months before high school graduation.

I met Danny in college. We were both sophomores. I'd seen him around campus for a year or so, and thought nothing of him. He'd seemed kind of douche-y actually—a typical frat boy, always with a Mets hat, and he may or may not have been on the rugby team. He had one of those ubiquitous faces that could easily be mistaken for literally anyone else with a light brown buzz cut and a polo.

We got together in the most anticlimactic, unromantic way possible. It was a frat party; he filled my red Solo cup with warm keg beer. We talked for maybe ten minutes about, well, warm keg beer, and he Facebook-messaged me the next day. That was back when I actually had Facebook. We were dating three weeks later. I had mono, and he was nice to me—that about sums up our entire relationship. He offered to give up his Friday night and came over with the first season of *Lost* and dining-hall frozen yogurt. So I felt like I sort of owed him my time, once I got healthy again and all. I never did get into *Lost*, though, which has always been the main issue in our relationship. Something he's never really gotten over.

"How can you feel *nothing* for these characters? *For the island?*" he'd ask, his voice prickly with pure distrust.

That should have been his first clue.

Two and a half weeks after my mono outbreak, I was back on my feet, drenching my spleen once again with copious amounts of vodka–Red Bulls. And then we had fun, Danny and me.

We still have an easy relationship. He pays the rent—well, his parents do, at least while he's finishing up law school—and we hardly ever fight. He's nice enough; pretty good-looking, too. My only complaint is that he still insists on having sex with his socks on.

But in my top desk drawer, tucked away beneath my folder

of suicide notes, are three carefully composed drafts of a breakup letter.

I hear his keys fumbling in the door. I sit up straight and try to act natural. He walks in, balancing the tray of coffee on his forearm, and I'm still not sure if I'll bother telling him about the call. But halfway through breakfast, I pull out the insides of my bagel and I tell him, without any sign of emotion, how she's dead, how she probably killed herself.

He stands up to hug me. "It's fine," I say, pressing my palms out in front of me. "We weren't close." He looks at me kind of funny and sits back down on the edge of the couch. "I don't even think I'm going home for the funeral," I say. "I don't want to anyway. It's just going to be miserable." This wasn't entirely true. I decided moments before that I'd at least go home for the week, if only to appease Karen and not look like a total asshole. I still wasn't sure about the funeral. That part was true.

"Do what you have to do," he says. He cocks his eyebrow and bites down into his sesame-seed bagel.

"What?" I put my own bagel on the coffee table and stare him down. He shrugs. "Why are you looking at me like that?"

"Nothing," he says. He's doing that thing where he shakes his head and sort of smiles, but only because he doesn't want to ruffle me up. But after a moment of silence, he at least attempts to say what he means, through a mouthful of bagel and cream cheese. It's gross, and I want to tell him to keep his mouth shut when he chews, but instead I just wait for him to finish his thought. It's always better to just get it over with. "I just think you should probably go, is all." He won't look me in the eye.

Instead, he stares intently at the bagel in his hands and chews with unnecessary focus. "It's the right thing to do."

The Right Thing.

"Well, Karen basically said I'm a heartless bitch if I don't go home; so I guess I don't have a choice." I take a sip of my coffee and wait for him to interject, to tell me it's okay, that I could never be a heartless bitch even if I tried, that I always have a choice.

But he doesn't.

"Your mom's kind of right," he says.

I pinch the bridge of my nose with my thumb and forefinger and close my eyes. I really can't deal with this all right now. The girl is a corpse and she still somehow manages to fuck up my Sunday.

I stare down at my half-eaten bagel.

I think she's cute.

I don't know, I guess. Cute, but kind of chubby.

I wrap up the rest of my bagel and stuff it back into the paper bag with the rest of the trash.

I can already imagine the sideshow that will be Rachel's funeral: her mother, weeping over a white veneer casket; her little sister, Chloe—who's got to be about sixteen now—chain-smoking in the parking lot; her stepfather, Jeff, leering at me from a shadowy corner.

I can feel it all. The uncomfortable silence when I walk into the church; all eyes on me, the best friend, the one she left behind; and a cosmic cloud of nauseating smells: flowers, too much perfume, and incense, the Catholic kind.

Ms. Price, our second-grade teacher, she'll be there for sure, and she'll pull me into her bony arms and tell me what a lovely young woman I've turned out to be, what a shame it was that we hadn't stayed close, how maybe then Rachel would still be alive. There would be hugs—a whole variety of them. Lingering embraces, one-arm-over-the-shoulder hugs, full-body hugs. I hate them all equally.

Ally and the rest of the old Seaport gang will be there, too, huddling in a corner, holding each other in a disgusting sob fest, stopping only to snap perfectly posed Instagram shots to show off their coordinated outfits—*#funeralchic*. There'll be Eric Robbins, clad in his marine uniform, the guests shaking his hand, thanking him for doing his part for this great country. Just the thought of it sends my stomach spinning and my throat tightens. I have to swallow just to keep from vomiting up my half-eaten bagel.

There will be sympathetic nods. And there will be Adam.

There will definitely be Adam, with his gray eyes and sloppy hair—his stupid face—always whining about something, always sulking.

I stand up and pick lint off my T-shirt. Danny pulls me into his chest. My face presses up against him at an awkward angle. My nose bends, I can't really breathe, and my instinct is to pull away, but I try and let my body relax in his arms, even if it's only for five seconds—which I think is my record. *One. Two.* He smells of cedar chips; he keeps his sweaters in an old chest at the foot of our bed. *Three. Four.* He releases me and I take a step back. My life with Danny is comfortable. It's safe. It's quiet. It allows me to go through the motions undetected, detached. And the idea of leaving it for a funeral on Long Island makes my guts ache.

I hold out my hands. "It's impossible to get a decent manicure around here. For twenty bucks, you'd think it would last more than a week." Danny looks at me like I'm crazy. I glance at the chipped polish and remember the name: *Wicked*.

Chapter 3

WHO PUT THE word "fun" in funeral? If you really think about it, funeral sounds like it should be synonymous with "carnival" or "funnel cake." But I can't think of anything fun about Rachel's funeral, except for the fact that she won't be there.

I sit on the stone stoop of a walk-up, four buildings down from our own so Danny won't see me. It's nestled between two oversized brownstones, just a few feet from York Avenue. It's humid, too hot for October, and my left temple throbs.

I suck on a Parliament and rub two fingers into my temple. I allow myself one cigarette a day—usually in the mornings before work—just to take the edge off. But this is my second. Rachel is dead, so I'm having two today.

Danny doesn't know I smoke, and I don't consider myself a smoker. I'm not a smoker, at least that's what I tell myself. I'm not a smoker, and *I'm not a cheater*. He thinks I only smoke when I'm stressed or drunk and says an actual smoker would be a deal breaker for him. But with the way he's been looking at me today, peeking over the top of his laptop, all squirrelly, I'm sure he wouldn't have anything to say about it.

It's only been four hours since I got the call, but I can already see through his probing suggestions like plate glass: *If you go home . . . When you decide if . . . If you're feeling up to it. . .*

I wish he would just ask me. Just ask me. *Are you going home for the funeral, Aubrey? I would like to know so I can plan accordingly.* I think I'd have to respect that. But until he asks, I will purposely avoid giving him an answer.

I do a lap around the block, slather my hands with Purell for thirty seconds, add a drop of lotion, spritz my hair with coconut-scented body spray, and pop a piece of spearmint gum. It's a ritual, and it usually covers the lingering smell.

Back at our apartment, I smell like a piña colada as I sift through some of my things, setting them on my bed one by one while Danny watches the Jets game. Underwear, a nearly empty bottle of Xanax, a couple of sweaters, not enough socks. Every commercial, I stick my head out the bedroom door to make sure he hasn't gotten up to check on me. Deodorant, face wash. He hasn't moved in an hour. I think he may have passed out. Toothbrush, yoga pants. I drag a sack of dirty laundry out from my closet—if anything, I'll get some clean clothes out of this debacle. In one swift motion, I swipe the contents off my bed into the laundry bag.

I e-mail my boss from my phone in the bathroom. I turn the shower on, letting the water drown out the sound of my fingers clicking the keys. The water sprays feverishly against the wall.

Hi Jonathan,

I just wanted to let you know that there's been a
death in the family, and I have to return home for a
few days. I'm sorry for the short notice. I will contact
you midweek after the services to let you know
when I will be returning to work.

   Weekly crime report is attached for edits.

Thank you,
Aubrey Glass

UpperEastSidePost.com
975 Lexington Avenue, 5th Floor
New York, NY 10021

The room fills with steam. I hope he fires me.

I'm in the wrong profession. I knew that from the start. Hyperlocal, online journalism—a type of reporting that requires a deep interest in the area you cover, an appreciation for the minutiae of everyday life, and little to no actual reporting, except for maybe a weekly phone call to the Nineteenth Precinct.

I'm not a reporter. At least I don't consider myself one. I'm an entry-level *content creator*, and I'm mediocre at best. My job is mostly programmed lists and copy and pasting press releases. I always thought I'd be a writer—a real journalist or a bestselling novelist—but after college, I realized I have nothing to write about, and I'm not passionate enough about anything, really. And isn't that the cornerstone of being a good writer? Passion? So as long as I have my father's credit card—or guilt

money, as Danny calls it—I don't mind the repetitive work and
low pay.

My most recent submission for the *UES Post* went something like this:

> *The Upper East Side's Nineteenth Precinct warns locals
> that there have been a large number of flashers on neigh-
> borhood buses, particularly along Third Avenue. Flashers
> are bumping into riders, and then revealing themselves
> as a distraction while their accomplice steals the victim's
> belongings. To combat such theft, NYPD recommends the
> following:*

- *Use handbags with zippers and locks, and never carry
  wallets in back pockets.*

- *Beware of loud arguments or commotions that may be
  staged to distract commuters as their pockets are picked.*

- *If you are unnecessarily bumped or crowded on public
  transportation, be aware that you might be positioned
  for pickpocketing and/or flashing.*

- *Never make eye contact with the flasher.*

- *If your pocket is picked or you are flashed, yell out immediately to warn the driver or conductor, and alert
  everyone else that there's a pickpocket/flasher team on
  board.*

My parents still can't get over the fact that they'll never see my name in print. I'll only ever have a Helvetica-font byline below the social-media share button.

I slip on a pair of black leggings, flats, an oversized charcoal cardigan, and pop a Xanax, before wrapping a black scarf around my neck and throwing a pair of Ray-Bans over my dry eyes.

When I know Danny is asleep, I leave a note on the coffee table in front of him, and drag my laundry bag out the front door. It's not quite the breakup letters I have stocked away in my desk drawer, but rather a toned-down version that promises I'll be back by the end of the week and asks him not to worry about me, to kindly respect my need for space at this *very difficult time.*

My heartbeat echoes and I start to get that shaky feeling in my hands. I walk toward Second Avenue to grab a cab and swipe my fingers over my hairline to wipe away the sweat. People stare. It's too hot for a sweater and scarf, but I can already feel my neck and chest rashing up. It always happens when I go home—this red splotchy flush of rouge—and I know Karen won't ignore it: *Oh my God. What happened to your chest? Are you allergic? Do you need Benadryl?* So it's better to just cover up than get into the fact that the thought of going home makes me break out in hives.

And though it's October and a freakishly warm day, I know once I get onto Long Island, the Atlantic breeze will lower the temperatures at least ten degrees. I suck the air into my lungs, but my chest feels too tight for any air to get through, and it's too late for a cigarette. I'll never make the train, and plus, I've already had two today. So I just walk and breathe, and try to focus on the gritty sidewalk in front of me. I know I just need to ride out this feeling until the Xanax kicks in and quiets this heart-pounding, head-throbbing panic. After a few minutes I feel it sweep through me, and my blood stops buzzing and everything feels very still.

Chapter 4

April 1997.

RACHEL HAD ALWAYS been fat growing up. Her beady little eyes would squint on her pudgy little face; her mouth would contort in this twisted little tyranty way; and I always knew to shut up and listen. She had this remarkable skill of getting my undivided attention—even at seven. We met in second grade when all that mattered was the newest Spice Girls album and whether or not a new episode of *7th Heaven* aired on Monday night.

That year, we spent most of our recesses indoors, seated around a kidney-shaped table with Ally Marlo. It was the most coveted table in the whole classroom—nestled in the back, against the unused chalkboard—but Rachel had laid claim to it sometime around November, and nobody ever challenged her for it. I guess it didn't matter anyway, since most of the kids preferred to spend recess outdoors.

It was one of those mundane weekday afternoons in April, and the three of us girls were huddled around a poster board, fumbling with markers, fighting to get our ideas onto paper.

Rachel sat in the middle of the table—in the alcove, her alcove.

"Everybody just shut up," Rachel said.

This was the year of As If, our up-and-coming girl band. Rachel said it best: if we're going to have our big break by fifth grade, we had to make sacrifices; and opting for indoor recess was essential to the cause of As If. And so, I was spending yet another spring afternoon inside a stuffy classroom, stinking of submission and broken crayons.

"Back off, you morons," she said. "Let me show you." With the yellow marker clutched in her sweaty palm, Rachel began to draw herself as the lead member of As If, clad in our album-cover outfits. It was a two-piece yellow nylon suit: a top, strongly resembling a training bra, and Adidas pants. The kind that swooshed and sort of make your teeth feel like they might fuzz together. I watched as she drew herself with such intricate detail. Funny, I remember thinking how good her body looked on paper.

"That looks amazing," Ally said.

"I know," Rachel said. Ally kept on nodding her head in awe, before suggesting matching belly-button rings.

LATER THAT DAY, we sat near the back wall on Ms. Price's Magic Carpet for afternoon story time where we were joined by Mrs. Gray's third-grade class from next door.

"Hey, Rachel, are you wearing a bra?" As the word "bra"

propelled from his lips, Eric Robbins reached over and tried to snap a bra that was not there. Rachel flinched forward, clasping her arms in front of her chest, protecting something that also was not there. This is my earliest memory of Eric, and at the time he was just a shrimpy third grader with freckles and two missing front teeth.

"Shut up. It's an undershirt," Ally said, pulling up the back of Rachel's shirt. Rachel hunched forward, her eyes cold and disinterested.

I tried to ignore the taunting and harassment, and traced the crimson alphabet carpet with my fingers. Eric's mother had passed away from cancer earlier that fall. That's how I remember him back then, as the twerpy little boy with the dead mother. Ms. Price told us that he was coping in his own way and we should all be understanding, which meant he got away with a lot. Maybe somebody should have taken this opportunity to teach him to keep his hands to himself. Maybe then things would have been different.

"Hey, Rachel," Eric said again as he repeatedly poked her on the shoulder. In some pathetic form of protest, she didn't turn around. "I heard you're not a virgin."

"Mom," I said in the car on the way home.

"Yes," she responded, uninterested and focused on the road.

"What's a virgin?" She shot me a fleeting glance out of the corner of her eye. She didn't say anything for a moment, but gripped the wheel with both hands and sighed a reluctant breath.

"It's a person from Virginia."

THE NEXT DAY, at lunchtime, Rachel called a meeting back by the coats and lunch boxes.

"Where's the book?" she asked, the question directed at Ally, who reached into her baby-blue JanSport backpack and pulled out the sacred As If journal.

To an outsider, it was just a marble notebook. To the sanctioned, As If girl band member, it was so much more. It contained partial lyrics to our two sure-to-be hit songs, outfit ideas, concert stage sets, and our album cover, which we believed was truly innovative in the world of nineties pop culture.

"We need to finish the lyrics to 'Don't Stop Lovin' Me, Baby,'" Rachel said. I had come up with the song title while riding the bus earlier that week. I sat, and listened, though I was more concerned with how I'd hide my American Girl doll's new haircut from my mother.

In her best attempt at a sultry, Mariah Carey–esque voice, Ally sang, "'Don't stop lovin' me, baby. I wanna make love to you, so I can get higher and higher.'"

"Yes," Rachel hissed, pumping her fist in the air. Ally scribbled down the new chorus in her chunky handwriting. I always tried to write like Ally, but my writing always looked sloppy and skinny, like a serial killer's.

I was deeply involved with the conception of our song, when I felt fingers press into the back of my shoulder. It was a sharp pain, surprising, and I swung around to face the culprit. And there was Eric Robbins, stoic, with his hands on his hips.

"Can we help you?" Rachel cut in.

"Your face looks like a hard-on," he said to no one in particular, but I assumed it was meant for me, since I'd been the one he'd thrust his fingers at.

"A what?" I asked. Ally stopped writing, stared, and waited.

"A hard-on," he said, again, slower this time. "Hard-on. Hard-on. Boner," he screamed, and he ran back to his friends. The three of us shrugged and went back to our song.

THAT NIGHT, MY five-year-old brother, Eli, still sat at the head of the table, sulking over his half-eaten steak and potatoes. My brother Marc was ten and flung pees at Eli's plate until my father finally lost his temper and sent them both to their rooms. I helped my mother clear the dinner table and softly hummed the tune to "Don't Stop Lovin' Me, Baby."

I picked up the cup of milk that I hadn't drunk and dumped it down the drain on the sly. I found that if I let my milk sit out during dinner, it got warm and developed a funky smell, but my parents would insist that I finish it, each night, regardless of temperature and odor. I carried a handful of dirty forks and knives over to my mother at the dishwasher.

"Mom," I said. "What's a hard-on?"

My mother stopped what she was doing, sighed reluctantly, and said, "Remember when I went to the tanning salon?" I nodded. "And I put the heart sticker on my chest to see how much color I got?" I nodded. "That's a 'heart-on.'"

THE NEXT DAY, I sat on the back corner of the Magic Carpet, my backpack and denim jacket still on. Rachel and Ally plopped down beside me. Rachel held a rumpled piece of paper.

"I finished the song last night and typed it up on Jeff's computer," Rachel said. I eyed it, and remember being impressed with how professional it looked. "It's awesome," she said. "I did such a good job."

I ignored the blatant fact that she took credit for the entire song.

"I want to show it to Ms. Lotus," she said.

"She'll love it, and I bet she knows people who can get us a contract," Ally added. Ms. Lotus was the Harbor School band teacher. We didn't have her as a teacher because only fourth and fifth graders were permitted to take band, and the fact that Ms. Lotus was so untouchable made her seem even more valuable to As If. The other girls, and undoubtedly a small part of me, were convinced she could make us famous.

"We should go now," Rachel said. "I'll show Ms. Price the song. She'll have to let us go see Ms. Lotus." Before I had a chance to respond, Rachel and Ally were off to show our teacher the first original As If song. I suddenly became self-conscious, a feeling that most second graders should not know. I'm not sure if I was just embarrassed by the situation, but I wanted nothing to do with the grand unveiling of "Don't Stop Lovin' Me, Baby."

I sank back against the wall and feigned distraction with the Koosh ball key chain dangling from my backpack.

I didn't see Rachel or Ally at morning meeting, nor did I see Ms. Price. As Mrs. Gray read *If You Give a Mouse a Cookie*, I didn't listen. I thought about what they could possibly be doing now. Maybe Ms. Price let them see Ms. Lotus after all. Maybe she loved the song so much that she'd excused them for the rest of the day so they could prepare for fame. Or maybe they were in trouble. Or worse, maybe they got sent to the principal's office. I couldn't figure out what could have been so offensive about the song. There were no curses. Maybe Ms. Price thought we wrote it during a lesson. I didn't know what to think, but I was worried. I was worried about my friends, I was worried about myself, and I really wanted a cookie.

"Hey you, look." Eric held up his hand in front of my face, waving his middle finger in the air. I guess he didn't know my name back then either. "I bet you don't know what this means." Within seconds, all of the third-grade boys were flashing their middle fingers at me.

Just as I convinced myself that Ms. Price had personally escorted Rachel and Ally to the band room, where they were all sitting around, planning our big break, I heard the thick wooden door creak open.

Rachel's head was down, her bangs and ash-blond hair flipped in toward her face, hiding an embarrassed sneer. The girls took a seat on the opposite side of the carpet. I couldn't see them from across the room, so I craned my neck, desperate for their attention. I wanted to know what had happened. I needed to know.

Neither Rachel nor Ally would look at me, but before I got a chance to creep across the carpet and find out just what went down, I heard my name. It was Ms. Price. She motioned for me to follow her. Mrs. Gray stopped reading, and all the other kids watched me get up and leave. As I stepped over Rachel and Ally, they giggled in a symphony of malicious intent. I can't prove it, but to this day, I am convinced that Rachel put her foot out to trip me.

Ms. Price led me into an adjoining classroom, known to students as the Blue Room. She told me to take a seat at the kidney table. I sat in the alcove. Rachel's alcove. She took a seat across from me, clasping the lyrics to "Don't Stop Lovin' Me, Baby."

"Does this look familiar?" she asked, sliding the paper across the table. I still can't watch an episode of *SVU* without flashing back to the legendary Blue Room Interrogation. I kept my hands glued to my lap, gave the paper a fleeting glance, and nodded. "I'm very disappointed in you," she said.

In me? My tongue swelled in my mouth. I couldn't speak, so I just sat there, stunned, silent.

"Rachel told me that you wrote this."

Me? I felt like I'd been sucker-punched right in the gut. Sure, I thought, now she gives me credit.

"The other girls told me this was all your doing. Is this true?"

I could have spoken up, told the truth, and ended Rachel Burns's reign right then and there, but I froze.

"I'm sorry," I said.

"Making love is not an appropriate thing to write about, and it most certainly is not an appropriate topic for school." I nodded.

"I'm sorry," I said again. "Please don't call my mom." I flashed her my best *who me? couldn't be!* face. "I promise I won't do it again," I added for good measure.

"Okay. Let's just forget this happened. I think you've learned your lesson."

When I went outside for recess, Rachel and Ally were huddled together by the tire swing. They saw me approach and vanished behind the metal slide. It took me a few minutes to gather my composure, but I sauntered over to them as if nothing had happened.

"What are you doing here?" Rachel sneered. She looked over at Ally and they giggled— that unnatural harmony that only resonates in creepy-little-girl-ghost movies.

"I didn't get in trouble," I said.

"Okay. Good," Rachel said. And that was it.

That day marked the untimely death of As If. Who knows; despite the fact that not one of us had a scrap of melodic talent, maybe we would have made it someday. If only we had gone straight to Ms. Lotus.

THAT NIGHT, AFTER my bath, I walked into my parents' room in my one-piece pajamas, the ones with the feeties and purple flowers.

"Mom," I said. She sat in bed doing her crossword puzzle.

"Yes," she said, still staring down at the paper in front of her.

"What does this mean?" I held up my middle finger, the way that Eric had at afternoon meeting.

She glanced at me over the top of her crossword.

"It means," she said, "fuck you."

Chapter 5

Sunday, October 5, 2014.

I JUST MAKE the seven o'clock train and slip into a three-seater near the bathroom. It's one of the old trains with the duct-tape-covered blue and red seats and no air-conditioning. It's crowded for a Sunday, mostly families, so I put in my headphones and turn up the volume on my angry-white-girl playlist—a medley of songs from the *Jagged Little Pill* album and a couple of Tori Amos classics.

If I wasn't feeling that swirl of anxiety before, I am now. My stomach has been bothering me all day—a sour, spinning cramp right in my gut, and I'm not sure if it's my breakfast or Rachel—but either way, I've taken more than the daily recommendation of Tums today.

I hold my BlackBerry in the palm of my hand. The tiny white envelope blinks, a reminder of the single voice mail waiting to be released. I close my eyes, but all I can see is a tiny, Polly Pocket–sized Rachel dancing, trapped inside my Black-Berry, clawing at the walls, trying to get out of my phone and into my head. Maybe I'm just stubborn, but I have no intention of listening. I have no intention of deleting it either. Knowing it's there, just knowing that her voice is wrapped up, neatly folded like a letter, is too much for me to deal with right now.

A robotic voice comes over the speaker.

This is the train to Babylon. The next station is Forest Hills.

Dusk settles in as we pass through Kew Gardens, and I start to get the thick feeling in my throat.

I hear the guy punching tickets from somewhere behind me. I hold out mine without looking up, keep my eyes closed, and press my face against the warm window. Someone pulls open the bathroom door, and a sickly smell wafts its way over to where I sit: toilet-bowl cleaner and possibly vomit.

"Seaport, right?"

I look up and see a vaguely-familiar face standing over me—shiny, oil-streaked cheeks and a slouchy, shapeless body, wrapped in the traditional MTA garb. It's meant to make him look dapper—respectable even—but there's something so damn doofy about it all. I nod, hoping he just spotted my ticket from afar with his supersonic vision and is just confirming my final destination.

"It's Aubrey, isn't it?"

I have no idea who this guy is or how he knows my name.

"Oh. Hey! Oh my God, yeah. How's it going?" I say with too much enthusiasm, hoping that if I dilute the conversation with enough words, he won't realize I don't actually know his name. His face comes into focus, and I think we could have gone to high school together. I can't remember his name, but he may have been a year or two older, maybe even in my brother Marc's grade, though we may have had a class together once.

"Pretty good, actually. You know after all that stuff a few years ago, I cleaned up and finally started working for the MTA this year."

His name might be Frank or Gary. The lines around his mouth stretch into a too-wide grin, and I notice that his teeth are coated with a thin layer of fuzzy film. I can just tell he has bad breath—that mothball-y scent of rotting meat.

"It's great pay. Great job. Things are finally going really well for me," he says.

I have absolutely no idea what he's talking about, but I nod and smile and act super happy for the guy.

"Oh hey," he says, his face suddenly going all somber. "Sorry to hear about Rachel. You guys were close, right?"

It catches me off guard. I didn't expect him to say her name, to even know her name. Which I guess is a ridiculous thought. Of course he knew Rachel. Everybody knew Rachel. But just hearing it, hearing her name again, makes me feel weak, like my bones might dissolve, and I'll just slide off the seat and melt into a puddle of warm piss on the floor.

I swallow the sickly feeling back into my throat and push my shoulders back. "Thick as thieves," I say. He tilts his head at me and yields a weak smile. I don't really think he picks up on my tone.

Louis. I think his name is Louis.

"So, I guess I'll see you at the funeral, then, right?" I shrug, smile back at him, and avoid giving any real answer. "Hey," he says. "The after-party is supposed to be pretty sweet. Everyone's talking about it."

"After-party?" I say. "Of what? The funeral?" He smiles and shrugs. "You're not serious," I deadpan.

"Yeah. So I guess you haven't heard, then? It's at O'Reilly's. It's sort of a memorial for Rachel. It'll be like a high school reunion. Should be fun."

A little boy shrieks from a few rows behind us. A papery old man clears his throat. Frank or Gary or Louis finally punches my ticket. *Click. Click. Click.*

I snatch the ticket from his pudgy fingers and slide it into my wallet. A high school reunion. A funeral. An after-party. Should be fun . . . eral.

I DON'T FEEL like having Karen pick me up when I get to the station. It's only a mile away, but the idea of sitting in the car with her, even for five minutes, makes me want to jump in front of the train.

The air whistles through the cracked window of the cab, and the streetlights blur as we speed through the back roads toward home—my ex-home. I'm not used to taking cabs on Long Island. It's different from the city. The driver seems to be in less of a hurry, and the car smells almost pleasant, like peppermint. I don't mind it.

I chew on a handful of raw almonds—the closest thing to the register at the Penn Station Duane Reade. It's all I've eaten since the hollowed-out half of a bagel from this morning. My stomach makes this horrific groaning sound, but I can't even think about food.

The front door is open when we roll into my driveway—my ex-driveway. The house looks different, but I can't figure out why. Maybe new shrubbery. I reach into my wallet for my credit card.

"Cash only," the guy mumbles without turning around.

"Seriously?" I say, pretending to scrounge around the bottom of my bag for cash I know I don't have. Unlike Manhattan, a five-minute cab ride costs twenty bucks. "You could have said something," I start, but then Karen comes trotting down the front pavement, her arms close to her chest, but her hands flailing, and I can't help but think of a T. rex. She's got a twenty-dollar bill in one hand and slips it to the driver. The perks of being back home. But so far I'm out eighteen dollars for the train ticket, and Karen's out twenty for the taxi.

How is a dead girl so effing expensive?

"You look thin," she almost sings it. It's the first of her many comments, and I can't help but feel a pang of self-satisfaction. She pulls me into her chest for one of those full-body hugs, and I keep my arms pinned stiff at my sides. I don't do hugs. "You feel thin," she emphasizes this time, grabbing me by the elbows.

My mother is blond, five-foot-eight with high cheekbones and a narrow frame—a height I never quite reached, and a body type I've still never been able to attain. Despite her obvious expectations, I never became a cheerleader. She signed me up when I was six, but I was clumsy and kind of a tomboy, not to mention suffering from undiagnosed ADHD. I have this memory of spinning around on a patch of grass and thrusting my tiny little body onto the ground while all of the good little cheerers were learning how to form the perfect pyramid. Karen stood off to the side, her thin lips pinched, assessing my grass stains, and realizing that her only daughter would never be that kind of girl.

The scent of stale coffee and my mother's Burberry perfume waft from my scarf. I notice her hair is straighter than usual today, sprayed into perfection, and I wonder if she spent extra time styling it just for me. Probably not, though.

"Are you eating?" Karen asks as I follow her into the house, tripping over a brick on the way up the walkway. Her thin arms hang from her sleeves, her elbows all knobby and bones. It isn't fair. Nobody ever asks her if *she's* eating. She's always been thin, doesn't matter what she eats or how little she exercises. But of course I inherited my father's short stature and wide frame. I have to work at it. I have to count calories and spend hours at the gym just to be considered *cute, but kind of chubby.*

That's it; the brick walkway is new.

Karen's arms swing to a stiff tune through the front hallway. "And why are you wearing gray?" she says, without turning around. "You look so pretty in colors." There's an open bottle of Cabernet on the counter, and I reach for a glass. A Yankee Candle flickers from the table—Midnight Storm or Harvest Moon—something strong and blue. "You know," my mother says, not missing a beat, "your face looks swollen. You should stop drinking so much." I roll my eyes. "You know, after college, it's called alcoholism."

I'm loosening the scarf from my neck, just enough to breathe, but not enough to expose the rash brewing beneath it, when she starts taking out leftovers and placing half-empty Tupperwares on the kitchen island.

"I've got cheese. I can make you a grilled cheese. There's salad. I can heat you up some soup." I don't give any indication that I'm hungry, but she keeps on laying out the contents of last week's dinners. I sit on the bar stool and spin my wineglass.

"I don't eat cheese, Mom," I say. "I'm lactose-intolerant, remember?"

"Huh? Since when?"

"Two years," I say, not counting the bagel and cream cheese I scarfed down earlier. I've been using the term "intolerant" loosely. Yes, for the past two years, I've been consciously avoiding dairy. And yes, I do get bloated and gassy when I eat it. But I make exceptions—and my bagel and cream cheese was an exception—even if I had to suffer through the throbbing cramp in my gut all day. And maybe if Karen acknowledged it, maybe if she had bothered to ask or show any interest in my dietary restrictions, I would have made an exception for her, too. But now I sort of feel like just being a bitch.

She suddenly gets quiet, stops with the food, and puts her hand on my shoulder. She's too close.

"How are you doing?" She tilts her head to the side, in that awful pitying way one does when they want to know how you are doing.

"I'm fine. I told you," I say. She breathes in real slow through her nose, something I'm sure her own shrink taught her to do, and I'm sure is a trick she passes on to her asshole students.

She breathes out through pursed lips and cocks her head to the side, like she's inviting me to spill my guts right here on the granite. I take a hard breath through my mouth. "Did you get your shit out of my room yet?"

She looks at me for just a second, shakes her head, and starts to put the food back into the fridge. She's slamming drawers shut now and snatches the block of cheddar from in front of me. "Don't forget to call your father and tell him you're home." Her voice is cold, and I know her hospitality is over. I nod, even though I have no intention of calling him. I can only deal with one parent at a time this week.

The television flashes from inside the den and some dramatic movie score blares through the surround sound speakers. I know it's my brother Eli and his newest girlfriend cuddling on the couch under my grandmother's knitted throw, and the thought nauseates me, so I take my wine and go straight to my room.

Karen kept her promise and moved all of her files, folders, and papers off my bed and onto my treadmill. I wasn't planning on any cardio anyway.

The room smells like citrus and dust, and I can just picture my mom swiping over each shelf and each individual Precious Moments figurine with a dish towel—the dust settling onto the hardwood floor before she sweeps it under the bed and sprays each stale, unused pillow with watered-down Febreze.

My room looks almost exactly the same as it did when I left it last. A shirtless Johnny Depp poster still hangs crookedly over my bed. On the adjacent wall, there's a *Breakfast Club* poster that I bought at the mall sophomore year. I'd only seen the movie once, but claimed it was my favorite film for the majority of high school.

My white wicker dresser is topped with an assortment of Bath & Body Works sprays and a jewelry box that I haven't opened in years, but I'm certain it's filled with tangled and broken necklaces from Claire's.

I remove a black cotton dress from my closet and hang it behind my bedroom door, just in case. I haven't worn it in years.

Cute, but kind of chubby.

But I feel like it would be appropriate to wear it, should I decide to pay my respects to Rachel. I still haven't decided whether or not I'll go to the funeral, but it's a good excuse to get a week off from work, and at least it will save me days of nagging guilt from Karen if she thinks I'm actually here for the funeral.

Danny's called only once since I left for Seaport. He left a message, just to let me know that he respects my need for space, but if I change my mind, he'll be on the next train. I listen to only half of the voice mail and hit delete.

I can hear Karen shuffling in and out of rooms, opening and shutting doors, like she's afraid I'll forget she's here. I swish the wine in my glass, and my gaze falls to the corkboard above my desk.

Rachel's muddy-brown eyes burn into me from the photo across the room. We were at the beach in Montauk during our senior year—before everything went wrong. We'd driven the hour-plus just to sit on the sand, something we could have done ten minutes away at Jones Beach, but there was always something about Montauk that made it worth the drive.

In the photo, we're sprawled out across this purple jersey knit sheet that she kept in the back of her car. I'm flat on my back, with her head on my stomach. She'd held the camera over us to snap the photo. It was a selfie before there were selfies—before it became an official word in the *Oxford Dictionary*. We look awful. The glare was too strong, and half of my face had been cut out of the shot. I barely make eye contact with photo-Rachel, pluck the thumbtacks out of the board, and let the picture fall behind the desk.

I reach for my wine again and feel silence out in the hall where Karen has just been stomping around. I lean into the door and know she's there. I can hear her breathing, contemplating whether to knock or come in. So I jerk the door open, and she stands there, her mouth hung open in a guilty smile. I swing the door open more, sort of an invitation for her to enter. She ducks in, sits on the edge of my bed, and fingers the pale blue comforter. I try to act busy, opening and closing my desk drawers and shuffling through my mail.

"So," she says. "I thought we could talk about Rachel?" She's using her guidance counselor voice, and I just know she's prepared a speech.

"What is there to talk about? I already told you." I eye her in the mirror. She focuses on the comforter, sighs, like she's about to say something, and then crosses her legs.

I tear open a credit-card statement. Not that I ever even look at them—no point really.

"Did something happen with you two? I mean, I know it's been years. But, Jesus, Aubrey, you're being a little extreme for two people who just 'fell out of touch.'" She bends her fingers to make air quotes. "Don't you think?"

"Nothing worth talking about," I say, and I mean it.

"She was your best friend!" Her voice squeaks, and I know she's lost all control over this practiced voice. I feel my chest tighten as the seconds tick away, and I think of all the things I could say right now. But I decide it's better to be vague.

"She wasn't a good person," I say, mentally checking off all of the shitty things Rachel had ever done/said/thought. My face reddens and twists, and I know I need to keep my voice steady. Karen has no idea. And there's no way she can ever know. It's the kind of thing she'd need to talk about, the kind of situation she's actually trained for—not the he-said, she-said bullshit of amateur bullying and catty middle-school cheerleaders. She'd cling to every word, and analyze my every move. She'd ask probing questions that I am in no way comfortable answering, and just the thought of it—just the thought of being treated like one of her pathetic students—makes me want to vomit. "I don't know what world your warped little mind is living in," I say, "where Rachel was this sweet little angel. She was not a nice person." I can see my mom's face start to furrow, like she might even cry, and I can't take the silence. "She was a bitch." She sighs again, holds her breath, and starts to refold the clothes from my suitcase.

There's another moment of silence. It's so thick, I think I can reach out and squeeze it.

"So what's new with you? How's work?" she finally says, her

voice shaky and distracted, and I can tell she's still obsessing over Rachel.

Karen had a baffling curiosity about Rachel's love interests—and just her life in general—all the juicy girlie gossip, things I guess I'd never really talk to her about. I'm sure Karen was a slut in her day, too, so maybe that's where the admiration stemmed from. But mostly, I think it was because Rachel was a cheerleader.

"Work's okay."

"Danny?"

"Danny's okay."

"Just okay?"

"I don't know. He got an A on his midterm. Do you really want to hear about that?"

"Law school isn't easy. Good for him. Everything else okay? You know, with you two?"

"Mom."

"Sorry. Sorry," she says. "I'll leave you alone now." She smiles, folds the last tank top on the bed, and stands up. "Well, let me know if you feel like talking."

She closes the door behind her, and I realize that I've been holding my breath. I sit down in the spot she'd been sitting in, the down comforter still warm from her body. I knead the covers until my fingers start to ache, feeling the guilty twist of my stomach. It's not like I want to be such a bitch. I wish I could be one of those girls—one of those fun-loving, carefree, open girls who giggle at everything and hug their mothers—the cheerleader kind of girl. The kind of girl who isn't afraid to show emotion, to show gratefulness. It's exhausting being this stiff, rigid empty shell of a human. I am appreciative. I am. I am fucking appreciative. But I can never say it. Even if I know that's all Karen ever wants to hear. The words get stuck, tangled, and twisted like damp bed sheets wrapped around my neck, like a noose tightening with each breath.

My phone starts to vibrate again from the nightstand. I grab it, noticing that another nail has chipped where I've been chewing at the cuticle. Assuming it's Danny again, I'm about to forward it to voice mail, but stop when I see an unexpected phone number—Adam's.

I stare down at the BlackBerry buzzing in my palm. Why is he calling me? Adam's number just sits there, and I wait for the phone to stop moving, but it just vibrates. What could he possibly want? To talk about Rachel? To offer his condolences? To see if I need a ride to the funeral? My heartbeat quickens, throbs really, from within my chest, and I wish I could just pound my fist against my sternum and make it stop. I can't imagine why he would call, and at the same time I can't imagine why he wouldn't, yet the thought of occupying the same room as Adam and Rachel unhinges me. Even if she will be in a casket.

The phone stops, and my heartbeat slows, and I hold the phone in my palm and stare, for maybe thirty seconds, until a message flashes on the screen: ONE NEW VOICE MAIL. TWO UNHEARD VOICE MAILS. I drop the phone onto the bed and fumble to my bag for another Xanax.

I'M BREATHING NORMALLY again by the time I get to my car. It's been sitting idle in the driveway for months, and I can't remember if I even put gas in it the last time I was home. I jam the key into the door, and a light flickers on from inside the house, as if on cue. I haven't had even a full glass of wine, but I can already feel a lecture coming on from Karen. *Make smart choices, Aubrey*, she'd say. *You're an adult now. I'm not going to tell you what to do, but make smart choices.*

I pull the key out of the door and stuff it back into my bag. I'm not in the mood to hear it tonight, and besides, Eli's new girl is blocking me in with her BMW. I brush past her shiny car—the black paint like a mirror, catching the light from the streetlamps. It's spotless, almost metallic in its perfection, and it makes my own white, 1990s Saab look sullied and cheap under the motion-sensor lights.

My car hasn't been washed in years. I don't see the point, really. It just gets dirty again the moment it hits the parkway. Either that, or it rains.

The air is still, and I can smell a fireplace burning somewhere on the other side of the street. I swipe my finger along the BMW and decide that I have the new girlfriend pegged already—assuming it's her car and not her parents'. She most likely commutes to some local college—probably Nassau—because her father bribed her with a shiny new Beamer if she swapped room and board for community college. Well, joke's on her. They got away with maybe a thousand dollars a semester in tuition in exchange for a $30,000 car, and now she's stuck at home in her twin bed, surrounded by Little League trophies and photos of friends she hasn't seen in two years. That car wouldn't even buy her a year at a private college, yet it's meant to be a symbol of wealth, a nod that says, *Hey, I make more money than you. I'm better than you.*

I catch my own reflection in the BMW door—I look squat and rotund—and I hope it's just the car, but I stand there an extra second too long and suck in my stomach and see if it makes a difference. It doesn't and so I walk, picking up pace on the sidewalk. I pull my phone out of my bag and stare down at the one new voice mail from Adam. I hold it to my ear and hit the button, and my feet are already carrying me toward Riverside Drive.

"Um, hey, Aubrey, it's me." His voice is deeper than I re-member, husky even. He clears his throat, as if contemplating whether or not I would still know who "me" is. "I'm just call-ing about Rachel. I figured you'd be in town. Anyway, call me back if you want." I replay, and replay again, his voice charging in my ear. I'm about to listen one more time when I realize I'm turning onto his block.

I stay across the street, and keep my hood up.

I can see Adam's house, clear across the street.

Um, hey, Aubrey. It's me.

A soft yellow glow emanates from the upstairs window on the right. It's Max's room. Or at least it used to be Max's room. I picture Adam up there now, cross-legged on the navy-blue carpet, sifting through the contents of his dead brother's desk. I wonder if Rachel's death triggered something for him.

I'm just calling about Rachel.

Of course Max's death had never been officially ruled a sui-cide, but I always had a feeling that Adam knew more about Max than he let on. And maybe the same goes for Rachel.

I figured you'd be in town.

I reach in my bag for a cigarette, but remember that I've already had my two today, so instead, I take three deep breaths and squint toward the upstairs window. I can't make out any shadows or figures or anything, so I sit down on the curb, a pile of wet leaves at my feet.

Anyway, call me back if you want.

I feel bad for Adam. Well, as much as I can muster up any sympathy after what he did. I hold my phone and hit the callback button. A deep, almost husky voice answers the phone.

Chapter 6

August 2005.

BEFORE THERE WAS Adam, there was Max. Sort of. We weren't a thing or anything. But I had known Max first. It was a sporadic, slightly awkward encounter that involved a mattress in the woods and a coffee tumbler full of tequila. It was the summer I turned fourteen, and just a month before Max was found dead in Clear Pond Park, hanging by the hood of his sweatshirt from a six-foot fence.

Everybody had their suspicions—he hopped the fence, got himself caught, and had been too drunk to wriggle free. I never really knew what I believed. I'd only met him once, but I remember the details of that day so clearly—how Rachel was already outside when I woke up that morning. How my window was open, and from my bed, I heard her chatting up Karen in the driveway.

Rachel had been spending a lot of time at my house that

summer. She lived with her mom, stepdad Jeff, and six-year-old sister, Chloe. It was weird over at Rachel's house, like they all had a bond, and Rachel was this outsider, like she was some drunk uncle, crashing on the couch every night. Even if her parents never said it outright, I could feel it when I went over there. Rachel was a reminder of her mother's mistakes, an extra expense, an intruder on the happy little biological family of three. Her home life had always been kind of screwy. Not in an abusive way or anything, just screwy. Her mother worshiped Chloe and would come home from work, toting a single cupcake with neon-pink frosting, or cute little princess outfits, while Rachel just sat there in her hand-me-downs from her older cousin Diane. And as a result, Rachel had some serious daddy issues. It didn't take a shrink to figure that much out. Her father left when she was a baby, and the only father figure she'd known had been Jeff, who was kind of a creep.

That afternoon, we were sprawled out in our bathing suits in my backyard over damp towels. I wore a one-piece, and Rachel wore a bikini that was too tight. The grass was flattened beneath my blue-striped towel. I had one of those aboveground pools, built into my deck, and we spent most of that summer dipping in and lying out. I never tanned well, though; my skin tone fluctuated between olive bronze and streaky red.

Rachel sat up and pulled her knees into her chest, her stomach bunching up into a single, thick roll. She realized, and pulled her knees in closer to conceal it. "You know her parents are sending her away, right?" she said, popping another piece of Trident into her mouth. She nudged her head toward the fence at my neighbor Tonya Szalinski. Tonya was a year older than us, but you wouldn't know it; she'd been left back in fourth grade and was a bit spacey. Karen called her slow. But I thought "spacey" was a better word.

"Where'd you hear that?" I asked. Rachel pulled on her shorts and a T-shirt. Her shorts were shorter than usual today. They were ripped denim, probably recycled from a pair of Diane's Levi's. The off-white jersey tee hung loosely off Rachel's pudgy shoulder. She was still sort of fat back then. Rachel had always been chubby growing up, but not in a typical fat girl kind of way. She held weight in her face, her shoulders, her gut, but she always had thin legs. And still she commanded attention everywhere she went. Self-esteem had never been an issue for her.

But at some point, earlier that summer, when I wasn't paying attention, she'd thinned out. Her stomach had flattened, but her shoulders still seemed too broad and her head too big for the rest of her body. And she still had that extra roll when she sat up in a bathing suit.

She flipped her hair to one side and casually exposed her bikini strap. She didn't have much to fill, on most days. Though, some days were noticeably bustier than others. I blamed Judy Blume. Once Rachel and I started reading *Deenie* and *Are You There God? It's Me, Margaret*—and more recently *Summer Sisters* and *Wifey*—all she started caring about were boys and boobs. Her stepfather, Jeff, noticed, too, and I think that's why she started spending more time with my family. He'd say things like, *You're really filling out there, girlie*, or *Maybe you shouldn't eat that second slice of pizza, you're gonna want to lose that baby pudge now that you got boobs.*

"I just heard," she said, her voice lowered to the edge of a whisper. "I heard that she got caught jerking off with a pencil in the back of the chorus room last year, and that Ms. O'Brien flipped out and called her parents, and that they're just sending her to some special school or something this year."

"Jerking off?" I deadpanned.

"You know what I mean," she said, flipping her hair over her shoulder again. This was also the summer Rachel's hair turned orange. Too much Sun-In and lemon juice had turned her ash-blond hair this awful unnatural shade of rust.

"You're such a liar," I said, stretching out on my towel. I reached down and pinched the damp nylon, snapping it against my stomach. I craned my neck toward Tonya's house. I could see her sitting out on the back deck of her high ranch, her thick black hair hung over her shoulder in a sloppy braid. She was strikingly pale, and I wondered how she didn't fry out there in the heat.

"I'm not lying," Rachel whispered. "Ally was in the class. She saw it." Rachel fingered her collarbone, a sick grin spreading across her face. She was most sure of herself when she was telling secrets. "Whatever. Don't believe me. Let's just go do something," she said, forcing her body up off the towel.

"Like what?" I pulled a white, cotton cover-up over my head. The dampness from my bathing suit seeped through.

"I dunno," she said, "but you're boring me."

I swatted at a bee, slipped on my flip-flops, and we started to walk through the gate toward the street. I hated myself back then. At least I hated the way I'd let Rachel tell me what to do all the time—no backbone to tell her to shut up. To tell her that *she* was boring *me*.

"We could go to the Jumps and watch the skaters . . ." she said, her voice trailing off in this dreamy singsong way.

"No," I said, before she could even finish the thought. I could see through her intentions like plate glass. Rachel couldn't stop talking about Brendon Shaw or how Ally Marlo had made out with a junior in the woods behind the Jumps. She'd recently begun making comments about my older brother, Marc, waving at him coyly, and saying things like, "I bet your brother has a huge dick," when he left the room.

She started to make a face.

"I don't want to go there," I said, a little whinier than I had anticipated. The thing about Rachel, though, she always got her way. We walked side by side, away from my house, and passed the Szalinskis' as she called out, "Put it away, Tonya!" Rachel sputtered in laughter, grabbed my hand, and dragged me out of sight toward the Jumps.

I hated everything about the Jumps. It was a sketchy clearing in the backwoods of Clear Pond Park that stank of dirt and gasoline. It was littered with garbage, broken glass, oversized tree roots—a girl in flip-flops' hell on earth. But mostly, I hated that it was where my brother hung around with his dirtbag friends.

I scuffed my flip-flops against the road, and every time we passed a parked car, I caught Rachel glancing at her own reflection.

"You know your brother's there, right?" she said, looking at me with what my mother would refer to as bedroom eyes.

"Obviously," I said. "Which is exactly why I don't want to go."

"Why not? You afraid they'll make you smoke a little pot?" She straightened her shoulders, pushing her chest out. "You know Diane's friend Leslie gave this guy a hand job there."

"No," I said, shaking my head. "I don't care what he does. I just don't want to go hang out with my brother. And I'm sure he doesn't want to hang out with either of us." I emphasized the *either of us* to shatter any delusion that she and Marc were pals. Marc hated her. Most of that grade did—especially the girls. Rachel was a flirt. And high school girls could not stand the idea of this slutty little soon-to-be freshman scamming on their men.

Rachel scoffed, and I rolled my eyes. At that point in our relationship, I could have made a full-length film solely of Rachel's scoffing followed by my eye rolling.

"God, Aub, you're such a narc." She nudged my shoulder and cackled. I wasn't in the mood, even if she was joking. I jerked my elbow into her ribs and walked out into the street. Rachel's face twisted and contorted into what appeared to be the onset of a tantrum, but she caught her reflection in a Volkswagen and composed herself. "God, I'm only kidding. Relax."

I kicked a rock into a sewer, and turned back toward my house. I had things to do. But before I could make it across the street, Rachel dashed over to my side and grabbed me by the elbow.

"No, wait," she said. "I completely forgot I had this. You're going to love me."

"What?" My stomach twisted, and I realized I hadn't eaten anything.

"First, tell me I'm your best friend." She used the same singsong voice and danced around me like a deranged elf—like the Rachel I now imagine to be dancing around inside my BlackBerry. "Say it! Say I'm your best friend."

"Okay. You're my best friend," I mumbled. I crossed my arms and waited.

She walked behind me, gripped my shoulders, and led me off the road into an area shaded by trees. "Here." She pulled out a pack of Camel Lights from her faded pink shoulder bag. I felt my tongue get thick.

"Where did you get those?" I had only smoked once before, when I was twelve. Marc let me share one with him in our garage, and I'd never told anyone but Rachel, but I sort of liked it. Growing up in the nineties meant suffering through hundreds of antismoking assemblies. So from kindergarten on, it was ingrained into our moldable little minds that smoking wasn't cool. It was rebellious. It was dirty. It was unhealthy. It was a gateway drug to other atrocities like booze and sex and heroin. And if you smoked, you would get cancer and then you would die.

"I found them in Jeff's dresser," she said. "Here take one. And don't forget that I'm your best friend." She said it almost as if she was reminding herself. She handed me a cigarette.

Rachel pinched one between her own lips like a pro. She had this small gap between her two front teeth. Of course she'd smoked many-a-cigarette with Diane. I craned my neck around toward the street. "No one's coming, narc." She smiled again.

Rachel stood a good two inches taller than me. I stared past her, to a spiderweb behind her head. She lit her cigarette first and shot me a fleeting smile. She coughed once, blew smoke out through the space between her teeth, and took another puff.

Smoke streamed off the end of her lit cigarette as she balanced it between her lips.

She lit mine with another match. My silver-and-sapphire mockingbird ring twinkled from my right hand—a gift from my grandmother two years earlier, and I hadn't taken it off since. But with the heat, the ring cut into my swollen fingers. I wished I could take it off, but I didn't have pockets or a bag. A tiny blast of sulfur struck my nostrils. I tried to be effortless, wanting so bad to do this better than Rachel had. But when I sucked in, I choked on the smoke, and dropped the cigarette onto the ground.

Rachel finished her cigarette and pulled a bottle of cheap perfume out of her bag. It smelled like baby powder soaked in vinegar, and she doused her hair and shirt. I could still smell the cigarette on my hands—feeling dizzy as we cut through the trees to the other side of the road.

That's when we saw them, Max and his two friends, standing outside the clearing of the Jumps—two acres of state-owned wooded area that backed the park. Rachel nudged me and started toward them. The boys spotted us and stopped on a small patch of grass between the woods and the street. There was a tall wire fence that barricaded the Jumps, and a crooked, reflective sign that read NO TRESPASSING. But to the left of the metal sign, there was a child-sized gap in the fence, like someone had pulled the wiring apart with a pair of pliers.

"So you ladies coming in?" Max asked, holding a piece of the metal fence back in this gentlemanly way.

Rachel narrowed her eyes at me, I shrugged, and we ducked through the fence and followed them into the woods.

It had been my first time drinking, and I remember that first swig out of the metal coffee tumbler full of tequila. The rusty-key-flavored liquid flowed through my esophagus and flared up like a burst of sulfur beneath my breastbone.

Rachel was sprawled out on her back like a starfish, right in the middle of an old, beat-up mattress that some teenagers had dragged out there earlier that summer. She had only taken a few swigs from the tumbler—less than I had—but she was rolling around and giggling, sloppy and hysterical.

"My God." She swooned, arching her back. "I'm actually drunk." Max Sullivan and the two older boys grinned at each other as Rachel kicked and writhed between them. "This is amazing, Aub." She leaned over and blew smoke onto my neck.

"Enjoying yourself?" One of the older boys smirked. I didn't see Marc anywhere, and I didn't recognize any of these guys as his friends. I was relieved, and it seemed like Rachel had forgotten about him, too.

"Just taking it all in," Rachel said.

I rolled my eyes, and caught Max staring in my direction. I looked away and took another swig. Each time the warm tequila hit my lips, I cringed, my face puckering. I remember trying so hard to act natural.

I rolled a piece of spearmint-flavored gum into a ball with my two front teeth and the tip of my tongue. It had lost most of its flavor and started to taste like spearmint-rusty-key-brass-flavored gum. I spit it out onto the cracked dirt and took a drag from one of the older boys' cigarette. Purple smoke ribboned above my head, and I let my body fall against the bare mattress.

The sun was low in the sky, but it illuminated the copper-colored earth with its dull, orange glow. Even though it was still August, dead leaves lay shriveled and curled, like dried fire around the perimeter of the mattress.

"Has anyone ever told you that you have the greenest eyes?" Max said as he fell onto his side and leaned over me.

I propped myself up on my elbow and leaned back to put some distance between us, but I think he took it as an invitation to come closer.

"Thanks, I guess," I said. He was hovering now.

"And I like your ring," he said, grazing my hand with the tips of his fingers. He lifted my hand to his face. "What's it supposed to be?" He traced the silver ring with his fingers. I tried to smile, but I could feel my hand shaking in his.

"A mockingbird," I said. "I think." I knew, obviously.

"Like the book?"

"No," I said. "I'm not really sure what it means. My grandma gave it to me for my confirmation."

"Oh, a Catholic girl," he snarked. "Too bad," he said. "I liked that book. And too bad, because you know what they say about Catholic girls." He looked at me hard, stoic and unblinking. "Hey," he said. "You know what my favorite book is?" I shook my head, unable to swallow, feeling the booze flow through me. He leaned in and whispered into my ear. "*Tequila Mockingbird.*"

I spit out that last sip of brassy booze and let out an awkward laugh. The lines around his eyes softened and creased, and he busted a toothy smile. It was at that moment when he leaned in to kiss me. His tongue flopped into my mouth—sloppy and hysterical.

I WALKED HOME at dusk by myself. Rachel stayed behind with The Guys. Two hours with them, and they were already *The Guys*. Funny, that would be the last time we'd hang out with them all together, ever.

A basketball bounced against a nearby driveway, and the whole street smelled of sweet, smoky barbecue as I walked home toward my house. I stared down at the cracks in the sidewalk, stepping around them, and practiced walking a straight line, heel to toe, just in case a cop car barreled around the corner and demanded that I prove sobriety. It was an unlikely turn of events—but a drunken habit that would stick with me for years.

I could see Karen's Cadillac in the driveway, and my throat began to thicken as I approached the house. We had a split-level home with white vinyl siding, and it looked out of place among all the high ranches on our street.

I cupped my hands in front of my face, blew out a breath of hot air, and sniffed. Karen would smell me the moment I

walked through that door—tequila and cigarettes—so instead
I headed over toward Tonya's backyard and peered over the
fence.

"Hey, Ton," I said. I don't know why I called her Ton. I
don't think I, or anybody for that matter, had ever called her
Ton. But it just felt real. I was smashed, and it felt real. "What
are you doing?"

"Painting shells," she said, so matter-of-factly that I felt
slightly dumb for not knowing.

"Oh," I said. The spaces between the wire fence started to
move like a kaleidoscope, and I slipped my fingers through the
green rubber holes. She walked up to where I stood. Up close,
she looked even paler, but she had these striking blue eyes—
celadon blue.

"Hey," she said, a look of confusion on her face. We hadn't
spoken in years, even if she did live just a few steps away. "I like
your ring," she said. "Is it a mockingbird?"

"It is," I said, tugging it off my finger and holding it in the
palm of my hand. "Here, you can have it."

She took it from my hand, slipped it over her finger, smiled,
and walked back to her shells.

Chapter 7

Sunday, October 5, 2014.

"Aubrey?" Adam's voice catches me off guard, and I swallow my breath before he can hear me on the line. His voice is deeper than I expect, even after hearing the voice mail. I sit silent, my voice caught in my throat. Part of me wants to answer him, part of me wants to scream into the phone until my throat is raw, but mostly, I just want to hang up and sprint down the street. I try to remember why I called back, but the reasons just swirl around in my head, and I'm starting to feel dizzy from holding my breath.

"Hello?"

It would be so damn easy for me to just speak, to just open my mouth, ask him to come outside, talk things out, maybe even clear the air. Maybe that's the key to all this—just talking it out. And it occurs to me that I don't even know what he looks like anymore. I still picture him as the shy, lanky boy with dark hair and a zip-up hoodie standing on my street corner. It's times like this I wish I had Facebook.

"Hello," he says one more time, and then the line cuts off. I stare up at the window and the light from Max's bedroom flickers off. I scoop up my bag, pull my hood back over my head, and take off down the street.

I'M WALKING, JUST walking, and I end up near the Seaport Diner. It looks pretty empty, so I slip in through the revolving door and seat myself in the far booth. There's a young family at one of the round tables, and a couple of teenagers at another booth, but other than that it's just me, and I'm relieved. I'm not in the mood to see anyone. I've had enough blasts from the pasts today to last me a year.

Yet I can't stop checking my phone. Adam hasn't called back, but part of me wishes he would just text me. It would give me the control I need right now. I've never been a phone person anyway, and I don't get why calls haven't become obsolete.

A thick-waisted waitress comes to take my order, and I realize I recognize her, but it's too late; I've been spotted. "Oh hey," she says. I force a smile. "How's it going?"

"Melanie, hey," I say. Her hair is pinned up in a half-up, half-down bun, and her cheeks are plump and red.

"How are you?" she asks again, and I guess now I have to answer.

"I'm okay," I say.

"I heard you're living in the city. That's so exciting." She speaks in this slow dreamy tone that sort of makes me feel hollow.

"It's not that great," I say. I pretend to read the menu, even though I already know what I'm getting, and I can feel her standing over me, too close, her hot bologna breath filling the space between us.

"You meeting the girls?" she asks, craning her neck toward the entrance, as if my high school posse is about to parade through the front door.

"What girls?"

"You know." She smiles. It's a nervous smile, and it bothers me for some reason. "The girls." She shimmies her shoulders and does a sort of dance. I know she means Rachel, Ally, and company, but I just shrug and go back to staring at the menu. I don't bother saying that I haven't seen "the girls" in years, or that Rachel is dead, *just in case you've been living under a rock, and despite your delusions, I don't actually have a gang of female companions who accompany me on late diner romps.* I'm probably just as lonely as she is.

"No," I say. "Just me." She seems almost disappointed, and I suddenly remember the last time I'd been at a diner. It was with Rachel. And it was the last time I saw her.

"Can I get a glass of red?" I say. "Whatever's cheapest."

"Sure," she says. "Can I just see your ID?" I look up at her, and realize it's the first time I've made eye contact with anyone tonight. She's sweaty and pink and swallows with her mouth open as she waits for me to comply.

"Are you serious?" I say. "You know how old I am." She tilts her head, and I can't tell whether she's embarrassed or reveling in the sudden power shift.

"Restaurant policy," she says. I make a big show fumbling

around for my ID. And as I hold it out for her, tilting my head and mimicking the same overenthusiastic grin from my driver's license photo, she finally drops the R-bomb. "Sucks about Rachel," she says, her voice going an octave lower. "She was an awesome girl."

An awesome girl.

I drop the license on the table. "Didn't she used to call you 'Melons'?" I say. It was fourth grade, and Rachel unsnapped Melanie's bra in front of the entire girls' locker room. She continued to call her "Melons" well into middle school.

"That was a long time ago," she says, swallowing again. She picks up the license and examines it for a bizarre amount of time, her bracelets clanking together around her thick wrist. She hands it back to me, swallows, smiles, and says, "So I guess I'll see you at the after-party?"

I start clicking the buttons on my phone, pretending to text, even though I realize I have nobody to talk to. "I don't think so."

When she brings me my wine—which is served in a plastic glass—she slams it down on the table, and thrusts her shoulder away from me. I eye her as she saunters over toward the hostess and whispers something in her ear.

I finish the wine in two gulps, throw down a ten-dollar bill on the table, and get the hell out of there.

THE NEW GIRLFRIEND'S car is still in the driveway when I get back. I slip in through the back door and go straight to the kitchen for a glass of water. I catch my reflection in the window over the sink—flushed cheeks and a purple-stained mouth.

When I open the cabinet, my stomach plunges to the floor, and everything feels still and limp. I see them, lined up, two rows of five on the bottom shelf.

Everything tastes better in a mason jar.

I'd forgotten about the jars, and how I'd come outside one winter morning to find them in a big white box cradled in Adam's arms. I'd used them as drinking glasses all through high school—way before Pinterest, hipsters, and gastro pubs. Mason jars had been a sort of obsession for me back in high school, but now the sight of them lined up in my mother's kitchen made my throat feel thick, and I wanted to vomit all over the granite.

I stumble into the den, forgetting that Eli is entertaining his lady friend. She stands up when she sees me, as if she'd been waiting all this time to make an introduction.

"Hoiiiiii, Awwwbry, I'm Ashley." Her accent is so thick and so Long Island that I know it can't be real. "It's so nice to meet you." I only catch a glimpse of her but I can tell she's got red hair, like Eli, and is wearing a Nassau Community College sweatshirt.

"Hi," I say, and nod at Eli, who's still sprawled out on the couch and looks stoned out of his mind.

"Where were you tonight? Mom's been asking a million questions."

"About what?"

He puts on his best Karen impression. " 'Where did your sister go? Did you talk to your sister yet? What's wrong with your sister? Why is your sister so sketchy?' You know. The usual." Ashley laughs uncomfortably, until she realizes that I'm not really amused.

I shrug. "I went out." He nods at me and sits up, planting his bare feet on the carpet.

"I ran into Adam," he says, so casual, and I instinctively catch my breath again.

"What? When?" He reaches into a bag of Doritos and stuffs a handful in his mouth, before wiping his hand on his basketball shorts.

"Earlier today at the bagel place," he says through a full mouth of chips, spitting bits of nacho dust.

"What did he say?" Ashley looks between us, as if she expects one of us to explain who Adam is, but I just stare down at Eli, waiting for an answer as he swallows.

"I don't know. Just asked me if I heard about Rachel."

"Did he ask about me?" I start, but Ashley cuts in.

"So sad. I heard she was a really cool girl." I catch myself midscoff, but it's too late, and this Ashley girl looks pretty embarrassed, but I don't have time to deal with this, so I smile, obnoxiously, and turn toward my room.

A really cool girl.

Chapter 8

August 2005.

MAX'S BODY WAS found almost exactly one month after he kissed me. He was my first and only kiss at the time, and it had been the last time I ever saw him alive.

The deli was pretty empty the morning they found him. Rachel and I hadn't been back to the Jumps since that day. She said she was just being elusive, didn't want to come off as desperate and immature. But I think one of the senior girls must have warned her to back off—that or she'd been too embarrassed to admit that Jason had never called her.

A rush of cold air hit us as we walked through the door. The girl behind the counter was in Marc's grade. I think they dated once. I flashed her a phony smile and noticed her eyes were raw and watery, like she'd been crying. Rachel scanned an issue of *Cosmo*, and I placed Strawberry Crush in front of the register.

"That it?" she asked, snapping her gum. I nodded, but when she tried to ring it up, the bar code wouldn't scan. She tried twice more, flashed me an annoyed smile, and went to get the owner.

"Hey," Rachel whispered, when the girl was out of sight. "Dare me to take these?" she asked, holding up a handful of Blow Pops.

"Are you insane?"

She raised her eyebrows in that Rachel way and shoved them in her shorts. At that moment the owner came out from behind the cans of pineapple juice. Rachel's face hardened as the man approached.

"Hey, girls," he said. He went to the other side of the counter and started typing numbers into the register. "Sorry about that," he said, handing me the Crush. Rachel stood stiffly behind, her hands cupped over the front of her shorts. The girl cashier came back and stood beside the manager and wiped her eyes with her sleeve.

I looked over at Rachel, and she shrugged.

"I guess you heard about Max, huh, Lex?" The voice came from behind us, where another guy in Marc's grade placed a bag of chips and a Coke on the counter.

The guy—I think his name was Pete—talked over us to the crying cashier as she rang up his bag of Doritos. She shook her head, wiped her eyes again, and he turned to us. "You guys know Max Sullivan? You know he was found dead today?

Saying it was probably a suicide." His name staggered on my tongue for a moment, in my mind, like I couldn't quite place him, as if he were some has-been heartthrob, once plastered all over my bedroom walls. "Right in the park."

The scent of smoke and perfume lingered as we came out onto Jackson Avenue and the heat made my whole body ache.

"That was close," Rachel said. I stared at the cracked sidewalk. She pulled the handful of lollipops out of her shorts and stuffed them into her bag. "And can you believe it? I can't believe Max is dead," she said, almost in the same breath. "You like made out with him, remember?"

The news hit me with a dull thud. The words swirled in the heat and felt hazy, and I felt hazy, and everything was just hazy: Rachel's voice, Max's death, our first kiss, my second cigarette. Rachel and I stood out on the hot asphalt, dizzy from the sun and news and fear. It felt like a dream, a dull, deafening dream.

"God, Aub," Rachel said. "You must have been a really shitty kisser."

WE DECIDED TO go to the wake. We sat in the back, wearing black silk scarves we stole from Karen; Rachel always had a flair for the dramatic. I couldn't help feeling like a funeral crasher, but it seemed the whole town had shown up. Max's body was set down in the open casket at the front of the room, his freckles muddled beneath a cakey layer of foundation, and his black hair styled in a wispy pouf. His family decided to bury him in his prom tuxedo. I guess that was his fanciest occasion, up until his funeral. How fucking depressing. His popped collar covered the markings on his neck.

I walked up to the casket, signed the cross, and imagined moving the collar aside and fingering the bruises that tracked across his Adam's apple, tracing the freckled white skin of his neck down to the gold crucifix that rested upon his unmoving chest. I could not remember the color of his eyes.

The Younger Sullivan—that's what we called him then— was our age. He went to the Catholic school in our town, so we didn't know much about him. Actually we knew literally nothing about him, except for that he was Max's younger brother. He stood stone-faced against the back wall, his suit pants too short, exposing a pair of black dress socks. I guess no one ever really has time to buy a new suit for a funeral. His eyes were fixed in the direction of his brother's casket. Green and white flowers, our school colors, decorated the area around the body.

A funeral is really the only occasion when it is appropriate to give a guy flowers. They're given to women all the time— first dates, the birth of a child, weddings. They're a symbol of love, given for every important event, right up until death, and even after a person is buried in the ground. It's the only gift you can really ever give a corpse, and people do it all the time. That's why I never understood guys who gave flowers on first dates—like, *Hi, I don't know anything about you, but everybody loves flowers. Even dead people!*

I watched as a few distant aunts and uncles approached the surviving brother—the women going in for a lingering embrace, their respective men offering a halfhearted pat on the shoulder. But in any encounter, his arms hung limp at his sides, his gaze vacant. When he was alone, he reached into his pocket, his wrist twisting against his pant fabric as he fidgeted.

I hadn't noticed at first, but I caught sight of Tonya sitting with her mom in the back of the room. I squinted, trying to see if she'd been wearing my ring. A small part of me wished I could ask for it back. Not because I didn't want Tonya to have it, but because Karen had asked me several times over the past month what happened to it. I didn't feel like explaining I'd drunkenly given it to Tonya Szalinski.

I started looking around the room for Rachel, when I watched the Younger Sullivan slip out the side exit. I slunk out close behind, hoping that I'd catch Rachel out back, smoking a cigarette with some of Max's friends, but when I pulled the door shut behind me and stepped outside, there was just Adam, leaning against the side porch. He shifted his weight away from the railing when he saw me, and I noticed the chalky, white, chipped paint had left the slightest stain on his navy suit jacket. There was no Rachel in sight, and I was standing face-to-face with the dead boy's brother. I didn't really have a choice but to try and strike up a conversation.

"Hi," I said.

His chest rose with breath as if he were about to speak, but just as quickly, he sank back into his slouched stance.

"Sorry about your brother," I said.

His jaw tightened, locking in his words, the muscles protruding just beneath his ears. His cold, gray eyes stared past me at the moths floating beneath the motion-sensor lights.

"You're a freshman this year, too, right?" I asked, feeling incredibly awkward. "Are you going to Seaport or St. Christopher's?" He took another deep breath, but stopped himself before the words could leave him.

"Look," I said. "You don't have to say anything. But I'm really sorry, and if you need someone to talk to, I live just over there." I pointed to the direction of my street, not that he'd have any clue where my house was, but it was a gesture and that was enough.

ON THE FIRST day of high school, the Younger Sullivan stood at the corner of my street—a blue, zip-up hoodie hugging his skinny arms and a saggy backpack slung over one shoulder. He was shy, raising his hand awkwardly at me, with an embarrassed half smile. He had black shaggy hair, and this cool, blue tone to his skin and lips, like he'd been out in the snow too long.

"Thought you might want someone to walk with," he said, nothing like the mute, broken boy I had met the week before.

So that's how it happened, Adam and me. And after all those years, he never even knew that I had kissed his dead brother.

Chapter 9

Monday, October 6, 2014.

I'M SORRY FOR *your loss.*

The response I get from Jonathan this morning. It's been almost twenty-four hours, but I guess I haven't bothered to check my in-box since I left for Long Island yesterday anyway. I wasn't expecting anything more. His e-mails are as detached as his managing skills, and I don't hate it, at least in this situation. But most times, it's just frustrating. I'll take five minutes to type up a thoughtful e-mail, minding the details, making sure to use just the right amount of professionalism with a touch of conversation—so I don't sound too eager. But whether I write a five-hundred-word paragraph or a simple question, he always responds with a curt one, two—or in the *I'm sorry for your loss* case—five-word definitive sentence.

Jonathan's got a thing for passive-aggressive periods. Even this one comes off as totally condescending. He's a big guy, with a heavyset chest, balding and always in a baseball hat. If I didn't know any better, I'd describe him as jolly, but his tone and use of the period just feel menacing.

> Me: Hi Jonathan! Just letting you know that I stayed late to make the Third Avenue fire edits. I think it came out well—given the deadline. It's attached. Please let me know what you think, and let me know if you need me to do anything else. I'm happy to stay late again!

> Jonathan: Thanks.

> Me: Hi Jonathan! I'm really sorry, but I'm not going to be able to finish the article tonight. I have the flu and need to head home. Please let me know if that's okay. Again, so sorry!

> Jonathan: Feel better.

> Me: Hi. Please see article I wrote on the dog park mugger. Let me know if it's okay to post.

> Jonathan: Do better.

I'm up early. It's a workday, after all, so I guess my body's just tuned to waking up at seven. I don't get dressed, though. That's the nice part about being here. I stay in my glasses, yoga pants, and throw a flannel robe over my ribbed tank top and set up on my backyard deck. Karen and Eli are still sleeping, but I can see into the kitchen in case my mother decides to rise and sneak up on me. I could get used to this. It's nice not having to drag myself down five flights of stairs just to get a cup of lukewarm coffee and risk getting spat on by the crazy homeless bitch on my corner.

My laptop rests on the glass patio table. I think about replying to Jonathan, offering some sort of explanation, but I'm not sure how one responds to *I'm sorry for your loss.* Do you say thanks? Do you let him know it's all right, we weren't very close anyway, or would he then turn around and tell me to get my ass back to work? Honestly, what I'd really like to say is something along the lines of *My loss? So now it's my loss? I haven't lost anything. Everything I lost happened a long time ago. There's no loss here. Nope. If anything, I'd call it a gain!*

I wonder what kind of response that would elicit from big old, jolly Johnny boy.

Okay.
See you next week.
Feel better.

I bring a mug of coffee to my lips. It's a Looney Tunes mug from Six Flags and must be ten years old, at least. I inhale— drop of skim, no sugar, sprinkle of cinnamon. There's something unsettling about autumn on Long Island. It's like the air is too thin, too perfect, too quiet. I even find the distant sound of a lawn mower unnerving.

So I gulp the coffee, taking a moment to just appreciate

the scene around me—the canal, the robin's-egg sky, the grass for a change. We don't get much grass in the city, not unless you make the trek to Central Park. It's not too bad of a walk from where we are, but on those sunny days, it's hard to find an untouched spot of grass without some obnoxious family picnicking within arms' reach. I lean back in my chair, stare at a metal rowboat bobbing against our neighbors' dock, but I don't relax. I'm starting to think that I just don't know how. I click out of Jonathan's e-mail and hover the mouse over the Google search box in the corner of the screen. It always starts like this—the hollow feeling in my gut, my blood buzzing like crazy. It's probably the most bizarre addiction that I'll never admit to anyone.

I type in his name. A few pictures come up—an old college lacrosse profile, Facebook, an article from the local paper naming those enlisted in the marines, army, etc. There's a mug shot from somewhere outside of Florida, but it's just a DUI. I know because I've searched the name too many times to count, each time hoping that some scandalous arrest would pop up on the screen. Some girl coming forward on a forum, calling him out as the piece of shit that he is. But maybe he's not. And maybe I'm wrong. I pick up my coffee too fast and the mug slips out of my hands, coffee splattering all over my lap.

"I THOUGHT I'D make dinner tonight."

I'm in my room—ex-room—with my back to the door when Karen's voice hits me from behind. "That's fine," I say.

"Anything special you're in the mood for?" She stands in the doorframe.

"Not really." I stand over my laptop, pretending to check my e-mail.

"Did you meet Ashley?" she asks.

"Who?"

"Eli's girlfriend. She's really very nice."

"Oh, right. She's okay," I say.

"I invited her tonight," she says, and I realize now this isn't just a casual family dinner, and the idea of socializing, even if it's with Eli's obnoxious girlfriend, makes me want to crawl between my sheets and fake the flu—which is already one of my backup plans for Thursday.

I wish my mom would get a hobby, and by hobby, I mean boyfriend. She doesn't date much, and she only brought a man home once, when I was in ninth or tenth grade. He took my mother, brothers, and me to Massapequa Bowl for a family Sunday-funday. He ordered a pitcher of root beer. I remember thinking that was weird.

I check my phone again. Adam hasn't called back. Danny hasn't called either. And I'm not sure which bothers me more.

Karen steps into the room and places a crumbling shoe box on my bed. "I found these in my closet," she says. "I thought you might like to have them."

I wait until she leaves to open the box, and the first thing I see is Rachel's gap-toothed grin beaming up into the sun. She looks about nine or ten, and her arm is draped around my slouched shoulder. I'm smiling, too. It was a Halloween parade. We'd dressed as hippies. We both wore blond wigs that fell to our butts and blue, tinted peace-sign sunglasses.

She wasn't all bad. On her good days, Rachel could make

me feel really special, and the girls in this photo were best friends. Sometimes I forget that. She never missed a chance to tell me that either—to constantly remind me that I was her best friend. Best friend. I was all she had, she'd say.

I heard Rachel talk about her family like that once, and that was only when I'd walked in on her sobbing over my bathroom sink when we were thirteen. We'd been having dinner at my house—pork chops and applesauce—and she'd gotten up abruptly in the middle of a conversation on how much I hated pork chops and applesauce. I hadn't realized there'd been an issue until Karen nudged me in the shoulder.

I had assumed Rachel locked the door, so my plan was to knock twice and wait thirty seconds before halfheartedly rattling the doorknob. Then I would report back to my mother that I'd at least made an effort and go back to picking apart my loathsome pork chop. But the door creaked open just as I was getting ready to pull back and walk away. Rachel had obviously wanted me to walk in on this scene, but she acted startled, splashed water over her face, and smiled through the tears.

I never could stand when people cried around me. It was never a secret. There was never anything that made me feel more uncomfortable and useless. And Rachel knew this, so when she saw me easing my way back out into the hallway, she reached out and pulled me toward her.

"You're my best friend, Aub. You know that?" I nodded, my body stiff in her embrace. "You're the only person who gives a shit about me," she said. "My mom wishes I were dead."

"Why would you say that?" I managed to mumble.

"She doesn't have to say anything, Aubrey. I'm not an idiot.

I see the way they look at me and the way they look at Chloe. You've seen it, too. I know you have." She splashed more water on her face, and I put my hand on her shoulder awkwardly. "You're so lucky to have your mom," she said. "Fuck my family, Aubrey. You're my family."

I bend the photo in my hands and wonder how such a young girl could hold so much power, how she could simultaneously make me feel so needed and so useless. I take a hard gulp of wine and scoff to myself, feeling a little bit like a survivor of battered-wife or Stockholm syndrome. *I survived. I survived Rachel Burns.* I should have a T-shirt made or claim my own color of a Livestrong bracelet. It would have to be black, like Rachel's soul.

It's easy to see now, how crafty Rachel had been with words, playing off my emotions, ever-so-elegantly tipping the scale of power in her favor. And yet, I continued to make excuses for the girl. Especially with Adam.

I don't understand why you're friends with her, he'd say. *Why do you let her talk to you like that?*

You wouldn't understand, I'd say. *That's why you have no friends.*

I thought you were my friend.

I'm your girlfriend. That's not the same thing.

Chapter 10

September 2005.

FIRST FRIDAY WAS a tradition in Seaport. It was on a level with homecoming, graduation, maybe even prom. On the first Friday of the new school year, the new seniors would throw a blowout. Location was a direct correlation between the social stature of the individual and the size of his or her family home. So the hotter you were, and the bigger your house, the better your chances of hosting the First Friday of your senior year. And that was a big deal. If you hosted First Friday, you could basically have your pick of fresh meat or senior ass for the rest of your high school career.

There were impostor versions around town, of course, and they took the form of low-key gatherings in smoky garages with cans of Bud and not enough cheese and crackers. But there was always only one real First Friday. And if you were a

freshman, then your level of sluttiness that night pretty much
determined your reputation for the next four years.

That first, First Friday was thrown by Jason Dowd, who
opened his sprawling three-story estate on the marina up
to the class of 2003 and the brave underclassmen who dared
to show up. Earlier that summer, I'd survived Freshman
Friday—a traditional day of hazing for the incoming freshmen on the last Friday of the school year. I'd gone with Ally
Marlo, and about twelve other girls in my grade, but Rachel
managed to dodge the day altogether, which didn't sit well
with the new seniors. It wasn't terrible. We were blindfolded,
loaded into the back of a truck, and dumped off at Clear Pond
Park, where we ran laps around the baseball field while the
senior girls doused us in mayonnaise, threw garbage at us,
and called us filthy, freshman sluts. The boys in our grade
had it much worse. Marc's friends spent the summer driving around, trawling the streets for freshmen, and when they
found them, they'd slam the shit out of their asses with a
paddle.

At the party, I took a drag of Rachel's cigarette while a
group of us freshmen stood on the dock. I held a Solo cup to
my lips, my arms crossed tightly across my chest. The September air was thick, humid, and smelled like wet wood and ash. I
could already feel my hair frizzing, sticking to the sweat on my
back, so I tied it back in a low ponytail.

I'll never forget the feeling of my first, real high school
party—the way my blood buzzed through my veins, the feeling of not knowing, of having absolutely no fucking clue
who I'd be for the next four years. I had an idea, though. I'd

announced to Rachel and Ally that I intended to stay single through high school—that I would not be tied down by any of the lackluster options in our town. A bold statement, because I think I was just worried no one would date me anyway. But as I stood on the dock, on that First Friday, passing the cigarette back to Rachel, I secretly hoped that some stubble-faced senior, on the verge of manhood, had already spotted my glistening back sweat from across the yard and had been so struck by my grace that he was already plotting our first kiss.

"What is this?" I asked, staring down into my cup—an endless pool of neon-red liquid that could only be vodka and Robitussin.

"Jungle Juice," Rachel cut in. "Pretty nasty, huh? Diane drinks it all the time." I raised my eyebrows at Ally and we shared a knowing smirk. Rachel had always used Diane to make herself seem a little less inexperienced. It had become somewhat of a running joke between Ally and me: *Blow jobs? . . . Diane showed me this awesome technique on a banana like five years ago. Cocaine? . . . How else would Diane stay so thin? What do you mean you never heard of Jungle Juice? . . . Why, Diane invented Jungle Juice!*

Neither Ally nor I had ever actually ever met this Diane. She was a legend—like Bigfoot or the Loch Ness Monster.

"So, ladies," Rachel said. Pulling our attention back to her. At some point when we weren't looking, she had situated herself at the center of the semicircle. "Who is everyone going for tonight? This is our night to lock our boys down." Her smile lingered as she swayed her head from side to side, making sure to include each of us in the conversation. That was one thing

Rachel was good at, making everyone feel comfortable around her. Must have made it easier for her to run the show.

"Aubrey here has sworn off men for the next four years." She winked at me, and she touched my shoulder, a gesture that felt oddly soothing. "Probably because the last guy she hooked up with hanged himself."

I felt my stomach twist, Ally and the other girls stifled a laugh, shaking their heads to feign disapproval, as if that made it somehow okay. Sasha Coyle crossed her pudgy arms over her chest and smiled up at me, her eyes cast down at her feet.

Sasha was Ally's new sidepiece. She was a hefty girl, who made up for it with an expensive wardrobe and a willingness to share her father's credit card. It was depressing to watch, but she seemed happy to be a part of the group.

"But," Rachel went on, "I think this is my year with Eric."

Rachel believed every year was her year with Eric Robbins, ever since he taught us what a virgin was back on Ms. Price's Magic Carpet. I never saw anything in him, even before he went and fucked everything up for us. He was a year older, stocky, freckled, with a space between his two front teeth that sort of made him look like a comic-strip character. But Rachel had been obsessed with him. Maybe it was his douche-y and aloof demeanor. Maybe it was his coveted spot on the lacrosse team that appealed to her. I couldn't tell you. I didn't see it.

"Well, I was thinking I'd try and go for a senior. Jason is kind of hot," Ally said, shrugging all cool and effortless.

"Yeah, right," Rachel said. "Never gonna happen." She laughed—a lascivious sound that prompted matching scowls from two senior girls on the other side of the dock.

"Take a picture," Rachel called out, before leaning back into our circle and muttering, "Bitches."

The other girls didn't know this, but Rachel had hooked up with Jason that day on the mattress in the woods. She'd drunk his tequila, and he'd felt her up and never spoken to her again—clearly not something to brag about.

"Who knows," Ally said, ignoring the senior girls. "Maybe I'll get lucky if I put out." She leaned forward and pressed her breasts together, exposing awkward, not quite developed cleavage. I looked up at Rachel, it was subtle, but something flickered in her eyes. I couldn't place it. "But I feel so bad for him," Ally went on, suddenly going all solemn. "I mean his best friend killed himself this summer." Rachel crossed her arms over her chest and took a sip of jungle juice, the look in her eyes fading, and then I knew. *Rejection.* It was Jason's rejection.

"Do you know what I heard?" Ally leaned in, her voice going real low. She looked around as if anyone else cared enough to listen in. "Well, I heard my dad on the phone, saying that some girl's father accused Max and Jason of, you know, taking advantage of her." She looked around again, all coy and shifty. "You know. Like right before Max killed himself." Ally's father was a cop, so her story could have been plausible, but that girl was always overhearing *something* he said on the phone to *someone.*

"Shut the fuck up," Rachel said, pushing Ally's shoulder. "Who said that? Who was the girl? Like take advantage how?"

"I don't know. I don't know." Ally shook her head, a huge grin splashed across her face, loving every moment of our eyes on her. "But then he killed himself. Like, who would say something like that? It's probably not even true."

"Probably some desperate slut," Rachel cut in. "Like some people need to get a fucking life." She shot another glance over at the seniors who had clearly already forgotten about her.

"Most of the time, it's not even true," Ally said matter-of-factly, like she was declaring there was no Easter Bunny.

"I mean I think it's mostly bullshit," Rachel said. "But Diane's friend said she knew this girl who was raped at college in like a parking garage or something."

Ally's face suddenly went all horrified. "I mean yeah. That's legit. But whoever said that about Max and Jay, I mean, she must have known them, right? So it couldn't have been *real* rape."

I HAVE ABOUT a million and one regrets. It's hard to prioritize them. I can't lay them all out in a neat little binder to go back to for reference on days I'm feeling particularly nostalgic. It doesn't work like that. Instead, they're all jumbled up in an awful knot, tangled together in my head, and when I think about them, I feel like I'm stroking out. I see spots, and all the blood rushes out of my face, right down into the pit of my chest.

I think that's technically the definition of anxiety. At least that's my definition. To me, anxiety is when my mind betrays my body, like I'm about to collapse in on myself. It starts in my chest, I get a dizzy feeling behind my eyes, my hands tingle. But when I think back to certain moments in my life, it's this conversation that sits on my tongue, an acrid, putrid taste; and I'm still waiting to spit out the words.

It's probably not even true. Get a fucking life.

I remember the conversation. I remember standing there, listening, appalled as the words flowed from their overglossed lips, nodding their heads at each other, sick smiles splashed across their faux-bronzed faces. I remember that guilty twist of my stomach, before I really knew what it had meant to feel guilty, and I listened, but I didn't say anything. Instead, I just stared down at my Jungle Juice.

I hear it reverberating through my veins as if from a megaphone.

It doesn't count. It isn't real. Desperate slut.

I HAD CONSIDERED telling the girls about Adam, but the conversation about Max and Jason and the mystery accusation sort of stole the show. Though, knowing Rachel, she'd be more shocked to know that I'd been walking to school every day with the Younger Sullivan than that his older brother was accused of some sort of assault.

I didn't expect to see Adam at the party. I felt like he didn't even really exist outside of our walks. It had only been a week, but I still never saw him in school, in the halls, in any classes. It was like he'd escort me to the main doors and then dissolve, just dissolve until 6 A.M. the following day, where he would be waiting like a loyal puppy—blue hoodie, empty backpack slung over one shoulder, and a halfhearted wave.

It was only when I left the dock to refill my drink that I saw him. He was standing next to the keg, talking to a sophomore guy. The sophomore talked with his hands, and only after seeing this interaction did I notice something about Adam. He never spoke with his hands, and it seemed so bizarre to me. I hadn't noticed when it had just been the two of us on our walk, but I saw it then, the way his hands hung limp at his sides, the way he spoke with an elegant grace. Adam had a calm energy about him, the kind that didn't warrant unnecessary gestures. I squinted in his direction. He looked taller. He nodded at me. I waved and walked away, toward the inside of the house.

I caught my reflection in the sliding glass doors while I shouldered my way back from the bathroom. My lips, teeth, and tongue were neon red. I stuck my tongue out to examine my reflection when I felt someone behind me.

"Nice mouth, Glass," he said. I spun around, and Adam stood there, his hands in his jean pockets. His shoulders were broad, but he was still skinny, scrawny even, like he hadn't grown into his limbs yet.

"So you do know my name?" We had walked together all week, but I couldn't remember ever telling him my name, and I couldn't remember him ever using it.

"Of course I do," he said. "You think I just walk random girls to school and don't even know their names? What kind of guy do you take me for?"

I opened my mouth to speak but let out a dumb laugh instead. I fidgeted with the cup in my hand.

"So you like that stuff?" he asked, nodding toward my newly refilled drink. He seemed ignited by the alcohol, in control, and handsome up close—something I hadn't noticed about him until that moment.

"It's not terrible, but it would be better out of a mason jar." I lifted the red cup toward him and immediately felt like an idiot for referencing mason jars.

"Mason jars, huh?" he said. "That could get expensive, especially with a bunch of clumsy freshmen who can't hold their liquor." He flexed his jaw and then let up with this crooked grin. "I mean can't you just see shattered glass everywhere?" As he said it, he pulled his hands out of his pockets and flung them outward, knocking my plastic cup to the ground. The glowing red juice splattered up off the cement, leaving pink stains on the bottom of his jeans. He didn't flinch, just kept on grinning, his arms still extended at his sides.

"Shit," I said, leaning down to pick up my cup and assess the damage to his jeans. His one hand gesture of the night, and of course he spills my drink everywhere. *Overcompensating much?* I wanted to say, but instead I just stared at the ground and began to apologize for the mess he made.

"Why are you sorry?" he deadpanned. "I did it on purpose. You know, to prove a point." I sucked in air through my nostrils, and a part of me wished I still had some of the drink left, so I could throw it in his face. I noticed then how white his teeth were. Maybe I only noticed against the contrast of his red-stained lips.

"Your jeans, though," I said. "They're ruined." No one else at the party seemed to notice our dramatic spillage.

"Don't worry about it, Glass," he said. "You know, you have crazy green eyes. Has anyone ever told you that?"

I shrugged. "Haven't heard that, no," I lied. He was still holding eye contact, his own gray eyes wide.

"So, don't you want to find your friends?" he asked, after several uncomfortable seconds of nothing.

I didn't, I said, and so we walked toward the waterfront. His lanky arms swung in sync with his legs. We stopped at a metal swing set nestled on the asphalt behind a row of covered-up boats.

He reached into his shirt pocket, pulled out a single Camel Light, and held it out toward me.

I shook my head. "No. Thanks. I don't smoke."

He cocked his head at me. "Well, neither do I," he said. "I saw you smoking with your friend, so I just assumed." He seemed relieved.

"Sorry," I said. "That was Rachel's. I was only taking a drag."

"Well, it's too bad, because I paid Jason three dollars for this thing." He held it up and flicked it into the water. The water rippled, and the cigarette lay, a limp, wet thing.

My lips went numb, and I started to feel the Jungle Juice flowing through me.

"So, Miss Glass," Adam said. "What's your favorite movie?"

"What's my favorite movie?" I looked at him, not really sure how to answer, not even sure if I had a favorite movie. "Is that what you ask all the girls?"

"Yes," he said. "Well, what is it?"

"What's your favorite movie?" I asked.

"Do you always answer a question with a question?"

"Yes," I said. "Do you?"

He flashed his teeth. "My favorite movie is *Homeward Bound.*"

"Like the dogs?" I asked, trying to hold back my laugh.

"And the cat. Don't forget about the cat." He looked so serious, and it was making me anxious. I needed him to smile, to laugh, something. "Sassy," he said. "Remember?"

"Okay," I said. "I can respect that." He squinted one eye at me, like he was taking aim. *The Breakfast Club*," I said. "That's my favorite movie."

He nodded. "I can respect that."

"What do you hate?" he asked. We were standing a few feet apart, neither of us knowing what to do with our hands.

"What do you mean what do I hate? What kind of question is that?" I said.

"There you go again with the questions," he said. "What do you hate? Who do you hate? There's got to be one thing or one person who you just can't stand." He gritted his teeth and scrunched up his face.

I took my hair out of the ponytail and ran my fingers through.

"Anne Hathaway," I said. "I hate Anne Hathaway. I don't know what it is. But there's something about her I can't get behind."

"Who's Anne Hathaway?" he asked. "Does she go to our school?" I shook my head and let out a dry, raspy laugh.

"No. She was in that movie *The Princess Diaries*. Rachel made me see it. It was pretty awful."

Adam nodded, stifling a smile. "Can't say that I've seen that one. But, God, you're pretentious."

"And you?" I asked.

"And me, what?" he said.

"What do you hate?"

"I don't hate anything," he said. "I'm not a psychopath." He spun around and walked over toward the swing. I stood with my hands across my chest. "What do you love?"

I sucked in a breath and realized I had no idea how to answer that. I loved my family, even if I made it a point not to tell them. I loved my friends. I loved the beach. But none of those things seemed like the right answer, so I said the first thing that came to mind: "Mason jars."

"Mason jars," he repeated. "What is with you and mason jars? God, you're weird."

I shrugged. I'd been begging Karen to switch out our drinking glasses for mason jars, but she refused. She said it was trashy.

"Everything is better in a mason jar," I said. "Seriously, think about it. You go to a restaurant, and you order a lemonade or an iced tea, and it comes in a mason jar. How excited are you?"

He half laughed and shook his head. "I don't know, Glass. I still think it's weird. Maybe you should consider changing your last name to Mason—you know instead of Glass." He shifted his gaze toward his pink-stained jeans.

"You know, I wasn't really expecting you to be like this," I said. The September air was still around us. Everything was still but the soft ripples in the canal.

"Be like what? Charming? Dapper?" He ran his finger over the chain and looked the swing up and down, assessing his next move.

"So talkative," I said. "You're usually so quiet."

"I'm not a morning person." His voice seemed to trail off as he looked up toward the metal pole, and then he looked at me, his gray eyes flickered with a cold, hard stare, and then just as quickly, the intensity dissipated and he was staring back up at the pole. I felt a chill, and not the romantic, gushy kind when a boy looks at a girl for the first time.

"Favorite show?" he asked. I was beginning to think he'd memorized a list of first-date questions before he'd left his house that night.

"Current or of all time?"

"Of all time."

"*Friends,*" I said. "Obviously."

"Obviously," he said. "But *Seinfeld* is better." He hopped up onto the swing. "Obviously," he said again. His sneakers pressed against the seat, and his arms stretched up toward the chains. "Sorry," he said, "but *Friends* isn't funny."

"I don't really think *Seinfeld* is funny."

"You just don't get the humor," he said, buckling his knees and picking up speed.

"What does that mean?"

"You see," he said. "You have to be intelligent to appreciate the humor in *Seinfeld. Friends?* That's mindless humor for dumb people. Like yourself. It's not realistic. Those apartments? Please. Don't they have jobs?" Before I could protest, or even register the fact that he just called me dumb, he swung through the air, let go of the chains, and landed hard on his feet, right in front of me.

"Okay," I said, pushing my hands into his chest. "Now who's being pretentious?"

"One more question," he said. "How do you take your coffee?"

"Guess," I said. He stood close. Too close. His shaggy black hair fell over his cold, gray eyes. He smelled like fruit punch and laundry detergent, and he rested his hand under my chin, and the first thing I noticed were his clean and perfectly clipped fingernails. I could hear my mother's voice pounding in my head as the seconds ticked away between us. *Clean fingernails and clean ears. Those are the first things to always look for.*

His hand stayed under my chin, and he brushed his thumb over my bottom lip, back and forth. He leaned in. I closed my eyes and braced myself for the kiss, my second kiss. I could feel his face close to mine, and then he leaned in once more and blew an icy breath into my ear. I could still feel his cool breath on my face when Rachel came barreling around the corner.

"I've been looking everywhere for you, slut," she slurred, and swung her hips from side to side as she walked toward us. She's been rehearsing that line in her head since the moment she realized I'd snuck off. I could just tell. She still held an overflowing Solo cup, and the neon-red liquid sloshed over the top as she stumbled toward us. She stopped in her tracks when she realized I wasn't alone. "Oh, hi," she said, peering through the darkness at Adam. The cool, confident Adam I'd just been talking to dissolved once again, and he nodded awkwardly at Rachel before making an abrupt exit back to the party.

I put my hands over my face to hide my smirk from Rachel.

"Um, what the fuck was that?" she asked, slapping me in the small of my shoulder. "Were you making out with the Younger Sullivan?" Her mouth hung open, waiting for my response.

"No. We were not making out. We were talking."

"Uh-huh," she said, her eyes wide.

"I swear. But I'm not saying we wouldn't have if you hadn't just come barging in here, you ho."

"Does he know you made out with his dead brother?" The look of sheer excitement on her face was disturbing to say the least.

"Um, no. It didn't come up." I shot her a *what the hell is wrong with you look*, and she shrugged. "And I don't anticipate it ever coming up."

ON MONDAY, THINGS went back to normal—shy Adam with his sagging backpack and blue hoodie. Only this time, he had a coffee in each hand when I met him at the corner.

"Splash of skim, sprinkle of cinnamon," he said, handing me the paper cup.

"How—" I started, but he cut me off.

"Since you were so sketchy about your coffee preference, I went ahead and guessed. Was I close?"

"Except for the cinnamon," I said. "I don't usually do that."

"Well, try it," he said. "I think you'll like it. And I take mine with cream, sugar, and cinnamon," he said. "FYI." He smiled, and the warm scent tangled between us. It was at that moment I began associating the smell of coffee and cinnamon with Adam Sullivan.

BY OCTOBER, I'D transformed into a morning person. I found myself looking forward to our walks and our coffees and just being. We didn't talk about much, just about the leaves, and classes, and what we'd watched on television the night before. But there was something about falling into step with Adam that got me out of bed each morning and gave me something to look forward to. I couldn't pinpoint it, and I still wasn't sure if I could see him as anything but the Younger Sullivan, but there was something about his serious face, and every time he cracked a smile around me, I'd claim it as a small victory.

Adam did actually smell like coffee, it wasn't just that I'd come to associate him with it. Coffee and cinnamon. And even though I started to drink the same concoction every day, it was his scent, not mine. It clung to him, and not like coffee breath either, but like the sweet smell of a freshly brewed pot emanating from his striped blue-and-gray sweater. I wanted to wrap myself in him. He looked cold, but warm, all at once. I walked beside him and sipped my coffee. The autumn wind swept dried leaves at our feet.

And then one late, gray October morning, he didn't show up. I waited ten minutes and then went on my way. I hadn't realized how much I'd been counting on him to start my day.

And for the rest of that week, he was MIA.

"WHY THE FACE?" Rachel said. She fell into step with me on the way to first period. She wore flip-flops and a denim miniskirt that crept dangerously close to her crotch. It was almost November.

"Nothing," I said. "Just haven't had coffee yet." She eyed me, jutted her arm through my elbow, and segued into our plans for the weekend. Jason Dowd was having a Halloween party.

"I'm going as a slutty pirate," she said. "You should come as my slutty parrot."

I pulled my elbow out from her grip.

"Come on, Aub. It's our first Halloween as high schoolers." She pouted.

I mumbled, "We'll see," and walked into class, leaving her out in the hall.

I LEFT MY house on Friday morning in a particularly sour mood. I'd overslept, I was late, and Karen was nagging me about the Halloween party that night.

"It's a senior party, Aubrey, I don't know," she said.

"So? Marc's going," I said. "You let me go to First Friday."

"Yeah, but that's different. That's tradition, like a rite of passage. Don't push it," she said.

I barreled around the corner with my head down, still reeling over Karen's sudden shift in parenting practices, and nearly body-slammed Adam. He stood on the sidewalk in a skeleton zip-up hoodie, with two coffees, and a shit-eating grin on his face.

"Well, well," he said. "You didn't dress up?" I shrugged and walked until he fell into step beside me. I quickened pace and he sped up. "Why no talk?"

"No reason," I said.

"Are you pissed that I bailed all week?"

"No." I took the coffee from him.

"I had a good reason," he said.

"I said, I'm not pissed." I was pissed. And disappointed and annoyed, but I'd always felt it was better to be a bitch than admit my true feelings.

"You are too pissed. I can tell."

"No you cannot tell. Because I'm not."

"Yes, you are," he said. "Your fists are balled up like you're gonna throw down." I looked down at my hands, released my fingers, and took a fierce gulp of coffee.

"So," I said.

"So, what?"

"So, what's your good reason?"

"I was sick."

I raised an eyebrow.

"Okay, fine, I wasn't sick," he said. "It's complicated."

"How's that?"

He let out a nervous laugh and looked down at his hands.

"Well, I sort of made a deal with myself," he said. "It's embarrassing."

"Well, now I really want to know," I said, but I wasn't sure if I did. He seemed nervous. It was awkward and unsettling. I knew that whatever he was about to say would be a game changer.

"So I promised myself I wouldn't walk with you anymore until I was ready to make a move. Because it's actually physically painful to be near you and not have the balls to." He sipped his coffee, and eyed me over the lid.

I took another gulp of coffee, unsure of what to do or say, and then he kissed me. It was awkward, and sloppy, and our teeth clanked together, and he pulled back right away, and began to stutter and apologize. We both tasted of coffee, and Adam's charming exterior had come unhinged in the moment of our first kiss—my second kiss. Without thinking, I put my hand around his neck and pulled him back toward me, pushing my tongue into his mouth. We stood like that, on the sidewalk, one hand gripping our coffees, the other, cupping the nape of each other's neck.

A fat kid in a vampire costume hobbled across the street, hollering and whistling. Adam pulled back and let out another nervous laugh. The leaves swirled around our feet. His shaggy black hair looked almost blue in the sun, I reached up and touched his dimple. He stared at me with those gray eyes.

That night, we ditched the Halloween party, and instead Adam snuck us in to *Saw II*. There hadn't been much movie watching, though. We fumbled at each other in the dark theater, our lips tangling. A college-age couple cleared their throats behind us, and we both broke out into a hysterical fit of giggles. It was only our first night together, and we were already a pathetic cliché. But at the time it didn't feel cheesy, it never does when it's happening to you. It felt real, and when it's real, it rarely feels cliché.

My Nokia buzzed from inside my pocket. Rachel. I forwarded it to voice mail and turned the phone off.

After the movie, he walked me home. The lights illuminated the streets, littered with relics of Halloween—smashed pumpkins, broken eggs, trails of shaving cream and silly string. A couple of straggling trick-or-treaters wandered around in Ghost Face costumes. Adam slipped his hand in my mine and pulled me toward a playground on the other side of the street. He sat on the swing, just like he had that night at First Friday.

He still wore his skeleton zip-up hoodie and an orange mesh hat. His shaggy black hair stuck out around his ears.

"So," he said, and he just said it. No buildup. "How many times am I going to kiss you before I ask you to be my girl-friend?"

I bit my lip, I think to keep from laughing at him, and stood in front of the swing. Gripping the chains, I swung one leg over and straddled him. He looked up at me, a nervous grin set on his face. I felt like for once, I was the one in control. And said, quite possibly, the most vomit-worthy thing that's ever come out of my mouth: "Just once more."

And then he leaned in and pressed his cool lips to mine. And that's how I became Adam's girlfriend.

I still cringe thinking about it.

Chapter 11

Monday, October 6, 2014.

KAREN'S DINNER IS going on as planned, and she's asked me to pick up some things from Pathmark. I've got nothing better to do, so I say okay. She's still trying to feel me out for the funeral, but every time she brings it up, I just shrug and walk out of the room.

Marc will be home for dinner, too. He lives in Long Beach now—just a few miles away, in a house with three roommates, all guys from high school. I don't know how he can stand it. He's twenty-five, and still actually *wants* to be around the people he grew up with.

I throw on some leggings, flats, and a baggy black sweater. It's cooler today—crisp, and the streets are lined with golden trees. A picture of perfect autumn suburbia.

My Saab belonged to one of my Cavanaugh cousins back when I was in middle school, and when he went to Berkeley, it just sat in my uncle's driveway, rotting away. He sold it to my mom for four hundred bucks. I loved that car, but Rachel always insisted on taking the wheel. She had this obnoxious yellow Pathfinder, that she affectionately dubbed "*the Bumble Bee*." She preferred to drive, said it helped her relax. But I'm pretty sure she just preferred control.

Empty Styrofoam coffee cups, a couple of crinkled plastic bottles, and a wad of Dunkin' Donuts napkins litter the floor of my car, and half a pack of Parliaments lay in the center console. I have no idea how long they've been there.

My eyes catch the bottle of five-year-old Listerine wedged into the passenger's-side door, and memory burns through me like a fever. Everything is just the way I left it the last time I'd been home, maybe last Christmas. A cord dangles from the tape deck and attaches to my open Discman, permanent marker scrawled over the top of the CD: *Spring Mix 2009*. I climb in and turn the key. It sputters for three seconds then plateaus into a static hum. Tracy Chapman starts to play through the speakers, and my instinct is to change it, it was our song, Rachel and me, but instead I crank it up. The oversized steering wheel vibrates under my hands. I plug my Black-Berry into the car charger and check for messages—still only one new voice mail. *Rachel.*

I close my eyes, take a sharp breath, think about deleting it, but picture the tiny Polly Pocket–sized Rachel again and throw the phone down on the seat next to me instead.

I strike up my one cigarette for the day just as I'm pulling into the parking lot, swinging the car into a spot near the doors. The lot is empty, and I remember the place looking much bigger as a kid—like this grand plaza at the center of town.

I unfold the shopping list, smooth out the creases, and try not to think about the last time I'd been here. My gaze falls toward the bottle of Listerine—an involuntary twitch—and I snap back to the list in front of me. *Focus. In and out. No bullshit.*

The Parliament dangles from my lips. *Chicken stock, rosemary, shallots.* I read through the list, mapping out the store in my head. I need to get in and out as quickly and efficiently as possible. There's only one supermarket in this town, and I can't risk a run-in. Not today. Smoke streams off the end of the cigarette and settles into the fibers of my sweater. I can feel the scent lingering in my hair, so I reach back and twist it into a messy bun on top of my head. *Six Yukon Gold potatoes, two organic tomatoes, romaine lettuce, cucumbers.* I dust the ash off my sweater and throw on a pair of Ray-Ban aviators before I go in.

The automatic doors glide open, and I push a clunky shopping cart through. A rush of cold air hits me, and I can already tell I grabbed the bum cart. The front right wheel swings at an awkward angle, screeching as it slides across the cheap vinyl.

I tear a plastic bag off the roll and reach for a cucumber, when I hear a shrill sound from behind me.

"Aubrey?"

Fuck.

I stop, and the air punches out of my stomach.

"Oh my God, Aubrey." I recognize the voice instantly—Ally Marlo. I turn around slowly to face her, my skin stretched around an unnatural smile.

She stands there, a glazed sideways smile on her face, like she's trying to drink me all in. She's with a much thinner Sasha Coyle, and they're each holding baskets full of butternut squash. *Be nice. Be nice. Be nice*, I tell myself.

"Hi! Oh my God. How are you guys?" I try to mimic their reactions, that raw enthusiasm that seems to come so damn naturally to everybody else, but I sound like a hyperactive moron, and as the words leave my mouth, and the skin around my mouth stretches harder, I know I'm not fooling them. Maybe it's the smell of day-old produce, the cold, stagnant supermarket air, or what happened the last time I stepped down this aisle five years ago, but I'm standing here, the elasticity of my face about to give out, and I just feel numb. Totally, completely, fucking numb. It spreads over me—still, stale, and empty, like I'm pumped full of helium.

My ears hum. I twist the plastic bag in my hands around the cucumber. All three of us stare at one another. Staring and smiling, like we're trying to outgrin each other. I break eye contact, let my gaze fall back to Ally's basket of gourds, and then feel her arms come down around me.

"I'm so, so sorry about Rachel," Ally says. She's got this baby voice, something that I know too well from high school. "I remember how close you two always were. *We all* always were," she corrects. I stand with my arms stiff at my sides. I don't breathe until she lets go. Her hands linger over my shoulders, though, and she pushes out her bottom lip. "I'm still so shocked." Sasha shakes her head in agreement, her lips all pouty.

"We haven't spoken in years," I lie, and blink nervously until I lose the image of Rachel's face, her final plea, in my head.

Sasha catches me staring at their baskets. "We're trying this new diet," she says. "All we eat is squash for five days. It's supposed to be, like, this new detox." I raise my eyes at her and smile, but I think it comes out more of a grimace, because she shrugs and looks at her feet.

"Sounds cleansing," I say, and I don't mean to, but I think of Rachel again.

She'd be standing here with us, her mouth twisted into that perpetual sneer, and when Ally and Sasha walk away, she'd turn to me and say something like, *God, Aub, butternut squash diet? Sasha didn't lose all that weight with butternut squash. Try trigger diet.* And she'd click her fingers toward her gaping mouth and gag, and then smile. That sweet, sneering, sickly smile. And I'd snicker and shake my head at her, and I would smile, but it would be real, because that's just how it was with Rachel and me. It was real.

Remember when I showed you how? she'd say.

And I'd be fifteen again, with the spins and a belly full of store-brand Cheez-Its and Franzia boxed wine.

You know you can make it stop? she'd said. *I can show you.* The room spun, just like it's spinning now, right in the middle of the produce aisle of Pathmark, but instead we'd be in my bathroom, Rachel holding my hair back—the swill of orange dust and zinfandel turning over in my guts.

Immgonnathrowup, I'd say. *Immgonnathrowup but I can't.*

Yes you can, she'd say. *Like this.* She'd lean down next to me, the sterile bowl smiling up at us, and she'd put two stiff fingers into her mouth. She'd take my own two fingers, limp and cold, and guide them to my throat. I would retch and pull my fingers out.

No, you have to commit to it. Just tickle the back of your throat with the tips of your fingers and don't stop till you puke.

So I'd push my fingers back into my throat, and thrust them against the dangly thing, till I felt the hot Cheez-It paste and cheap wine splash back up at me.

Nice, she'd say, stroking my hair out of my eyes.

The produce aisle comes back into focus. "So," Ally says. "You're going to the funeral, I assume, though, right?"

The cucumber becomes deadweight in my hand. I want to say no. I want to say, *No, Ally, I'm not here for the funeral. There's no place on this earth I'd rather be less than the funeral, except for maybe standing here with you.* But I don't say that. I just smile, and say, "Of course." Her face stretches into an obligatory grin.

"Oh," she says. "I almost forgot to tell you. Sasha, Adam, Eric, Ellie, and I are in charge of the after-party. We could really use your help." Before I can even process the fact that another person has confirmed that this after-party is actually a thing, she's going into all of the grisly details: "It's at O'Reilly's—right after the cemetery. A bunch of us are getting a limo. You can get in on that, but I honestly just don't know if there's any room left. I have to pick up the decorations, the shot glasses—oh my God, we got the cutest shot glasses with her name engraved—you know instead of those stupid prayer cards that everyone throws away anyway. Rachel would have wanted it that way. And oh, oh my God, T-shirts. They are adorable. I had Jimmy screen-print her face onto them."

She pauses and takes a breath. "It's just so intense, planning everything, you know? Like a total mindfuck. But it's going to be so amazing to see everyone."

Her words swirl around me, and I pretend to listen but all I can hear is his name.

"Sounds fun," I say. She clicks her tongue, like I'm totally out of line for using the word "fun" to describe a funeral.

"Oh, it's all for Rachel. It's what she would have wanted."

I smile and nod, and start to think of an excuse to leave, when she's got her arms around me again.

"You know, why don't you come over tonight. We'll have a girls' night. You know? Like old times." Sasha nods way too enthusiastically at her side.

"I really can't," I say. "I've got this dinner thing—"

Before I can finish, she cuts in. "That's fine. We'll wait up. Come by at like ten?" I want to say no. I need to say no. "I'll pick up some vino," she sings, and I'm about to decline, but the pushover in me comes out and I just smile and nod.

I LEAVE MY cart at the end of the aisle and run out to my car as soon as Ally and Sasha are out of sight. I'm in my car, the windows closed, sucking in hot air until I stop seeing those floating black spots in front of my eyes. My hands shake. I hold them in front of me and try to keep steady. I count to three, a trick I learned years ago. I figured out that if I steady my hands for three whole seconds, then the shakes usually fade, and I'm back in control. *One.* I can feel my back drenched beneath my sweater. *Two.* I hold my breath. *Three.* Nothing, so I fumble for a cigarette, my hands still shaking.

"Fuck. Fuck. Fuck," I say, and then, "Breathe. Breathe. Breathe." It actually helps to say the word, even if it means I'm not actually breathing. I roll the window down with my free hand, a cigarette dangling from my lips, and scrape the bottom of my bag for a lighter. The tips of my fingers graze crumpled receipts, lip balm, but no lighter. "Fuck," I say again, and then a bottle rattles from inside my bag—the Xanax. I look over my shoulder out the back window. Sasha and Ally would still be shopping, buying out all the squash in the place, but I can't stop shaking, and my breath still feels stale and sharp. My knuckles whiten around the bottle. I pop open the top, crunch a pill between my teeth, and swallow hard with no water. I turn the ignition, and the car sputters, shakes, and rumbles.

I see the automatic doors slide open from across the parking lot and I sink into my seat, still fumbling for that lighter. *Please don't see me. Please don't see me.* I know it's not Ally, but the thought that any person in this twisted town could come gliding out of those doors makes my whole body ache. I sink even lower and close my eyes, and finally grab the lighter. *One.* I hold out my one hand again. *Two.* With my other hand, I flick the lighter. *Three.* My hands stop shaking, and I strike up my second cigarette for the day.

I pull the smoke into my lungs and blow it out through my nose. Maybe it's all in my head, but I think I can actually feel the Xanax sweep through my blood, calming my veins, and somehow in the midst of my meltdown, I manage to make it out of the parking lot and onto a side street. My Saab idles, and I blow smoke out the cracked window. I'm hollow and weak, like you feel after a fever breaks. I need to compose myself and pull it together, think of something believable to tell Karen.

Sorry, Mom, I lost your list; forgot my wallet; had a massive panic attack in the middle of a crowded supermarket.

Though the truth is not an option here. If I tell Karen about the panic attack, I'll have to tell her about all the panic attacks, and I'll have to tell her why they're happening. And one of two things will happen: she'll cry and make a huge deal about it and insist I seek professional help, or she won't. And I'm not sure which I'm more afraid of.

"Fast Car" plays again, low through the static of my speakers, and I can't figure out what triggered me this time. Maybe it was Ally. Maybe it was hearing the way she casually dropped his name, like he'd be the florist or the caterer. Maybe it was just being in that place again—the cold rush of the air-conditioning, the smell of produce and dirty mop water. Maybe I was just too sober for that sort of encounter, or maybe it was Tracy Chapman. But whatever the reason, for the first time since I got home last night, it all starts to hit me.

Chapter 12

December 2005.

ADAM'S MOM STOPPED going to church after Max died—at least that's what he told me years later. He thought that's why she didn't fight him when he said he'd wanted to go to public school. She just shrugged, offered a tired half smile, and said, "We'll sign you up next week."

I was stretched out on his basement floor studying for my French midterm. Adam was watching some cooking show on the Food Network, the volume turned down low. This was our routine those first few months. We walked to and from school together, and studied together, but I never once saw Adam open a book. He said he just liked to sit with me, even if I was *actually* doing work. So he watched his cooking shows and mentally took notes on *amuse-bouche* recipes that he'd never actually make.

His mother's soft footsteps padded over the carpeting upstairs. I avoided her. I never knew what to say to her. Adam never talked about Max then. We'd known each other nearly five months—together, officially, for two. It was just before winter break of freshman year, and I could tell he was bummed about the holidays, like he didn't even know how to bring it up with his parents, didn't know the protocol of celebrating. When I'd asked him to come Christmas shopping with me, he'd changed the subject and made up some half-assed excuse, like he had to cook or catch up on his English homework. But like I said, I'd never seen him open a book.

"What about Vermont?" Adam asked, his voice cutting into the silence, except for those footsteps overhead. He was sprawled out over his black leather couch in a pair of flannel pajama pants. "Vermont's nice, right?"

"Sure, I guess it's okay. Why?" I asked without looking up.

"I mean for college. Would you go with me?" I felt my eyes flicker, but I caught myself and focused on the textbook open across my lap: *Mon frère monte le train.*

"Ad, that's like four years away."

"Yeah, so?" He reached down and twirled a strand of my hair. The floorboards creaked under his mother's footsteps, and the television cut to commercial. I tried to swallow.

"What makes you so sure you won't dump me by then?" I wished I'd sounded more sure of myself.

"That won't happen," he said. I stared down at the same line: *Mon frère monte le train.* "But you can't tell me you don't think about college, Mademoiselle, with your AP French." I snapped the book shut and faced him.

"Are you calling me uptight?"

"I'm calling you slightly, tightly wound," he said, his face stretching into a slow smile. "But I can fix that." He rolled off the couch, and fell into place beside me.

I felt his breath on the back of my neck as he kneaded his hands into my lower back and pressed his cool lips against my shoulder. I twisted around to kiss him.

"Or Canada," he said. I pulled back and looked into his gray eyes. "Anywhere I can live quietly. Just you, me, and the snow."

"I hate the snow," I said, stretching out again and resting my head against his crotch. "I'm more of a beach girl."

"Are you now? Well, that's disappointing." His voice stayed flat, the way it always did when he teased me. Adam had one tone—pure deadpan.

"Yup. I'm a beach girl, so I guess we were doomed from the start, then." I nestled my head into the crook of his stomach, feeling his body rise and fall with each breath. "But my dream school is Brown, so I may have to deal with the snow anyway." We stayed like that for minutes, but I could feel him thinking, his blood pumping in rhythm with that brain of his. And then he spoke.

"Brown, huh? Why does that not surprise me?" He paused and I felt his body relax. "Do you believe in heaven?"

"Sure, I guess so," I said, without realizing the context of the question. "I mean I'd like to think there's something after all of this. Not just worms and dirt, you know?" I regretted the imagery as soon as the words left my mouth. "I didn't mean that," I stuttered. "I don't think that's—"

"It's okay," he cut in. "You don't have to be like that with me."

"Be like what?"

"Like I have a dead brother." I turned to face him, but kept my eyes fixed on his gray cotton T-shirt. He twirled the same strand of my hair around his finger. "Max was a Catholic school dropout, and I was a good boy—or at least that's what my mom would say. 'The good boy,'" Adam scoffed, like the thought of him and the word "good" in the same breath was just the most preposterous thing. "So that's why I decided to go to Seaport. I didn't want to be *the good boy* anymore." His face fell into a weak smile. "But now I'm just the dead kid's brother."

"No," I said, still focused on his shirt. "Nobody thinks that." There were nine hundred things I could have said—I should have said—but I'd never been good in these types of situations, and as if he'd read my mind, Adam just smiled.

"I know this must be excruciating for you," he said.

"Why?"

He just shook his head and smiled.

"Are you calling *me* unemotional?" I asked, a poor attempt to grasp any levity left in the conversation.

"I'm calling you slightly detached." He stared at me, blank-faced, and in one swift motion grabbed at my sides until I collapsed against him, my body convulsing as his fingers prodded against my only weak spot. "And I'm also calling you ridiculously ticklish." He let out a dry, raspy cackle.

"Stop making me laugh during serious conversations, Sullivan," I said.

"Stop being so fucking cute."

"Stop making me want to puke." He let go, and we both

sprawled out over the floor again. We sat in silence, breathing. Adam cleared his throat.

"No, but seriously," he said. "I didn't cry at Max's funeral. How fucked up is that? I didn't even cry at my own brother's funeral."

I shrugged, a knot twisting in my stomach. He furrowed his brow, deep in thought, desperate for validation.

"Crying is overrated," I said, and I meant it. I'd never cried at a funeral—not that I ever had a comparable loss—but I couldn't imagine how I would even react if I found out Marc or Eli were dead. I mean, in a perfect world, I'd cry, I'd mourn, I'd act like a normal, *feeling* human being—like people expected me to act. But I couldn't imagine a scenario where I would burst into tears at the news and throw myself into Karen's arms. Maybe I'd tear up a day or two later when I was alone in bed, or driving, and it really sank in, but I couldn't picture myself sobbing at their funerals, showing weakness in front of literally every person I ever knew. I couldn't even imagine consoling my own mother. Now how fucked up was *that*.

"Yeah," he said. "But how could I be sad knowing that I never would have met you if he hadn't done it." The words hung between us, sticky and hot, like I could reach out, pluck at them, and shove them under the couch.

"You don't mean that," I said. Even though I'd thought that too.

"My mom used to talk about heaven a lot, you know," he said. "She'd be all like, 'Anyone worth knowing again, you'll see them in heaven, Adam.' But I haven't heard her say that since Max." He stopped, sighed, and sat up, pulling his knees into his chest. "I guess she just stopped believing—doesn't want to get her hopes up or something."

Adam cleared his throat again, and I could still hear his mother's footsteps pacing overhead.

"If there's a heaven, I can't picture it," he said. "I just imagine white space. Nothing but this huge white space, and all the Catholics I'd ever known standing around in a circle dressed in their Easter best. You know what I'm talking about?" He grunted, half laugh, half embarrassment, and I nodded. "But if that's where being a good Catholic boy would get me, well, I don't really want to be a part of that." I shook my head, more in understanding than agreement. I never really knew what I believed in. I once read that religion is where your love is, so I guess I believed in Adam—as much as anyone could have believed in another person.

With anyone else, I would have felt my tongue get thick, mumbled something, and changed the subject. But with Adam, I felt like I could handle it. Like I wasn't stiff and awkward talking about *feelings*. "What would your heaven be like?" I asked. And I wanted to know. I really wanted to know.

"Snow," he said. "Just snow falling like stardust into an endless dark place."

Adam looked at me with that crooked smile, that sad and beautiful, crooked smile.

"That sounds perfect," I said. I put my arms around his neck, looked into his gray eyes, and kissed him on the lips, firm and quick. "But I'm still more of a beach girl."

HE WALKED ME home that night, still in his pajama bottoms, his pea coat pulled over his chest. We were fourteen—fourteen and dumb, as if we'd reached the end of our little fairy tale with happily-ever-after spread out before us into an endless dark space. We walked up my driveway, past the hay-colored grass—all brittle and stiff—past the plastic snowmen sprouting out of the snowless earth. White Christmas lights dangled from my porch awning. He grabbed my hands and pulled me into his arms. We stood like that for what could have been a full minute. My porch light went on, and I saw Karen's face peering out from behind the front window.

"Guess I should go," I said. "Warden is watching." He turned toward the window and waved. She waved back with the enthusiasm only a middle-school cheerleading coach could pull off.

She knew there was someone I'd been sneaking off to see, but I'd managed to keep Adam a secret, and I wasn't quite ready for him to meet my mother. It had to be planned, and it had to be formal. Karen was like a cold bath; you had to jump right in, because if you tried to ease into a relationship with her, you'd never stick around.

A few months earlier, Marc had brought a girl home late one night after a party. I think her name was Lilly or Layla or Lucy. Karen was supposed to be asleep, so he came in through the back door and led the girl down into the basement, where he'd promised they could watch a movie, and no one would ever know. But ten minutes into their little rendezvous, Karen came barreling down the basement stairs and then asked to speak with Marc upstairs—privately. And as if that wasn't humiliating enough for the poor girl, Karen—very audibly— began to voice her dismay with the situation, starting with, "What kind of girl would just show up at a strange boy's house in the middle of the night? With *his family* asleep upstairs?" Marc had grumbled something about keeping her voice down just before she sent him up to his room and showed Lilly/ Layla/Lucy to the front door.

"I look forward to seeing you again," Karen had said as the girl scampered down the path to her car.

Needless to say, no one ever saw Lilly/Layla/Lucy again. Not that Karen hadn't asked about the girl for months. *Whatever happened to*—Lexi. Her name was Lexi—*whatever happened to Lexi? She seemed like such a nice girl!*

I started to walk up toward my house, leaving Adam with a brisk pat on the shoulder. The sky was navy and I could see my breath in front of me.

"Hey," Adam called. He grabbed my elbow and spun me back to face him. He grinned hard, puffing icy breaths between his perfect teeth. "I didn't want to do this in front of your mom." He nodded his head at the window, where she hid stealthily behind the curtains. "But, I love you, Aubrey." The words left his mouth and I swore I could see them suspended between us. "So fucking much," he said. "I just thought you should know that."

I stood facing him, a huge grin splayed out over his face, even as I mumbled, "Thanks" and stumbled back up toward my house.

"HE DROPPED THE L-bomb," I said to Rachel. It had been two days since he told me he loved me, and I hadn't told anyone yet.

"What?" Rachel stopped in her tracks and dropped her Abercrombie & Fitch shopping bag onto the mall floor. We were supposed to be Christmas shopping, but so far she'd only bought clothes for herself. Karen had dropped us off two hours earlier and promised to be back for us by six. I clutched my own bags—a Yankee Candle for Karen, a sweater for my dad, cologne for my brothers. I still didn't know what to get Adam.

"Are you that shocked?"

"Well, yeah," she said, her mouth gaping, eyes wide in that Rachel way. "I just didn't think you guys were like that serious."

"We are," I said, too defensively.

"Well, I didn't know," she snapped. "I guess I just didn't think he was that into you. And like, you could sort of do better if you actually tried."

"Well, he is, and we're fine."

"Well, did you say it back?"

"I said 'thanks,'" I deadpanned, and she sputtered in a raspy, exaggerated laugh. "Whatever, I was nervous," I said.

"Well, do you?"

"Do I what?"

"Love him?"

"I don't know," I said. "Maybe. I think so." I could feel myself start to smile, but stopped. Showing any form of weakness would just leave an opening for Rachel's cruelty It had to be casual. It always had to be casual.

"Okay," she said, grabbing her bag off the ground and walking away. I was meant to follow.

IT WAS MORNING a few days later—Saturday, maybe Sunday. And I'd been in my bed reading *The Great Gatsby*. It was for school, but I was kind of into it. I think I just liked that it was set on Long Island. I was in my robe and a pair of shorts, with a steaming mug of coffee on my nightstand. It had to be before ten when I heard something rattle my window. It was one of those icy winter mornings, so I assumed it was just the wind, and then I heard another rattle, and another.

Obviously my initial instinct was Rachel just being Rachel and finding weird shit to do on a random Saturday—or Sunday—morning, but when I pulled aside the curtain, I saw Adam standing on my lawn.

I came down and pulled my robe closed over my chest.

"I wanted to give you your Christmas present," he said, with a Cheshire grin. His hair was falling in front of his eyes. He was holding a box with both arms and tossed his head to the side, shaking the hair out of his face.

"You got me a Christmas present?" I still hadn't decided on a gift for him.

I never had trouble with breathing back then. It always came easy for me. I didn't even have to think about it. But that was before Adam and all the shit that came after him. I stood on my porch, with my robe wrapped around me. The icy air between us. I should have invited him in. A normal person would have invited him in, but I just stood there and watched him, and his arms wrapped around that big, white box.

He wore a soft gray-and-black plaid shirt. He looked taller.

"Here." He handed me the box. "I have to go, though, so why don't you open it inside." He thrust the box into my arms. It was heavier than it looked, and I nearly dropped it before I caught it from the bottom.

"Thanks," I said. He was already walking away, his lanky legs and arms swinging in sync.

"No problem," he said, without turning around.

When I got the package up to my room, I tore it open with a pair of those awful awkward, left-handed scissors—safety scissors. They must have belonged to Eli.

I pulled the flaps back and removed a layer of Styrofoam. And there, stacked side by side in absolute glass perfection, were ten mason jars.

IT WAS JANUARY when he met my mother, officially. New Year's Day. Karen invited him for dinner, and I think that was really the first time I ever considered us a couple—even though he'd told me he loved me. Maybe it was just Rachel's voice in my head that made me doubt the validity of our relationship. But either way, now it was real, and I was nervous for him to meet my mom. So was he, I could tell.

"These are for your mom," he said when I opened the door. He held pink and yellow carnations, tied together with a cheap, red lacy bow. I could tell he had just picked them up from Pathmark on his way over. I stifled a smile. Karen hated carnations.

But before I could even let Adam in the house, Karen was

hip-checking me out of the way and cupping his hands in hers. The flowers hung limp to one side.

"You must be Adam," she said. "I was so sorry to hear about your brother." Her eyes lingered on him, all sad and somber, and I felt a swell of panic in my chest. *Seriously, Karen,* I was dying to scream. *You had to bring that up* now. But Adam just did what he always did when people brought up Max—smiled politely and nodded a gracious thank-you. This was around the time I stopped calling Karen "Mom." It was a smooth transition, effortless, and it just sort of happened one day when she asked me to take out the trash. *Okay, Karen,* I said. I'd been testing it out, and when she didn't make a fuss, I just went with it.

I thought about what it would be like to meet my girlfriend's mother for the first time, and all she could do was feel sorry for me. It must have really fucking sucked.

I cleared my throat, and Karen averted her lingering eyes from Adam.

"Those are for you," I said, annoyed that she hadn't acknowledged the bundle of cheap carnations in his hand.

"Oh my goodness," Karen said, feigning surprise. "That is so sweet. Thank you." She took them from Adam and stuffed them into a turquoise vase already filled with water in the middle of the set dining room table. I could tell she was disappointed.

Dinner was one of those stiff, formal kind of meetings. Karen kept asking questions about his family, his classes, all that icebreaker kind of shit. I sort of wished he'd ask ques-

tions, too. I wished he'd ask those probing, nosy questions that
would make Karen cringe—like why she wasn't married to my
father anymore, and if she realized her son was blazed out of
his mind, or whether or not any of her students ever talked
about suicide, and if so, what she did to change their mind.

I twirled spaghetti around my fork.

I'd already warned him. My mother was a talker.

"She's going to try and shrink you," I'd said on the phone
the night before. I was sprawled out over my own bed, the
cordless phone propped between my neck and shoulder.

"Well, she can give it her best shot," he said. "I'm unshrinkable." It was true, I later learned. His mother had sent him to a
shrink once when he was twelve, or so he said.

"I got in a fight once, you know," he began. I could feel him
smirking over the phone.

I'd tried not to laugh. "Oh yeah? How'd that work for you,
tough guy?"

"His name was James Riley, and he had flaming red hair,
but that's not why I punched him out," he said. "I was on the
bus home from school, reading, like really into this book, and
the funny thing is, I don't even remember what book it was."
So he did read, I'd thought, nodding my head for him to keep
going, as if he could even see me.

"But I was into it, and I was just having a shitty day. James
was in the seat behind me. I kept feeling his knees jut into the
back of my seat, and then he was like hanging over the seat—
just flicking me in the back of my head."

"What did you do?" I asked, trying to sound more interested than I actually was, though I was curious how scrawny Adam Sullivan managed to knock a kid out.

"I ignored him," he said. "But then he reached over and ripped my hat off."

"What a dick," I said.

"I'm not finished. Then, before I could even react, he swooped in and ripped the book out of my hand. The cover tore and everything. He was all like, 'What are you reading, faggot?' Meanwhile, this kid had *flaming red hair.* So I waited until we were off the bus. He was walking with his little cronies, and I'm pretty sure he'd already forgotten about me, but I walked up behind him, real calm, and threw him down into the snow. He fell to his knees, and I just started to pummel him. Right in the face."

"Well," I said. "Remind me never to piss you off." Adam had laughed, in his husky deadpan way.

"Kid wasn't in school for a week, and I was ordered to undergo mental evaluation. Turns out I was normal. At least that's what my shrink said." I could just picture him, grinning on the other end of the line, and I wondered if he really was all that normal, or if there was something dark and brooding beneath the surface that his therapist had overlooked, even then.

And as I sat next to him at my family's dinner table that next night, I searched for a sign—anything that might give him away. I couldn't understand, after everything he'd been through with Max, how he could act so relaxed. I had a feeling it was an act, but we hadn't known each other long enough. So Adam just sat there, eating his spaghetti, casually answering

Karen's questions, as if he'd prepared the night before with flash cards.

"So how do you like Seaport High?" my mother asked. "It must be a change from Catholic school?" He finished chewing his food and nodded.

"It's great. I like the freedom. You know, not having to wear a uniform. And plus, I got to meet your daughter." Karen smiled, and she seemed almost embarrassed. But maybe it was charm. I could never tell the difference. When she reached over the table for more salad, Adam turned to me, subtle as ever, and winked. Or at least he tried to. It came off more as a facial tic.

"Is it tough, being around all your brother's friends? I imagine that can't be easy." I felt like kicking Karen under the table, but I closed my eyes, mortified, and swallowed a mouthful of salad.

"It's okay," he said. "It's nice to be around people who knew him."

"What about at home? Is everything okay there? Do you live with both parents?"

"Both parents, yup," he said, methodically chewing his food before speaking. I shot Karen a sharp look, but she kept her eyes focused on Adam, her head tilted in that guidance counselor way. I half expected her to reach across the table, touch his hands, and say, *This is a safe space, Adam.* "It's definitely hard for them. But they're getting by. Everybody has been really supportive."

"Do they have any idea what happened? I mean I've heard some things, but I couldn't imagine any of it to be true."

"Mom," I finally snapped, slamming my fork down onto my plate. "Seriously?" I turned to Adam.

"No, it's okay, Aubrey," he said, smoothing the napkin over his lap. "Everything is delicious, Mrs. Glass. Did you use paprika in the sauce?"

"You know, Adam," Karen said, "I did. I ran out of red pepper flakes and wanted to give it a kick. That's so funny you noticed. Do you like to cook?" She beamed and finally stuffed a forkful of spaghetti into her mouth. I felt my body start to relax. Adam reached under the table and patted my knee. It was true. He was unshrinkable.

Chapter 13

Monday, October 6, 2014.

WHY DON'T I take baths more often? My body drifts and floats, cutting the surface of the murky blue water. I'm still cursing myself for agreeing to girls' night. But at least there'll be wine.

A single flame flickers from the corner—"Fresh Linens" or "Cotton Ball Ocean"—something blue and detergent-y from Karen's closet. Definitely a Christmas gift from me.

A few limp bubbles linger before falling flat into white patchy amoebas, and I feel relaxed. It feels off, like maybe this isn't what relaxed feels like, but rather low blood sugar, or I've finally crossed the threshold into complete numbness.

The reflection of the water dances with the flickering light on the ceiling, and I think for a moment that it's mocking me, but then I remember to relax.

I raise my hips to the surface of the water. I see the tattoo and reach for the soap. I wonder if I scrub hard enough will it just disappear, wash away like squid ink into the bathtub. I trace my finger over the *heartigram*. *My heart-on.*

I hold my breath and let myself sink—my ears fill with water, muffling the silence—except for the toilet running and the vague sounds of the television in the other room.

I can't stop thinking about Adam. But I won't see him. Why should I? I don't owe him anything. And besides, it wouldn't be fair to Danny. I may be a lot of things. I may be cold, callous, manipulating. I may be a liar. But I'm not a cheater. *I am not a cheater.*

I'm all warm and pruney, and I think if I was ever going to do it, if I were ever going to kill myself, it would be like this. Floating, drifting, my body bobbing with the buoyancy of a bloated fish as my veins empty into the murky blue water. Rachel killed herself sometime after 3:00 A.M. on Saturday. It was Chloe who found her, or at least that's what Karen said when she called. She'd taken pills, something prescribed for sleep or anxiety. I wasn't really paying attention when she told me; I was too busy picturing Rachel bloated and purple on the bathroom floor. She'd taken too many, and they were pretty sure it was suicide, but it also could have been an accident. She didn't leave a note. Only a voice mail—but nobody else knows about that.

I wrap myself in a fluffy maroon towel. The heat lamp overhead warms my body. I can smell the chicken roasting from the kitchen. I'm not hungry, but I can't think of anything else to do with myself, so food just seems like the easy answer.

KAREN MAKES A big to-do about having us all home for the night. She even sets the dining room table with candles, a tablecloth, her holiday dishes, and that empty turquoise vase that once held Adam's carnations. She brings out a bottle of wine and sets it down in the center of the table.

Eli's new girlfriend sits in my seat. I don't say anything, but it takes everything in me to keep my mouth shut. I'm sitting in my father's old seat, and it feels weird, and I'm getting all restless, like all I want to do is sit in my chair, but she's all smiley and nervous, so I suck it up. She wears a purple floral dress with a white cardigan. Karen makes sure to note how beautiful she looks in *such vibrant colors* before glancing at me and suggesting that Ashley take me shopping.

Ashley smiles at me. "That would be fun," she says.

Ugh.

I wear a charcoal-gray sweater and black yoga pants. My hair is in a ponytail, and I wear my black thick-rimmed glasses— hipster glasses, as Danny calls them. I'm saving the contacts for girls' night. Right now my eyes need all the oxygen they can get. My glasses are Gucci and the sweater is cashmere, but for some reason, Karen thinks I need to take fashion advice from Forever 21's number one customer.

"Can I get you anything, hon?" Karen says, mostly to Ashley, and it reminds me of how she used to speak to Rachel— *Can I get you something, hon,* or *sweetie,* or just *Rach.* She never calls me anything but Aubrey.

"I'll have a glass of Jack," I cut in.

"Whiskey?" she asks. "You want whiskey with dinner?" She shifts her eyes around the table.

"Yes, I'd like some whiskey, please. And a Diet Coke." I unfold the cloth napkin and smooth it over my lap. "Please," I say. "But I know your one-can-of-soda rule, so don't worry, I'll only have one," I cock my head and give my best sweet smile. "Coke, that is."

My eyes follow her to the cabinet and she reaches for the bottle of Jack Daniel's.

"Ice?" she asks.

"Yes. Please."

She shakes her head, still looking over at Ashley, as if to say, *Please excuse my rowdy daughter. I just don't know what's gotten into her!*

Karen steadies the bottle of Jack over one of my mason jars, letting it splash to a quarter full. It's weird that she kept those jars after all of these years, especially since she once called them *trashy*. And then Adam floats into my mind. It's sudden and dull, like a bad headache—his carnations, his polite answers to Karen's probing questions, and his white box full of mason jars. It's hard to swallow, and I'm starting to feel weak and full of panic, so I eye Karen at the counter as she tries to visually measure out the Jack with the diligence of a nursing-home bartender.

"More," I say. "Please." She sighs, and pours another splash. "More. That's not even a full shot."

"Aubrey," she snaps. I smile, and that's when I see it, dangling by a single magnet, front and center on the freezer door—the picture of Rachel and me from the Halloween parade in our matching hippie costumes. I want to rip the photo off the door, hold it in front of Karen's face, and scream. Not only did

she go back into my room, uninvited, to dig it out of that old
shoe box, but now she displays it like some trophy right in the
middle of dinner.

She sets the glass jar in front of me and slams a cold can of
Diet Coke next to it.

Ashley smiles, looks over at Eli, rubs his shoulder, and then
shifts in her seat.

"I'm sorry," I say, hiding my urge to laugh. "I'm so rude. Do
you want?" I hold the glass out to her, but she shakes her head,
looks over at my mother, and smiles again.

"We don't make it a habit to drink hard liquor with dinner,"
Karen says.

Eli winks at me from across the table, and Karen shifts her
eyes between us, like we're hatching some sort of a plan. "So,
Ash, can I call you that? Or is that weird?" I pop the can open
and splash a drop into my glass. The ice clinks and I take a
hard gulp.

"Yeah, sure. That's what *awll* my friends *cawl* me anyway."

"Perfect," I say, taking another swig. There's this thick
silence at the table, and then she speaks again, and I can't
tell if she's nervous or feels right at home. In either event, it's
unsettling.

"So," she says. "Eli tells me you're a reporter? That's so
cool." I scoff, and take another gulp. The Jack burns my throat,
but it quiets the throbbing thoughts swimming in my head. I
catch the photo again out of the corner of my eye.

"I prefer the term 'hyperlocal journalist,' it just sounds
more professional, you know?" I say. "It's not as glamorous as
it sounds, though. Technically, I'm just a content creator." I

take a sip and keep talking. "What are you going to school for? Nassau is pretty competitive, I hear." My mother shoots me a death stare from across the table, but I'm sure Ashley doesn't catch my tone. I finish the drink, and wipe my mouth with the back of my hand.

"Yeah, but I seem to be doing pretty well this semester," she says. She takes a tiny sip of wine. I squint at her, gauging whether or not she actually drinks it. "I'm not really sure what I want to do yet, maybe psychology or teaching."

"Oh," I say, standing up and walking over to the kitchen island, where the bottle of Jack stands half empty. I pour myself another glass, but don't add soda this time—Karen's rule. "Well then, I'm sure you know *Miz Glass* here is a stand-up school psychologist. I'm sure she's just a plethora of information." I swig again, and swish the Jack around in the glass. The hot whiskey burns the back of my throat, and I wince; but it's a good kind of pain, like running too fast or getting a tattoo. "I bet she'll let you pick her brain. Right, Kar?"

My mother nods, smiles at Ashley, but never takes her eyes off of me. The front door opens, and Marc's heavy footsteps bring my mother to her feet.

"Having fun?" Eli says when my mother leaves the room.

"A blast," I say. Ashley looks uncomfortable and rubs Eli's shoulder again.

"She's going to kill you, you know," he says.

"Looking forward to it," I say.

KAREN BRINGS OUT the roasted chicken on this fancy stainless steel platter. She got the recipe from *Barefoot Contessa*, her all-time favorite show. I wouldn't be surprised if Adam watches that these days. Last I heard, he was still working in the kitchen at Jason's father's restaurant at the marina.

My temple starts to throb around eight; T minus two hours until girls' night. I'm still trying to think of a way to talk myself out of it when Marc cuts in.

"Are you really not going to go?" he asks. "To the funeral. Mom says you're being a real bitch about it." Everyone gets silent. I shovel a forkful of chicken into my mouth. Karen stands up and heads into the kitchen. I roll my eyes. "I mean, I feel like even I have to go. Everybody is going. At least to the after-party."

Something pinches inside my lungs. I swallow, open my mouth, and remember to breathe.

"My God," I say, too loud. "What the hell is with everybody and this after-party? Am I the only person in this town who thinks it's outrageous?" Marc just laughs, and Karen pokes her head back into the room and lets out a heavy warning sigh.

"It's going to be sick," he says. "Bobby is DJing." I take another breath and try to remember that it's a funeral. A fucking funeral. Not a party. It's not just me. It's everybody else.

"Why would you go to the funeral, anyway? What, did you hook up with her or something?" I ask, only half serious.

"Not really," he says, and I nearly spit out my drink.

"Not really?" I stare at him, waiting for him to crack a smile, say he was joking, anything. But then I think, *Why wouldn't she have hooked up with my brother? She hooked up with everyone else I knew.*

"It was just this night at O'Reilly's like two years ago,"

he says. "We were both drunk." His voice gets low so Karen doesn't hear. "We did a line in the bathroom. We made out a little. That was it."

"That was it," I repeat. "And you?" I look to Eli. The thought of Rachel going after my baby brother—even if we are only two years apart—makes me want to put my fist through a wall.

"No way," he says, patting Ashley on the back for reassurance. "But we're definitely going to the after-party."

I let out another breath, and find myself another reason not to go.

"Aubrey," my mother finally says. "Can you help me in the kitchen for a minute."

I know where this is going. I grab my jar of Jack and follow her out of the room.

"What is your problem?" she says through clenched teeth.

"What?" I snap. "Am I not being a good little host?"

"Keep your voice down," she warns.

"No," I slur; I'm just realizing how drunk I am. "Am I embarrassing you, Mother?" She comes toward me, and I stumble back. "Fuck off," I say. Karen gasps and grabs my arm. I laugh, a husky cackle that sends spit flying at her face.

"Sorry," I say, still sputtering. "Relax. Jesus." She grabs my arm again. "Seriously, let the fuck up." She's looking at me like I've absolutely lost it, and I'm wondering what Rachel ever did that was so fucking great. I remember the night I found her sobbing over my bathroom sink, stammering some bullshit about how horrible her own mother was, about how lucky I was.

You're my family, Aubrey.

I sat down with her on the cold tile, letting her cry, until Karen came in, scooped Rachel off the floor and up in her arms, and led her to my bedroom. *You're always welcome in our home, Rach*, she said. *You're part of our family.*

"You are going to this funeral," my mother says, her voice stern, her hand still clutching my elbow. "Show some respect."

"Bet you wish it was my funeral, don't you?" I stare hard. I don't mean it. I don't know why I say it, but she just stares, a dumb look on her face. "Right? You and Rachel, 'Oh, that spark plug!' The perfect mother-daughter team you could have been. The perfect, fucking cheering duo."

"Aubrey," she says. "Calm down. You need to stop."

"I need to stop?" I'm screaming now. The words scratch my throat; my hand tightens around the jar. "I need to stop?" I say even louder. "I'm not the one who swallowed a bottle of fucking pills. That's spark-plug Rachel for you. Couldn't make herself happy and so she kills herself. Or tries to. Because God knows how much that girl loved attention."

"Aubrey," she says, her eyes going all teary on me, but this just fuels my rage.

"Are you seriously crying now?" I say. "Please. Stop trying to make me feel bad. You have no idea what she did to me."

Karen takes a sharp breath. "So tell me," she screams, but before I can even process the thought, I'm slamming the mason jar of whiskey onto the granite floor, and the glass shatters at Karen's feet.

Chapter 14

February 2009.

FUCK HIM.

I kicked the curb, stubbing at least three toes, dropped his jacket in a parking-lot puddle, and walked back inside. I already felt better.

Fuck him.

Adam was going through an emo phase: tight jeans, band tees, hair in his eyes, and a vintage denim jacket which was now soaking up parking lot grit. But with this new phase came a new level of brooding. I could see him in the back of the concert hall, crushing a can of Coors in his hand, unsteady on his feet. He leaned up against the wall and jerked his head to the side, flipping his hair out of his eyes. He was flirting. A short chick in a pair of Chuck Taylors and a pixie cut giggled up at him. I could feel myself scoffing, shaking my head, waiting for him to catch my eye. And he did, a cold smirk set on his face.

His gray, icy stare pierced through the crowd right into me. I glared back, and we held each other's eyes. She wasn't even pretty and she definitely wasn't his type. She smiled, laughed nervously, and kept her arms crossed over her chest. He was intimidating her. I could tell just by the way he hovered over her, smiling and nodding, but never taking his eyes off me. She checked her phone, and in his smug Adam way, he lifted his hand and waved at me. Not a friendly wave, but a tight, slow villainous wave.

Lesson learned: never trust anyone who says he'll be designated driver, especially if he's driving your car.

Adam had gotten the tickets for my birthday, which was the biggest joke of all. It wasn't really my scene, it was his thing. He'd always been the one to drag me to shows of bands I'd never heard of. But I went along with it. This time, though, it was Jimmy Eat World, a band I actually liked. He jumped at the opportunity for a mutually beneficial birthday gift. Kill two birds with one stone, I guess. But he justified the gift by buying three tickets. Two for us and one for Rachel. It was my seventeenth birthday, so I should celebrate with my best friend *and* my boyfriend, he'd said, even if the actual show was five months later.

Things had been tense lately, so the third-wheel scenario wasn't actually a terrible idea. Rachel had made it very, very clear that I'd been spending too much time with Adam, that I'd been ditching her for years now, that all I cared about was my boyfriend, and it was *pathetic*.

"What am I supposed to do, Aub? This is supposed to be our *senior year*. All you two do is fight anyway." It was true, we fought a lot. But I also only told her about the fights, never the good stuff. I didn't tell her how the week before, I'd had to pull an all-nighter for my AP lit paper, and he'd shown up at my house with Starbucks and Magnolia Bakery cupcakes, which he'd driven all the way into the city to get.

So the tickets were a birthday gift, five months after my birthday, a night out, which started out fine, where I didn't have to feel like I was choosing between him and Rachel.

The show was at Stony Brook. Rachel and I took turns swigging Jack and Diet Coke out of a Poland Spring bottle in the back of my Saab. Adam sat in the driver's seat, drumming his fingers to "Pain." Rachel took a long sip, wiped the corners of her mouth, and straightened her shoulders. I caught her peering over her shoulder and smiling at a group of college guys tailgating a few cars away.

"Rach, you're drinking whiskey and soda out of a plastic bottle. Stop trying to be classy." I meant it as a joke, but her face twisted and contorted into a classic, pissy-Rachel face.

"Seriously," she said, pushing the bottle back at me. "You should talk."

"Okay," I said. "I was joking."

"Whatever," she said. I took a swig and handed her back the bottle. She snapped it out of my hand and pulled herself up into the passenger's seat next to Adam. "Here, why don't you drink. You're gonna need it. Your girlfriend is a real bitch tonight." She turned back to me.

"He's driving," I deadpanned, my arms crossed tight over my chest. "And I said I was joking. Jesus." Her face softened and she smiled.

"I know. So am I," she said. But I still couldn't tell. I never could with her. She propelled herself back to the backseat next to me and took a strand of my hair in her hands. "You should wear your hair up," she said. "You actually have a pretty face. You'd look so much better if you let me do your hair." I felt her hot whiskey breath on my neck. "Right, Adam?"

"I think she's perfect the way she is." He craned his neck and winked at me—again it was more like a facial tic. All the years we were together, he'd never perfected the wink. Rachel dropped my hair, turned, and pressed her face up against the window, and I can't be sure, but I swear I heard her sigh.

I climbed into the front seat next to Adam. "Konstantine" started to play through the static of my speakers.

"Our song," he said, grabbing my hand, and he started to sing in an exaggerated whiny voice.

"Oh my God, gross," Rachel scoffed, and promptly opened the car door, stepping out into the dusky February air.

" 'It's always you,' " he sang, loud and off-key. " 'In my big dreams.' " I shook my head, and he quirked a crooked grin and turned off the car.

We were feeling pretty good when the show started. Rachel and I hung back in the outskirts of the mosh pit, dancing with ourselves, while Adam dove into the mosh, slamming his body into a sea of limbs that stank of sweat and gymnasium. A group of college-age guys stood off to the side with cans of Coors in their hands. I could feel their eyes on Rachel, and apparently so could she. She swung her hips, and turned to face them, flashing her famous *bedroom eyes*.

During "Work," one of the college guys, a short stocky kid

with a receding hairline, moved in. He held Rachel's hips and swung his own stiff body awkwardly behind her, burying his face in the back of her neck. They moved like that for a while, rocking their hips back and forth out of sync.

Rachel grabbed my hand and pulled me toward her. I saw Adam out of the corner of my eye; we made quick eye contact and he disappeared back into the mosh pit.

Can we take a ride? Get out of this place while we still have time.

"Dance with me," she shouted over the music, the stocky guy still grinding up behind her. Rachel held my hands and we moved together, imitating stocky guy's awful moves. She leaned into me, her breath against my ear.

"Is he hot?" she shout-whispered.

"Not at all," I said, still dancing. Rachel threw her head back, almost knocking the guy right in the teeth, and busted into a husky cackle.

And then I felt a pair of hands fall onto my hips. I swung around and my face was in this guy's chest. It felt like seconds, it must have been seconds, but Adam was already grabbing my elbow.

"What are you doing?" he said, his voice sharp. The guy stepped back and disappeared into the crowd. Rachel kept on dancing, her eyes closed, head back, pretending not to notice, but she had this smug, satisfied grin on her face.

"Nothing." I jerked my elbow away from his grip. "He just grabbed me. Relax."

Adam's face was slick with sweat, his hair soaked. "I saw the whole thing. Don't give me that shit, Aubrey."

"You clearly did not see anything if that's what you think you saw." He grabbed at my arm again, and I jolted him back. He wobbled on his heels and came back at me with a shove. It wasn't hard, but just enough to call attention from the bouncers.

"Is this guy bothering you?" one of the security guards asked.

"No, I was just leaving," Adam said, before thrusting his denim jacket at me and storming off toward the bathrooms.

So fuck him.

Adam's precious vintage jacket was now drinking puddle water, he was chatting up some pixie-cut little slut, Rachel had disappeared with that short guy, and I'd been drinking water for the past hour trying to sober up enough to drive us home. Happy birthday to me.

I texted Rachel for the fifth time. *Where are you?* I knew she wouldn't answer, she never did, but I needed to look distracted. I couldn't let Adam win.

It wasn't until the band started packing up, and Adam was on what appeared to be his seventh beer in two hours that I finally cracked.

"I'm ready to go," I said. The pixie-cut girl looked up at me, a mix of surprise and disappointment on her squinty face. "Sorry to break up your little party." Adam shrugged at the girl, nodded at me, and walked toward the exit in silence. I followed him, grabbed his shoulder, and swung him around. He stared, cold and hard.

"He grabbed me," I said. "I didn't just spend the whole night flirting with some fifteen-year-old."

"Whatever," he said. He smelled of sweat and beer. He shivered when we got out into the parking lot but never asked about his jacket. "Where's Rachel?"

"I don't know. Probably off blowing that short guy. She's not answering."

"Of course," he slurred. "What the hell else is new?" Rachel never answered her phone during her drunken disappearing acts. It was like she was testing me. I was sure of it. She'd ignore my texts and calls so I'd have to spend the night tracking her down, and God forbid I went home without her.

"My phone was dead," she'd whine. "I can't believe you ditched me. I would never do that to you." But her phone wasn't dead. She'd turn it off; it was her way of controlling me while she was off getting hers.

"Keys," I said, my voice bitter and cold. He reached in his pocket and jammed them into my open hand.

It was nearly midnight, and the air was thin, in the high thirties. We walked side by side through the parking lot, neither of us speaking.

"Hey, Sullivan," a nasally voice called from near a red Jetta. Adam turned toward the group of guys, tall and muscular. Someone shotgunned a beer while the others leaned against the car smoking cigarettes.

"I hate that guy," Adam said under his breath, lifting his hand in a reluctant wave, but the guy was already walking over to us.

"Long time no see," he said, eyeing Adam then shifting his gaze to me. "Who's your girl?" Adam shook his head and kept walking. The guy stepped in front of us.

"I'm Greg," he said, offering his hand to me. I took it, but he didn't shake, just held my fingers limply. "Me and Sullivan here went to elementary school together."

"Come on, Aubrey," Adam said, grabbing my hand from Greg's and dragging me toward my car.

"Oh man," Greg said. "You gonna let this guy tell you what to do like that?" I shrugged and followed Adam. "Guess it runs in the family," he said. Adam stopped and swung around.

"What did you just say?"

"Let's go, Ad," I said.

"I said, it must run in the family. You know, rapists." Greg let out a dry cackle; his buddies at the car grinned and kicked the parking-lot grit with their sneakers.

I let go of Adam's hand, and he launched himself forward. It was swift and sudden, and before I could react, he was tackling the guy to the ground. A bone cracked, but I couldn't tell if it was Adam's fist or Greg's jaw.

"Let's go," I shouted, dragging him to his feet. The other guys were too stunned to do anything. Greg sat up, his hand cupping his jaw.

We got into my car, and Adam's knuckles were already swollen and purple.

"I think I broke my hand," he said, and then he lost it, burying his face into my chest. I could feel his body convulsing under me, his sobs dampening my shirt.

"It's okay," I said. "I can take you to the hospital if you want." I rubbed his shoulder, my own body stiff. I was never good in these situations, but I traced my fingers through his damp hair until his breathing slowed. I felt my body relax, and my breathing fall into pace with his.

When I look back on our relationship, it was in this moment that I loved him the most. Out of all our memories, quips, our secrets, it was here, with his head in my lap, that I felt my love for Adam swell up in my chest and swallow me. Maybe it was his vulnerability, maybe it was mine, but it felt nice to be needed—to be trusted. And for a moment, just a moment, I let myself believe that I needed and trusted him, too.

"Do you believe it?" he said, his eyes still wet. We'd been sitting like that, with his head tucked into my lap, for a half hour.

"Believe what?"

"What they say about Max. That he was a rapist?" I took a breath and sighed. I didn't really know what I believed. When I knew Max, he was intimidating. But only because I was so young. We kissed. And that was it. I only have good memories of that day. My first kiss. My first drink. My second cigarette. I could have told Adam this. I could have told him that I knew his brother, and that he had only been gentle with me. But I didn't. It didn't feel like the right moment. We'd already been fighting, and now he was opening up to me for the first time, and part of me admired that. Part of me resented him for it. But I didn't want to say anything that would make him regret trusting me. It didn't feel right to take advantage of that.

"Does it really matter what I think?" I said. "What any-body thinks? He was your brother, and you loved him. What does it matter now?"

"I try not to think about it," he said, his jaw locking. "I mean, I know Max was no saint, but I don't think he would have done something like that. He was a good guy."

"Well, maybe he was a good guy, and that's why he couldn't live with himself. People make mistakes," I said. "And that's why he did it. Killed himself, I mean." I shouldn't have said it. I knew the second the words left me. But Adam didn't say anything.

He just sighed and said, "Maybe."

"Do your parents ever talk about it?"

"No," he said. "But Max gave me something right before he, you know. I think it might have belonged to the girl. It was jewelry. Why would she give him that? I don't know," he said. "It just seems weird for a girl to give a guy their jewelry." I nodded. It did seem weird. So maybe he took it, and maybe he did hurt her. That's the only reason I could think of. But I didn't tell Adam that. We just sat like that for a few minutes, until my phone buzzed from the dashboard. Rachel.

"Answer it," he said. I pressed the phone to my ear.

"Where are you?"

"Aubrey," she slurred. "I'm at the beach. I need you to come pick me up."

"You're at the beach? How the hell did you end up there?"

"Just come pick me up. Please, Aubrey. I need you."

Adam sat up in his seat.

"It's fine," he said. "I'll be fine. Just drop me off." He closed his eyes and leaned back in his seat, cold and detached, like he hadn't just been sobbing in my chest about his dead brother.

I PULLED MY Saab up to the opening of the tunnel that separated the parking lot from the shore. The headlights illuminated the Atlantic, all black and foam. I flashed the brights three times—two quick and one long. A sort of Morse code, hoping she would just come and get into the car without a struggle. Two quick, one long, and no response. So I shifted into park and started down the tunnel—the headlights glowing behind me. The wind swept through the hollow path—dust, sand, and even particles of snow swirled at my feet like crawling ghosts. Ahead, I could see the Atlantic, a fog clinging to its surface. My shoulders twitched and I pulled my coat closer to my body.

When I reached the other side of the tunnel, the moon slung against the black sky like a slivered hangnail, and I could see Rachel's shadow, small and unmoving about a thousand feet away. When I got close enough to see her face, I could tell that her lips were kind of blue and she was breathing slow, like a whimper almost, her knuckles whitening around the neck of a bottle of Pinot Noir.

"What happened?" I asked, plopping down in the sand next to her.

"Nothing," she said. "That guy was a jerk-off. I gave him head and then all of a sudden he had to go," she slurred. "Fuck that. I said I'd find my own ride home."

We stood up and started back toward the car lights, but she'd stop every few steps, the bare balls of her feet pressing into the sand, and her head tilting like it was on a swivel. Her hair stuck to her Pinot-stained lips.

"You're my best friend, Aubrey. I love you so fucking much," she said.

"I know. But it's freezing, so let's go." She fell back into the sand and let out a maniacal giggle that morphed into a high-pitched squeal.

The February wind swept the sand into my face, sharp particles stinging my hands. I reached over Rachel and into my coat pocket for my gloves.

"Did I ever tell you about my first kiss, Aub?"

"With Frank?" Rachel had made out with Frank Webber in eighth grade at Ally's birthday party.

"No," she said, still giggling. "My actual first kiss. I was twelve," she said. "I met the guy online. In a chat room. Remember those? You know A/S/L?"

"Um, no," I said. "I never heard about this."

"He said '18/m/Queens.' I said '16/F/LI.' We were both lying, I think."

"Jesus, Rachel," I said. "So what happened?" My voice cracked and got really low, and I'm not sure if she even heard me. I wasn't sure if I wanted the responsibility of hearing the answer, but she went on with her story anyway.

"We talked for a week, or so. Every day after school, when my mom was still at work." She sounded amused as she recalled the details with such a casual, drunken elegance. "I just really wanted to kiss someone, you know? Or at least to say that I kissed someone. I kind of thought that was a normal thing to want." She pulled her coat tighter over her shoulders and let her body fall back into the damp sand. "So we made plans to meet up. He said he'd pick me up in the movie theater parking lot. I honestly thought that I would get into his car, we would kiss, and I would leave. And that would be it. We'd both be happy. Maybe we'd see an R-rated movie or something and kiss some more. I remember *The Exorcist* was playing that week, rereleased. How stupid was I?"

"Rachel, you were twelve. Why didn't you tell me?"

"Twelve and stupid," she slurred. "Anyway. I was really lucky." She scooped a handful of sand. "I got into his car. He had the radio on, it was something grungy, like Nirvana, but not Nirvana. If I heard the song, I would know." She opened her fist, and the sand sifted through her fingers. "He seemed really confident, and I felt really sick. Like, as soon as I shut the door behind me, I just felt like I'd really fucked up, you know?"

I nodded.

"He had pockmarks in his face. Like acne scars," she said. "And his hair was greasy. Yeah, I remember his hair being greasy. I just felt really gross but I couldn't just leave, you know?"

I nodded. The ocean looked black.

"He kept shaking his leg over the gas pedal, and every few seconds he'd press too hard and the car would rev up. So we both just sat there awkwardly for a long time. And he was chewing gum really loud, and eventually he just leaned in and said, 'So are we going to hook up or what?' And then he kissed me. His tongue was limp and cold, and he just sort of licked my teeth and then darted his tongue in and out of my mouth, until I finally pulled away."

"That is disgusting," I said. It was the only thing I could say.

"Tell me about it," she said, still amused. She sat up again and stabbed the sand with her fingers. "So I panicked, got out of the car, and just ran home."

"And you never told anyone this?"

"Nope." She seemed to be smiling again. "Who was I going to tell?" she said. "I felt like such an idiot. I couldn't tell you."

"You could have told me," I said, lifting her to her feet. "But let's get out of here. I'm freezing." She stood up, steady this time, walked to my car, and never once thanked me for the ride.

I STOOD IN Rachel's kitchen, refilling the same glass of water over and over until I felt the nausea wash away. I had gotten her home, into bed, and wiped the puke off her face. I called Adam on the way back to Rachel's, just to check up, but he didn't answer. Must have been sleeping, I figured. It was nearly 3 A.M.

I chugged another glass of sink water, and that's when I saw him. Big, hick, Nascar-loving Jeff, with nothing on but a pair of tighty whities. I didn't see him lurking in the shadows, so I jumped, knocking the bottle of Palmolive into the metal sink.

"Whoa, there," he said. "I didn't mean to scare you." It was dark, but the moonlight shone through the sliding glass doors, perfectly illuminating the outline of his crotch. He opened the refrigerator and pulled out a can of Busch. "Want one?"

I could only shake my head to keep from vomiting all over the cheap linoleum. He was balding, and his gut protruded over the elastic band around his waist. He leaned against the kitchen counter, his hips jutting out toward me like he was showing off.

"Rough night?" he asked, popping up the tab. "Heard you two come in. Sounds like Rachel-girl is one hot mess tonight." He let out this throaty chuckle, and I caught myself glancing at the wiry black hairs on the tops of his thighs.

I watched the microwave clock change to 3:07, then I awkwardly mumbled something about the bathroom, stumbled into Rachel's room, and locked the door.

Chapter 15

Monday, October 6, 2014.

THE STREETLIGHTS SWELL around Ally's house—her parents' house, and it looks the same as it did back in high school, except for what might be a new slate stoop. I park across the street and sit in my car, still feeling my buzz from earlier, my head still pounding from all that Jack.

Ally doesn't live near the water, she lives east down by the Seaport Diner. I shouldn't have driven, but once that jar shattered on Karen's kitchen floor, I had to get the hell out. I can't get that look on her face out of my head, like everything just clicked for her, like she finally realized what I really am. Bat-shit crazy.

I didn't stick around to clean up or apologize, just fled, grabbing my car keys on the way out. I hadn't realized that I'd left my phone behind until I started the car. I expect at least forty missed calls upon my return. There was a commotion in my wake, I'm sure: Ashley consoling my hysterical mother while Marc and Eli swept up the broken pieces.

I linger in my car and watch the shadows of three or four slim bodies behind the shades. I have no idea who to expect at this gathering and I'm not so sure I want to find out.

I reach in my bag for a cigarette—my third of the day— and that bottle of Xanax, then slink back into the seat, rolling the window down an inch just to air out. I crunch a Xanax between my teeth and swallow before lighting up.

It's been more than five years since I've been here—the First Friday of my senior year. It had always been Ally's dream to host First Friday, like some people dream of making captain of the swim team or getting into an Ivy League. Ally's dream had been simply to host our senior First Friday, as if that would hold any sort of merit post–high school. And I remember feeling oddly proud of her.

KEEPING UP WITH our First Friday tradition, Adam and I had ducked out of the party just after midnight with a bottle of Jack. It had been one of those warm September nights. We took turns swigging from the bottle, the hot whiskey dribbling down my chin and staining the front of my tank top. Karen was staying with my grandma in Connecticut and Eli was staying at our dad's, so we had the house to ourselves.

Ally would have been heartbroken if she knew that I'd

skipped out early on her big night, probably the most important night of her life to date, but I think she was too busy scrubbing the semen stains off her parents' five-hundred-thread-count sheets.

Adam had carried me home on his back. We hardly made it through the front door, when he pushed me up against the hallway wall, his whiskey lips dancing over my neck. I pulled him by the collar of his polo, and dragged him to the staircase. My back pressed into the carpeted steps, and he was on top of me, writhing against my drunk, limp body.

I'm not sure how we got into the shower. Maybe I blacked out, maybe I was just too caught up in the moment, but one second we were fully clothed, grinding up against each other on the stairs, and the next we were both naked, standing under a waterfall of hot steaming vapor.

We didn't touch. We stood at least a foot apart. It was the first time he'd seen me without my clothes on and it didn't feel right. It didn't feel wrong either. Just unsettling.

His eyes were fixed on me, and he sank his tongue into mine. His warm body pressed into me. I let my arms hang around his neck, and he hardened against my bare thigh. He moved up against me in a quiet rhythm until a groan escaped from the back of his throat.

I THINK ABOUT leaving, about speeding off down the street and crawling back into bed—texting Ally in the morning with some half-assed apology, but then I see someone peer out from behind one of the shades, and then another set of eyes; suddenly there are three or four bodies waving emphatically at me from inside the house.

"Shit," I mumble. "Shit. Shit. Shit," and put out my cigarette in the car's ashtray before anybody sees me.

I stumble out of the car, smooth my gray cashmere sweater over my stomach, and wave back at them, slinging my bag over my shoulder and smiling until my jaw aches.

The door swings open just as I'm coming up that possibly-new slate stoop.

"Finally," Ally says, draping her arms around my shoulders. I can already tell she's wasted. "I'm so happy you're here. We thought you wouldn't show."

They stand around the doorway with weak smiles. There's Ally, Sasha, and two other vaguely familiar faces, but for the life of me, I cannot remember their names. I can't tell if it's the liquor or if my memory has just been shot to shit, but either way, I realize I'm more slammed than I thought as I steady myself into the foyer.

The air is too hot, the family photos on the wall look fake, and I feel the cashmere start to stick to my skin as my back dampens. And then I see it: the dining room table covered with the props for Rachel's funeral, assembled in a perfect line. Ally wasn't lying. There are shot glasses, at least sixty of them, with Rachel's name, birthday, and date of death engraved into the frosted glass—and T-shirts, at least thirty plain white tees, with Rachel's grinning face print-screened, slightly off-center. Whoever made them did a pretty shitty job. I take a step toward the table and finger the cotton fibers.

Ally pours me a glass of Pinot Noir and I sit down on the couch next to one of the plain-faced girls—Ellie—it's Ellie Martin. "So you're still dating that guy?" Ally starts. She crosses her legs and leans in toward me.

"Danny," I say. I take a sip and nod my head. The wine warms my throat—earthy and rich—and I can feel Ellie's eyes on me.

"Tell us about him," Ally says.

"I don't know. He's okay?" I say, and wonder why they even care.

"Just okay?" She lets out a high-pitched snort and looks at the other girls. "Don't you guys, like, live together?" Ally's cheeks are flushed, and her mousy-brown hair falls down the middle of her back. She's wearing too much bronzer.

"We live together," I say. I nod again and swirl the Pinot in my glass.

"Well, so it's serious, then?" Maybe it's the way her voice gets all somber, but I start to get that guilty twist in my stomach, and I can't figure out how she has all this information. It's not like I have Facebook or anything—and it's for reasons like this I like my privacy.

"I guess so. We've been together a while." I feel myself getting defensive, and I hate that I feel the need to prove something to these girls. Sasha, Ally, Ellie, and the Girl I Can't Remember all sit on the couch, facing me like a panel of judges, leaning in, soaking up every word of my dull, monochromatic life. "He's a nice guy," I say. My ring clanks against the wine-glass, and I realize that my hands are starting to shake again, so I gulp down the rest of my wine, put the glass down, and shove my hands under my thighs.

"Mm," Ally says, a smug look on her face as she sits back into the couch. "So have you seen Adam yet? You know he's helping us with this stuff, right?" His name rolls off her tongue, but it's like she spits it at me. I feel my face go hot, pull my hands out from under my legs, and reach for my empty glass. "That must be awkward for you. Seeing him."

"It's complicated," I say, my voice cold.

"I mean," Ally starts, glancing at the other girls. "We heard some things." Everything stops. The room starts to spin, and I swear the lights somehow dim.

"What are you talking about?" I say. I know.

"I heard you did something bad," she slurs. She almost sings it, and the other girls stifle a laugh.

I stand up. Too fast. I'm dizzy. So fucking dizzy.

"So, Ally," I say, the room spinning with a dull grace. "What's going on with you? You're still living at home. No boyfriend? Still working at the mall?"

"You really weren't there for her were you, Aubrey?" Ally stands up and walks toward the table of funeral swag. "She could have really used her best friend in the end." I want to speak. I want to bring my arm across that table of shot glasses and shatter them all, like tiny grenades at Ally's feet. But I don't. I just stand there. My hands shaking. The numbness clashing with cold, hard panic—a nauseating combination. *What about me?* I want to scream. *I could have used my best friend in the end, too.* But I don't say it. I don't say anything, I just stand there, the wineglass stem clutched in my sweaty palm.

"We'll all miss her, though. Such a shame, isn't it?" Ally

says. She wobbles away from the table and stands in front of me, too close, and brushes the hair out of my eyes with her finger.

"I don't miss her at all," I say, the words rolling off my tongue, smooth and effortless. I can smell the wine on her breath. And the room stops spinning. It stops spinning, but it's quiet now. Stale and silent. One of the girls clucks her tongue like she's about to speak out, but they all look at each other, and nobody looks at me. Not even Ally, who's practically standing on top of me.

"Why would you say that?" Ally says, her eyes fixed sideways at Sasha, Ellie, and the Girl I Can't Remember—who are all huddled together by the sofa now. I pick up the bottle of wine and take a swig. It feels warm and bitter going down. I swallow.

"Why are you all pretending to care?" I ask.

"Come on, Aubrey. You don't mean that," Sasha cuts in, her voice low and unsure. It's the first thing she's said since I got there.

"Um, yes. I fucking do." I take another swig, and wipe the dribble off my chin with the back of my hand. I can feel it again, the words bubbling up inside of me. "She was an attention-whoring-whore." The words come out slurred and wet. "Give me one example of one time where she wasn't being a horrible bitch," I say. "I dare you. One time." I eye the row of shot glasses, and it's like they're winking at me, taunting me, willing me to backhand them onto the floor in one swift motion. But I sit back down onto the couch, exhausted. "You guys are a buzzkill," I say.

"You're here for a funeral. What did you expect?" Ally says, still standing where I left her. The room is quiet, except for the soft sounds of Adele playing from an iPod dock across the room. It's the first time I've noticed the music.

I take the half-empty bottle of Pinot, stand up, and shove my purse under my armpit.

"I'm not here for the funeral," I say.

Chapter 16

March 2009.

RACHEL SWUNG HER bright yellow Pathfinder around in front of the school, grazing the curb on the way in. I stepped back, waiting for her to brake, before climbing in, hoisting myself up into the passenger's seat. It was a Friday afternoon in late March. She handed me the coffee before my ass even hit the seat. Drop of skim, no sugar, sprinkle of cinnamon. She knew how I took it. That's one good thing I can say about her. With Rachel, it had always been the little efforts that actually meant something—knowing how I took my coffee, being the first to wish me a happy birthday every year, picking me up when I stayed after school to work on the newspaper.

Rachel sucked down her iced caramel Frappa-something, one hand turning the wheel away from curb. The slush slopped down her wrist, and she lifted her arm to her face to lap at it—her tongue drawing spitty lines around her purple Livestrong bracelet. The sticky sweet smell of slush-caramel-flavored-coffee-saliva made my guts roil, and I reached into her glove compartment and handed her a stack of coffee-stained Dunkin' Donuts napkins.

"So? Any word on your man friend?" She didn't waste any time.

I shook my head and tried to act unfazed.

It had been eleven days since our fight. It was stupid, really. It had started with some playful wrestling, nothing out of the norm for Adam and me. But we had been together for all of high school, and tension was building on the whole sex conversation.

"CHRIST," HE'D SNAPPED. We'd been on my bedroom floor, the door open. It was earlier that month.

"What's wrong with you?" I asked. I knew. Adam sat up, adjusting his jeans.

"Either do it or don't. Stop fucking around."

"Or start?" I said. He hadn't said anything. "Or what?" He'd clenched his jaw, and his gray eyes burned through the hardwood floor. I stood up and walked toward the door. He was still pouting. Staring hard at the ground, like he was on the verge of spewing out some nasty remark.

He'd filled out over the past month, since the concert. His chest and back had broadened, almost overnight. He'd started lifting weights, and he'd been working at the marina restaurant for Jason Dowd's dad, busing tables and lifting boxes. He was still dark, brooding, and somewhat hypothermic-looking with those thick bluish lips, but when he kissed me, it was never cold, and when he hugged me, I rarely pulled away.

"Adam," I'd said. He didn't look up, just drew circles on the floor with his finger. "Hello?" Nothing. "So you're just going to sit sulking there, then?" He smelled like french fries and seawater, with a hint of coffee. "Okay."

I stood in the doorway of my own room. It's not like I hadn't been accommodating. The year before, I'd given him his first hand job; six months earlier, his first blow job. Most nights, he would climb on top of me and grind up against my thigh for ten minutes until a small wet stain would seep through his jeans. I didn't really mind. It was better than letting him do anything to me. I had a strict nothing-below-the-waist rule at the time—my waist, not his.

"What does it matter at this point anyway?" he said.

"What does that mean?"

"You know you're gonna end up leaving. So what's the point?"

"I never said I was going."

"Do you really think your mom will let that happen? You're going to Brown. I know it. You know it. So if you don't do it with me, you're obviously just holding out for some jerk-off frat guy who'll only want to get inside of you for a night."

He sat on my bedroom floor, sulking, drawing stubborn circles on the hardwood with his fingers. "You know that's not true, Adam," I started. "What would possess you to even say that?" He didn't say anything. He didn't even look up. I let out a breath and waited, feeling the weight of his words bubble up inside me. At the moment they were just words. Cruel, empty words, a telltale sign of his own insecurities; but the more I stood, and the longer I waited, the harder it was for me to stay calm.

I had no intention of dumping Adam. That was never

even an option for me, and I didn't understand how going to college—something that I'd always been meant to do—could provoke such a tantrum. It didn't seem fair. I'd worked hard. He'd known that. And I'd gotten into an Ivy League school, despite Karen's professional opinion. That was huge. He should have been celebrating with me, not guilting me. As I turned his words over in my head, *holding out for some jerk-off frat guy*, I felt the sudden urge to punch him in the face, to grab him by the shoulders and shake the doubt out of him. But I didn't do any of those things. Instead I kept cool, like I always had, and with an even, dull voice, I said, "Go fuck yourself," and walked out of the room.

I didn't go far, just to the bathroom, where I stared myself down in the mirror, clenched until my back muscles spasmed and my whole body shook. When I came back, he was gone. I sat on the edge of my bed, my hands on my knees, my chest seething with each breath. I didn't want to text him. I didn't want to be *that* girl. I had nothing to apologize for and he had everything to.

I'd known it was coming. I had felt it brewing in the thick space between our words for months: his moods, his condescending tone, the way he threw himself into work. I felt stupid for not seeing this shift for what it was. I was leaving. I was leaving and he was staying. No Vermont. No Canada. No snow falling like stardust into a dark space where Adam and I would live out our fairy-tale ending. Our heaven. None of that. Just one last summer on Long Island.

My first text was a passive-aggressive test, just to give him a chance to apologize: *So this is how it's gonna be, Adam?*

My second text was a peace offering: *Call me.*

My third text was slow-burning fury: *No, really, GO FUCK YOURSELF.*

"HE'S RIGHT, AUB," Rachel said as we drove out of the school parking lot. "You'll regret it if you don't do it now. At least you *love* him."

"What does that even mean?"

"It means," she said, "that once you get to college, no guy is going to love you like that. Nobody wants a relationship in college, you know. You're gonna end up losing it to some random guy."

"That's not going to happen," I said. Rachel raised her eyebrows and sipped her coffee drink through the straw. "He won't even talk to me. It's his birthday tomorrow. What am I supposed to even do?"

"Oh, for Christ's sake," she said. "Just do it."

"That's pretty hard if he won't even return my texts."

"Tonight. Everybody will be at O'Reilly's. You'll definitely see Adam, and you can tell him to his face. Sort of like a 'Surprise! Happy birthday! Here's my vagina!'"

"It's the principle," I said. "I don't want to just give in."

"Oh, come on," she said. "Now you're just being stubborn. You know you were going to do it anyway." She was right. I was. I'd planned on it at least. But I'd also planned on staying with him, and the lack of trust my own boyfriend and best friend had in my ability to show some self-control was sort of obnoxious.

Most of the college kids were already home for spring break, and O'Reilly's was the place to be—whether you were still a senior in high school or part of the *I'm too cool for this town but still not twenty-one* college freshman crowd. It was just a dive bar, nothing fancy, strung up with white Christmas lights, and built against the train station. And as bland as the place was, Rachel was right; it was my chance to straighten things out with Adam.

I let my body relax back in my seat and lifted the tab of my coffee, careful not to spill on my white sweatshirt.

"Fast Car" started to play. I reached forward and turned up the volume.

"Really?" I say, acknowledging the song.

"You know you love it," Rachel said. "It's our song."

"Yeah, but I just didn't expect to hear it after 'Milkshake.'"

Rachel grinned, her cigarette between her teeth. "I made you a copy," she said, nodding to the dashboard. I opened the clear, plastic case, and true to her word, there was a burned CD that said *Spring Mix 2009*. I slipped it into my bag.

"So how was the paper brigade?" Rachel asked as we pulled up to a red light, and I hated the way she said it, the implications of shame.

"Oh, you know, the usual," I said, veiling the tiny bit of self-reproof she'd put onto me over the years. She never really gave me her blessing when I started writing for the *Seagull*, but she hadn't been trying to get into Brown either. Extracurriculars were never really her thing, unless, of course, it was cheerleading, and even her own days as a cheerleader were numbered. She showed up late to practice, if at all, and her coach caught her cutting class to smoke cigarettes on the great lawn. The first time she got a warning. The second time she was suspended from the squad for a week. Next time she's off for good.

Rachel accelerated onto Wantagh Parkway, and we careened past a blur of trees—lush and green and broken and brown, all at once. The colors of South Shore Long Island. As far back as I can remember, the grass never grew along the beach parkways, no matter what time of year. Just dry, cracked dirt along the side of the road surrounded by thick shrubs and shades of green, so many shades of green, everywhere but the ground.

We were cruising, and cold air streamed through my cracked window. I rolled it down all the way. The wind rushed in and tangled my hair.

"So what's our game plan for tonight?" Rachel asked. I shrugged. I hadn't thought about it.

We rumbled over the first drawbridge, over the silver stretch of bay beneath us. I stared out toward the marshes. It'd been too cold for recreational boating, but a few brave Jet Skiers and fishermen zipped around in the distance. I could see our town sprawled out against the marshes—the marinas, boatyards, and a few massive homes at the edge of the bay.

I breathed in the cool, salty air—the unmistakable smell of the ocean. It was like our own slice of paradise, away from the suburban blight of high ranches and split-level homes lining every neighborhood, Italian delis, nail salons, bagel joints, and pizza places in every shopping center. All of that faded away once you hit the parkway. It was like the landscape changed. The grass grew differently; it was all sedges, Salix, and sometimes a subtle burst of color—a single hibiscus, goldenrod—but it was all a blur of green as we drove through. Green and thorny.

"You haven't thought about it at all?" she asked. I shrugged again and gulped the last sip of my coffee.

"Not really," I said. "I was just sort of planning on going with the flow, you know?" The road narrowed as we rolled over the second bridge, and I squeezed into myself. The amphitheater came into sight up ahead.

"First," Rachel said, "we need to get you liquored up. You're gonna want to be numb. Trust me." I agreed. I had heard tales from Rachel and Ally—tales that involved tearing hymens and significant amounts of blood. Liquor sounded good.

We made the loop around the Jones Beach Pencil—a Long Island icon—and pulled into Field 4. I reached behind me into the backseat for the crumpled jersey-knit sheet. The wind came in hard off the Atlantic as the sun went down. We smoothed the sheet out a few feet back from the tide and sprawled out with our oversized sweatshirts and equally oversized sunglasses.

It was March 31, the first real spring day of the year and our first trip to the beach. I sat up, dusted the sand off my leggings, and clutched a plastic water bottle full of gin and tonic in my hand. The beach was empty, except for a couple of power walkers and a lone cyclist up on the boardwalk.

"So, are you nervous?" Rachel asked.

"Not really," I said. I was. But not so much about the planned dual deflowering. How bad could that be? Rachel had done it—or so she claimed. Ally had done it. Adam and I were in the

minority as V-card carriers. So it just felt like going through
the motions at this point. But it was the possibility of rejection
that ignited my nerves—the fear of giving it all up and learning that's all he'd been after—the *what happens next* in a relationship that maybe isn't going anywhere after all. Things had
been tense with Adam lately. But things had always been tense
with Adam. He was just an intense kind of guy, and I liked that
about him. It balanced out my blatant lack of intensity.

"Well, while you're off doing *that*, I'm thinking about hook-
ing up with Eric tonight," Rachel said, her voice muffled as she
lit the cigarette pinched between her lips. "I mean, if you're
getting laid, then I probably should, too, yes?" She flashed a
Cheshire cat grin around the cigarette. "But if you're gonna do
it," she said, "you gotta show a little more boob." She grabbed
at my chest. I swatted at her hand and reached for her pack of
Parliaments.

"Do what you have to do, Rach," I said, lighting up. "But be
careful, people are going to start to think you're a slut."

"Hey," she cackled, throwing the crumpled plastic bottle
of gin at me. "You're lucky I like you." She took a long drag
off the Parliament, and her face got all serious. "I mean, I've
wanted him since like second grade."

"Right," I said. "Ever since he taught us all about hard-ons."

"Speaking of *heart-ons*," she said. "How's the tat?" She lifted
up her own shirt, pulled down her pants just to her crotch line,
and peeled off the gauze. Her skin was still raw and red, and
the black ink still raised and bumpy. We'd gotten them the
week before, when she turned eighteen. I peeled down my own
bandage to show her, the cigarette hanging from my lips.

"Looks good, right?" I mumbled, smoke streaming out of the corners of my mouth. It hadn't hurt too bad. I actually thought it had felt kind of good. But it had itched and burned that whole week—no matter how many times I slathered my hip with Lubriderm.

We'd successfully hidden our new ink from both of our mothers. *I just had to make it to college*, I thought. Just make it through the summer. And when I came home for Thanksgiving break, she'd think I had just gotten it at college. Rachel, on the other hand, was going to Hofstra and living at home. I don't think she was too worried, though; her mom pretty much ignored her anyway.

"You think I can pull it off? With Eric?" she asked.

"If that's what you're into, go for it. I don't see it, though," I said. And I didn't see it. Eric was stocky, with bad teeth and too many freckles.

"I forgot you like them scrawny and brooding," she said.

I felt my face go hot and my tongue swell, the way it does when Rachel says just the right thing to make me want to knock her teeth in.

"Rachel," I said. I said her name because it adds a condescending element that you just can't get without saying the person's name before a statement. If you ever want to make someone feel incredibly stupid and small, then start a sentence with their first name. "He's had a pretty fucked-up life. His brother fucking hanged himself, remember? Give the guy a break."

"Oh, right," she said. "The brother you sucked face with right before he offed himself. Are you still withholding that little piece of information from lover boy?" Her tone remained sarcastic, playful even, but I still wanted to smash her face in.

She must have sensed it because she took another drag of her cigarette, let out a self-satisfied snort, and said, "Relax, Aub. You know I'm only kidding."

I lit another cigarette and shook my head at her. "Not okay."

"Fine," she said. She winked and put her cigarette out in the sand.

Rachel's dirty-blond hair fell just below her shoulder blades, and her bangs swooped over to one side. She'd thinned out around the middle of ninth grade, just around the time I'd started to thicken around my ass and thighs. Her cheeks were dusted with freckles, but you'd never know. She hid them well.

"We should go to Montauk tomorrow," she said, her voice raspy. "To celebrate."

"Montauk. Mon-tawk," I said, twisting a hollowed stick into the sand. "This is why we talk like this. Montauk. Wantagh."

"Yeah. Walk the *dawg* and get some *cawfee*," Rachel said. "Blame the Indians."

"Ugh," I said. "I could go for more coffee." I clutched the almost empty Poland Spring bottle of gin and tonic and swished it around. It had tasted like a dream, what I imagined clouds might taste like, dry and airy, but I cringed at the thought of that last little gulp and poured it into the sand.

Chapter 17

Tuesday, October 7, 2014.

COME WITH ME, *come with me, he says.*

I wobble on the balls of my feet, twisting my car keys in the door. It doesn't open. Smoke streams off the end of my lit cigarette. It's clenched between my teeth.

It won't open, I say, my voice muffled. I collapse into a hysterical fit of giggles. I'm on the ground, my sweater lifts up and the asphalt scratches my bare back.

Come with me, Aubrey, the voice says. Let me take you home.

There's pressure under my arms—hands, I think, lifting me back on my feet.

The streetlights buzz, the keys rattle and fall to the street. His hand comes down and swoops them up. I can't stand, I feel my weight start to shift, and Ally's house stands like a giant pink elephant on the cul-de-sac.

The streetlights spin, I let my face fall into his chest. I breathe in coffee and cinnamon.

Let me take you home.

My car, I say. I think I say it. My car. But my insides spin and the streets swirl around me and I feel my center of gravity churning up from my guts, up through my chest and lodging in my throat. I fall to my knees, and retch: Karen's roast chicken, Jack, and half a bottle of Pinot splatters onto the street.

The hand rubs my back. The keys rattle in his pocket. He's lifting me to my feet.

THE SUN SHRIEKS through a crack in the curtains. My insides feel hollow and dried out. I open my mouth, and the air hits my tongue. It feels like I've been chewing on sand, puke-flavored sand. A thick, groggy fog envelops me, and for a moment I don't remember where I am, or why I feel like shit, and then it hits me like a bag of bricks, and panic sweeps over me.

I'm in my own bed.

I can barely read the digital clock on my nightstand, but if I squint, I make out a blurry outline: 7:51. I'm almost sure it's 7:51. And the light streams in through the window; it's the bright, unnatural morning light, the kind that comes all at once. I groan and roll on my side. I'm simultaneously hot and cold, drenched in a dizzy sweat. I kick the covers off, but feel exposed in a Brown T-shirt and shorts; I don't remember putting on either. So I pull the blanket back up over my head, will myself to just vanish into the sheets, and retrace my steps from last night. I can't see the clock, so my contacts are out. That much I know. At least I'd been somewhat responsible. But other than that, there's nothing—just a black hole of nothing and this throbbing pain in my temple.

And then it starts to come back to me. Piece by piece. There was dinner.

There was Ally's.

I remember falling, vomiting, and that smell. Coffee and cinnamon. There's only one person I know who smells like that. So that part must have been a dream. I'm sure of it.

I need water, but I'd rather shrivel up and die before walking out into that kitchen right now. There's no doubt in my mind that Karen is setting up an intervention at this very moment. I can just see it now: Eli, Ashley, and Marc seated around the living room, Styrofoam cups of coffee lined up on a folding table, the kind reserved for holiday parties and beer pong. They will each have prepared a speech, how my sudden erratic behavior has affected them in some way.

I know we hardly know each other Awwwbryy, I can just see Ashley saying, *but I feel like we really have a connection. You know? And I want to help you.*

Maybe even Ally will have come down. If she even cared enough to see if I made it home all right. Which is doubtful. She didn't follow up five years ago and she won't follow up now.

I turn over to face away from the window, my head still throbbing, and I see it. It's there on the edge of my night table—a mason jar, filled to the brim with water.

Chapter 18

March 2009.

RACHEL LEANED UP against the bar, sulking. She kept staring over in Eric's direction, but he was too busy talking to his lacrosse buddies to notice her. A local college band tuned up on the stage. She whipped around, flagged the bartender for a shot, and sighed, hard.

"He's not even looking at me," she said. "I don't get it."

I shrugged and nursed the Bud Light in my hand. I already felt unsteady on my feet. We'd been drinking all day. I checked my phone. Still nothing. I smoothed my dress over my thigh.

I had worn a dress to make the whole seduction process a bit more methodical. I bought it from Urban Outfitters back in January with my Christmas money, but the weather hadn't been warm enough to wear it yet. It was simple—black cotton, with a sweeping neckline, and it fell around midthigh. There was a thin string that I tied around my waist.

"You look so hot," Rachel had said when I tried it on.

"It's seventy dollars," I said. "I mean, it's just a black dress."

"Shut up," she said. "It's actually flattering."

So that night, I wore the dress with a dangling heart necklace and cheap black, sequined, mesh flats that I'd bought from a bin in Chinatown. Rachel picked me up at six and we parked at the train station, right next to the bar, and sat in her car, downing Monster energy drinks and gin. It tasted like pine needles and chemicals. I winced with each gulp, but could feel my blood start to buzz.

"What if he doesn't show?" I said, after a particular sour swig.

"Then fuck him," Rachel said. "I mean, not literally. Just fuck someone else." She wore a light green tank top that squished her breasts together, black skinny jeans, and bright pink come-fuck-me pumps. Her ash-blond hair swooped over her face and fell into flat waves down her back. She looked thinner than she had earlier at the beach, but I didn't tell her that, I just eyed her when I climbed into the car and said, "Nice shirt."

Adam still hadn't responded to any of my voice mails. "Ad. It's me. Want to talk," was all I'd said. I wanted to wait until we were in person, for him to see me, dressed like a lady, ready and willing. I couldn't wait to see his tongue swell up in his mouth, like the first time he saw a pair of tits in *Titanic*. Yet, it was nearly midnight and I was standing in the middle of this crappy bar so that Rachel could make eyes at Eric and his buddies.

I stepped outside, half expecting to find Adam arguing with the bouncer about his fake ID.

O'Reilly's was right beneath the Seaport train-station platform—easy access for South Shore bar-goers. From where I stood, I could faintly make out the voice from the loud-speaker overhead.

The eleven forty-five to Babylon is operating on time.

A furious ball of frustration began to spool in my gut as I concealed a bottle of Bud in my bag and halfheartedly nodded to some junior girls fumbling in their patent pumps. There was nothing to do but wait, and I risked missing Adam altogether if I went back inside. So I checked my phone again. Nothing.

The eleven fifty-three to Penn Station is operating on time.

In seven minutes, Adam would turn eighteen, and I couldn't stand the fact that he wasn't celebrating with me.

"I want that one," Rachel said, when I shouldered my way back toward the dance floor. She was still leaning against the bar, swaying on her feet. She pointed, subtly, though not quite subtle enough, at some guy. "His name is Rod," she slurred, and then busted into an hysterical fit of giggles. Rod stood next to Eric. We'd never seen the guy before, and decided he was one of Eric's lacrosse buddies from upstate. When Rod caught Rachel sloppily pointing in his direction, he approached. Ally, Sasha, and Ellie signaled to me from the bathroom line.

"What happened to Eric?" I asked.

"Like I said, I'm saving him for a special occasion," she crooned. "Besides, maybe this will make him jealous." Rod had a shaved head, hard eyes, and a weak chin.

"I want to go," I said. "I'm bored. And Adam clearly isn't coming." I reached into my bag and felt a damp wad of cash that had been soaked by the beer I snuck outside.

"Relax," Rachel said. "Why don't you have fun for once? As far as I'm concerned, you're a single woman."

The band started up on the stage and began to play a slow emo version of Pat Benatar's "Invincible."

Rachel waved me away and put her own arms around Rod's thick neck. I watched their fluid movements on the dance floor. Rachel's hips swung to the tired beat of the song.

This bloody road remains a mystery.
This sudden darkness fills the air.

"Hi." The voice startled me. I whirled around, the bottom of my dress brushing up against my midthigh.

"Eric," he said, pointing at himself. I knew who he was. He'd schooled me in hard-ons, the middle finger, and virgins, but it was okay, because he had a dead mother. He had graduated two years earlier, and from what Rachel said, he now went to some preppy college upstate on a lacrosse scholarship. He lived near Adam. I passed his house each time I walked there, but we hadn't actually spoken since that time he gave me the middle finger in second grade.

His navy ribbed sweater seemed outdated, and his sleeves were rolled up to his elbows, exposing his thick forearms. The tiny hairs on his arm stood up, and it reminded me of this time when I was ten. I had been sitting on my living room couch, sulking, waiting for Karen to take me to soccer practice or softball practice, or whatever season it was. We were already late. The tiny hairs stood up on my legs, and that's when I decided it was time to start shaving. That night, with my father's razor, I sliced a chunk out of my knee, a scar that would—over the years—fade into a tiny white film, barely noticeable.

"Hey?"

"Excuse me?" I said, realizing again where I was, the hazy air of the bar swirling around me like exhaust from a car. He said something barely audible over the band.

"That's your name, isn't it?" Eric said.

"No," I said. "It's not." I took a swig of my beer and craned my neck, looking for another familiar face. Rachel winked at me from the wooden dance floor, and the song played.

"Do you want a drink?" he asked. "I'm getting a drink." I shook my head and stared at the door. Still no Adam. Eric shrugged and walked toward the bar. His body moved with a cold indifference.

I waited for Rachel to make eye contact again and signaled for her. She whispered something into Rod's ear and shouldered her way toward me.

"You okay?" She put her free hand on my shoulder.

"I guess," I said, and took a swig out of the bottle. "Just bummed it turned out like this. I think I might just go home."

"Don't go home," she whined. "Give me like an hour, and we'll go home together. Okay? Besides, your bag is at my house, remember?" She smiled, her sickly-sweet Rachel smile, draped her arm around my neck, and pulled me into her. "Please," she said. Her hot breath tickled my cheek. I wanted to say no. I should have said no, but part of me still thought Adam might saunter in through the wooden doors.

"Go ahead," I said, and pushed her back toward Rod. She

smiled and threw her arms around me, smacking her lips into my face. I wiped my cheek with the back of my hand.

I SAT, PERCHED at the high-top table near the door, peeling the label off the bottle of Bud. I'd lost sight of Rachel more than an hour earlier, and my phone was about to die. Ally, Sasha, and Ellie were dancing. I'd given up on Adam, and was about to call it a night, when I felt the weight of the table shift.

"Shots?" Eric stayed standing and leaned into the table. He placed two glasses of tequila down in front of me. "You can have them both." He wasn't smiling, but he seemed amused, in a dry, deadpan way, and it reminded me of Adam. He smelled different from Adam though, more artificial, his sweater doused in a cheap drugstore cologne.

"Thank you, sir," I said, eyeing him as I threw one back and the brass-flavored booze burned my throat. He wasn't so bad up close, and for a moment I thought I saw what Rachel saw—sharp blue eyes and just the right amount of composure.

"You look bored," he said, his voice straining over the music. His chest was broad up close, too—something that Adam had always lacked, no matter how many push-ups he attempted. Part of me wanted to reach out and touch him, just to know what actual masculinity felt like for once.

"I *am* bored," I said. I leaned in and took the second shot.

"Me, too." He grinned, and he signaled to the bartender for another shot. "Well, I was."

"I think our friends ditched us," I said. He leaned into the table, still standing, and held his phone up to my face. I squinted and read the text: *Rachel's phone is dead. We're back at the house. Bring her friend.*

"From Rod," he said.

"So typical," I mumbled, and threw down the rest of my drink.

"Then why do you put up with it?" He took another shot, and I shrugged. I didn't know why, and I wasn't about to delve into it with the guy who flipped me off in second grade.

"She likes you, you know." I don't know why I said it. I knew Rachel would have killed me, but the words sort of just fell from my mouth. I shifted in my chair, feeling the tequila start to buzz through me.

"Oh yeah?" he said. "Well, what about you?" His gaze stayed stoic but playful, and again he reminded me of Adam. I shook off the thought, and stared at his sharp blue eyes.

"What about me?"

"Do you like me?" And then his cold face broke, and he sort of smirked, and shrugged, and pulled himself up onto the stool.

"I have a boyfriend," I said.

OUTSIDE, I KICKED at the curb with my heel. Eric pulled his truck up to where I stood.

The one fifty-three to Babylon is operating on time.

I stood on the sidewalk in a circle with Ally, Sasha, and Ellie. We passed a joint around the circle, the air hazy and cool.

Eric lurked on the sidewalk. He'd seemed bothered by my presence once I dropped the boyfriend bomb, like he'd promised to play wingman while Rod did his thing. If only Rachel knew, maybe she would have encouraged me to go for Rod instead.

"Are you sure you don't want to come back with us?" Ally asked again, eyeing Eric, who was now holding his passenger-side door open and tapping his foot impatiently on the sidewalk. I handed her the joint. She put it out and stuffed it back into her bra. I felt the weed hit me all at once.

"You know Rachel—the master of Irish exits." I shook my head and stumbled toward Eric's car. "I promised I'd go back with her. My stuff is at her house anyway," I said. "Are you sure you're not too drunk to drive?" I asked Eric, not really caring. He'd promised to swing by his place, pick up Rachel, and take us back to her house. I just wanted to get into Rachel's bed, and text Adam a defeated Happy Birthday note.

Maybe he'd feel bad. Maybe he was testing me. Maybe if I just spilled my guts, told him how I really felt, how I was sad and disappointed and *hurt*. Hurt. Quite possibly the most pathetic word of all.

Eric nodded, and I waved Ally away. I smoothed the front of my black dress and hoisted myself up into Eric's car. I felt unsteady, but shook off my first wave of the spins and focused on the dashboard in front of me. It was cold, and I was starting to regret not bringing a jacket. That was Rachel's idea, too.

I chewed on the corner of my lip until I broke the skin. The truck rumbled and sputtered against the dark back road. The metallic taste of blood distracted me, and I didn't notice when he pulled into his driveway.

Eric cut the engine, and it was silent. He looked over at me, his mouth stretched into a thin line. It was so silent that the air felt thick, like it was pressing down on my chest.

"You can just drive me home if you want. I can pick Rachel up in the morning if that's easier." I didn't know what else to say. I felt like more of a burden at this point, and Eric wasn't the kind of guy who played wingman.

"No. Whatever," he said. "We'll figure it out." I was starting to feel like some kid who'd gotten dumped on his stoop.

He didn't turn on the lights when we walked into the foyer. It was dark, but I could hear voices from the kitchen, and I imagined a group of guys all seated around the table with a deck of cards.

"Wait here," he said.

"Where's Rachel?" I said, reluctant to step into the house. It was drafty and smelled like old cedar and cigarettes. I didn't recognize any of the voices from the kitchen, but it sounded like some sort of after-party in the works, and I wasn't in the mood to be social. "We're not staying. I just want to find her and leave. Okay?"

"Okay," he said, flashing me that patronizing smile again. "Just sit tight." He pushed me down onto an armchair, and I suddenly realized how drunk I was.

He was gone for a while. Minutes—maybe ten. But the voices from the kitchen were low, husky, and casual. I couldn't tell how many people were in there, but it was definitely not Rachel.

"I think she's cute," I heard someone say.

"Yeah, I guess so. Cute, but kind of chubby."

I put both hands over my stomach, which wasn't in such bad

shape, I thought, and sat up straight as if to march in there and defend myself. But the room started to spin, and my tongue felt too thick to even speak. I fell back against the armchair and closed my eyes.

It may have been more minutes—seven, eight. It's hard to tell because when he shook my shoulder, I jolted awake.

"You can't stay here," Eric said. His hand was still on my shoulder.

"Okay," I said. I was groggy, and not fully awake, my body weighed down by sleep. "I can leave."

He laughed, a dry, husky laugh. "No. I mean you can't stay on this chair. Come on. Rachel'll be right on that couch. I'll find you somewhere else to sleep. Cool?"

"I guess," I said, and followed him up the stairs. He opened the door to a drafty room. There was a couch—somebody already curled up on it, his back to us—and an empty full-sized bed.

"How about you just sleep here, and I'll find somewhere else to crash." He smiled, nothing like that arrogant prick he'd been at the bar. I almost felt bad for being such a bitch. My body hit the bed and I felt sleep take over again. Relief.

"This is fine," I said. I rolled onto my side and faced the wall. He disappeared into the hallway. I must have drifted off into that drunken realm between sleep and wakefulness, when I heard the door creak open and a strand of yellow light streamed in through the doorway.

"There was nowhere else to go," he said, his voice low. I felt his body come down next to me, his bare chest pressed against my back.

THERE IS NOTHING worse than the weight of a man on your chest: the stubble of his face scratching your cheek, the rough pads of his fingers prodding, his unyielding tongue drawing spitty lines all over your neck.

I felt my own body shake in the cold drafty room. Maybe it was the weed, but I was sure I was about to split. I was sure my torso would crack and my insides would spill out onto the hardwood floor.

"Be quiet," he said, and nodded in the direction of a shadowy figure sprawled out on the couch.

"Stop," I said, too softly. My hips raised beneath him as I tried to wriggle out from under him, but he took it as an invitation.

"Relax," he said, and his hand pressed down gently over my mouth. *Relax. Relax.* What a vile word. He reached under my dress and moved my underwear to the side, his fingers grazing against me. I wore lace. I borrowed the pair from Rachel. It was supposed to be for Adam.

The reflection from the streetlamp against the cheap panel wall attached to my eyes and spun with a dull grace. *Relax.* But all I could think about was the beach.

We were young, Rachel and me—maybe eight, Eli was around six. The three of us spent the afternoon digging a hole. It was one of those holes that you find at the beach as a kid and reuse, because it's such a waste to fill it in. But we hadn't wanted anyone to enjoy our hard labor, so we buried Eli up to his neck. When we were finished, and he couldn't wriggle free, he started to cry, panic really. The lifeguards had to come and dig him out with a special shovel. Later, Karen lectured us on

how we could have killed him, how his chest could have collapsed.

Now, as I lay on this bed with this man on my chest, I knew
how it felt to be buried in the sand.

I STARED UP at the ceiling. The streetlight still buzzing. How
could anyone sleep with that sound? His boxers were scrunched
next to the bedpost.

My dress hung limp over my body, but Rachel's underwear
was gone, tangled somewhere between his white down comforter and the starchy bare mattress.

He was beside me, his back turned to me, curled up in the
fetal position, breathing. Peaceful.

Chapter 19

Wednesday, October 8, 2014.

I'M ON MY knees, my body wedged into my closet, and I pull out a single black pump and fumble around for the other shoe. I probably won't need them, but I'd like to have everything ready just in case. It's the night before Rachel's funeral. It's also the night of the wake. Visiting hours are from seven to nine. It's six thirty now, and instead of getting ready or even entertaining the idea of making an appearance, I help myself to some of Karen's wine.

I'd been camped out in my room since yesterday—except to use the bathroom—and I didn't venture out until I heard Karen's car edge out of the driveway around noon, and that was only to refill my glass with water and snag an unopened box of cereal.

I sit on the hardwood floor, outside of my closet, with a

glass of Pinot Noir. I can hear her heels clicking on the hardwood in and out of the hall bathroom.

Monday night's dinner fiasco and everything that followed at Ally's burn like a fresh wound, and the words keep spinning around in my head.

I heard you did something bad. She really could have used her best friend in the end.

I've spent the past two days buried beneath my covers piecing together that night—every word, every smell, or at least what I could remember of it. I heard my door creak open at around ten—Karen must have been checking in to make sure I was alive—but I kept my face hidden in my pillow and feigned sleep. She hasn't tried to talk to me yet, and I've been brainstorming a way out of the conversation for more than forty-eight hours. I've never been good at these types of conversations.

I take a sip of wine and continue fumbling around my closet for the missing black pump. I pull out other mismatched shoes, a couple of rumpled designer bags, and an old shoe box. The box is torn, watermarked, and coming apart at the edges. It's filled with notebooks, photos, and birthday cards. I take a wad of photos in my hand. There are a few pictures of Rachel and me; Adam and me; Rachel, Adam, and me, but nothing worth keeping. I throw them all into my garbage can.

It feels okay, though. Not liberating or anything, just okay.

I swish the wine in my mouth, swallow, and shuffle through more of the shoe box. I start to toss some old school notes into the garbage, too, but stop to look at the top book, a black Marble notebook with the words *As If* etched out in pencil on the white part of the cover.

"Shit," I say out loud, opening to the center of the book. And right there, taped to the page and printed in faded purple ink, are the lyrics to "Don't Stop Lovin' Me, Baby."

I reach for my wine in pure amusement, my eyes locked on the poorly spelled rendition of our almost breakout hit. I'd forgotten that I'd kept the book after the infamous framing incident. I had lied and told Rachel and Ally that Ms. Price had confiscated it. I don't realize that I'm smiling, and for a second, just a second, I almost, almost wish I could call Rachel and tell her what I found.

I take another sip of wine. It's sweet and earthy. Karen raps three times on the door.

"Yes?" The door creaks open, slow and dramatic, like she's waiting for me to scream or throw a dish at the door. "Yeah?" I say again. Karen pushes the door open, and I see she's wearing a black pantsuit.

She's actually going to the wake. Without me.

"I'm leaving. You're really not coming?" Her voice sounds tired, and she doesn't take her eyes off the bottle of wine open on the floor.

Memories are a funny thing. I think of Rachel, and I think, Narcissistic slut, judgmental bitch, sadistic psychopath, weak. I see her throwing me under the bus at seven years old, calmly telling Ms. Price how I'd been responsible for "Don't Stop Lovin' Me, Baby." And then again at thirteen, as she politely explained to Karen how I'd been the one who stole the bottle of whiskey from the liquor cabinet. I see her driving around in her yellow truck, a cigarette dangling from between her thin lips. I see her prepping me to lose my virginity and then walking out the second some dick with a guy attached looks her way. I think of her while I was lying in Eric Robbins's bed, his back to me, his boxers scrunched up next to the bed. I see her when I look at myself in the mirror, every time I go to the bathroom. I see her carved into my hip for the rest of my life. And I see her with Adam.

And my whole body aches again.

And all of the rest of it—the long drives, the secrets, the inside jokes—all of the rest of it falls away. It just doesn't matter anymore. They're just hollow shells scattered at my feet.

I start to say something, but Karen cuts in. "At least for her family, Aubrey. Whatever little spat you had with Rachel that was so awful, you can show some respect to her mother and sister." Her voice is cold and accusing. My fingers tingle. It spreads up my hands, arms, and chest like pins and needles. This is what numb feels like. I want to tell her to mind her own business. I want to tell her to get out of my room and leave me alone, but instead I just reach for the glass and raise it toward the ceiling.

"Cheers," I say.

I propel myself back into the closet one last time, and finally emerge with the black left pump. The dress I picked out still hangs from behind my bedroom door, it's shadowy and menacing, and it probably won't even fit right. I've lost a good deal of weight since my *cute, but kind of chubby* days. But, even if the dress is a tad loose, I think the whole outfit will look nice pulled together—a classic black dress, patent fuck-me heels, maybe even a bit of red lipstick—*#funeralchic*.

I'M HALFWAY THROUGH the second bottle of Pinot when that dull pain starts behind my eyes, and my chest starts to tingle again. I know I will start to feel it if I don't get the hell out of this house.

I throw on an old gray sweater and step outside. I suck in the autumn air, drawing it into my lungs, trying to reach that place where my breath never seems to touch.

I walk around the side of my house and sit down on the curb, my feet sprawling out on the street in front of me, a cigarette pinched between my shaky fingers.

A middle-aged man with a receding hairline rounds the corner. A small white dog stumbles a few feet ahead, tugging at the leash in the man's hand.

He slows up, a bit, in that neighborly way, and nods his head at me, like he's waiting for me to ask to pet his dog. I press my lips together in a reluctant smile and shift my gaze toward an empty beer bottle nestled against the curb across the street.

"You're way too pretty to be smoking," he says. He has this jocular smile that lingers for an extra uncomfortable second.

I suck in the smoke, trying to fill that hollowed place again, and blow it out the corner of my mouth.

"No," I say. "Not pretty." Gray ash burns and falls from the tip of the cigarette, settling onto my leggings like stardust. "Cute. But kind of chubby."

Chapter 20

April 2009.

THE DUGOUT WAS cold and wet, and the rain seemed to be suspended in the morning sky—collecting in the sagging gray clouds. The bench gave off a thick metallic scent. I held a cigarette between two fingers and sat between the red-painted walls. I didn't inhale all the way. I never did and I wouldn't until college. Until this point, I had never really smoked without Rachel. But that Wednesday morning, I sat like the shady class cutter that I'd become, holding the smoke inside of my puffed-up cheeks, hiding in the baseball dugout. Smoke streamed off the end of the lit cigarette, creating invisible designs on page ninety-seven of *The Bell Jar*, a red paper clip was placed gently in the center fold. The smoke twisted and twirled like hair on a finger.

I'd read *The Bell Jar* twice before. Once in ninth grade, to see what all the hype was about, but I didn't get it. I was unimpressed—don't even think I finished it. And then again for a women's lit class in eleventh grade. I remember liking it then, finding the prose quite beautiful actually, but retaining nothing. But this time, it was as if the words crawled off the page, like tiny spiders, and onto my skin, and I hated myself for it. I'd become like those pretentious, dramatic, *feeling* girls I swore I'd never be. Those girls at school who quoted Sylvia Plath for no other reason than to sound edgy, dark, and complicated.

It hadn't really sunk in until Saturday, late afternoon. I didn't sleep at Eric's house. I'd just stared up at the ceiling while the tequila and weed pulsed through my veins. I waited until he was asleep before I finally forced myself to get up. I pulled my dress down toward my knees, but each time it sprang back up to midthigh. It seemed shorter than before. I felt more exposed. But I guess that's just what happens after. Or at least that's what they always say. I needed to get to the bathroom, to make sure I wasn't bleeding. I could still feel his hand jamming into my crotch.

My flats glided against the wood floor. Downstairs, a dull glow from the den soaked up some of the darkness in the hallway. There was no sound, just the phantom shadows of the television. I fell back into the armchair and pulled out my phone. Nothing. It was after four, and a news segment started on the television. I read the caption: *April, 1, 2009, April Fools' Day.*

I sat there for a while. Minutes. Maybe ten. Maybe fifty. Time didn't really make sense anymore, but from where I sat, I saw two bodies tucked under a blanket on a pullout couch just across the room. I could see her ash-blond hair spattered out over the couch pillows. I slipped out of the door before she woke up.

"So," Rachel sang from the third-base line. The hard sound of her voice scared the shit out of me and I slammed *The Bell Jar* shut. "A little light reading, Aub?" she said, but before I could answer, and as I shoved the book into my backpack, she went on into the real reason she'd found me. "You never called me back, bitch."

Sunday, Monday, and Tuesday stood like a barricade of bricks between that last night at O'Reilly's and the two of us on the empty baseball field.

I had managed to fake an ongoing migraine the first half of the week, a believable ailment, genetically shared with my mother. Karen's sympathy hadn't been an issue. I skipped two days of school and spent them lying in my bed, staring up at the ceiling, feeling stagnant and empty. Worse than any migraine I'd ever had. A dull pain spread across the back part of my skull. My ribs ached with a fatigue that I couldn't shake. Sometimes it would seep into my lungs, a crushing sensation that pinched my breath.

And then there was the nausea. Constant. Lingering. I couldn't eat more than a few forkfuls of whatever was on my plate before I'd feel it rising up in my throat. I'd been sticking to iced coffee and frozen yogurt, making excuses at dinner— I'd had a late lunch, my stomach hurt. Karen looked at me and shrugged. I think she thought I might drop some baby fat before college.

I've heard that anxiety can manifest itself as physical symptoms. That what's in your head can spread through your body like poison. And I felt full of poison.

I managed to avoid both Adam and Rachel. Not that avoiding Adam was too hard; it was becoming clear he wanted absolutely nothing to do with me. Rachel was the real issue. She'd been calling nonstop since Sunday morning.

"I wanted to tell you about my sexcapades," Rachel said, snatching the cigarette from me and taking a long drag. She put her other hand on her hip, pausing slightly, as if she just now remembered hearing me come back into the house with Eric. This look of hers—the way she raised her eyebrows at me in suspicion, sparked that crushing sensation in my chest. I sucked in air but tried to keep my face still. "Wait a minute," she said.

I held my breath. The air suddenly felt warm. Way too warm. I stammered, about to change the subject before she could bring up Saturday night, but she just stood there, her hand on her hip, and said, "Since when do you smoke?"

A lull swam over me. I exhaled, my muscles eased up just a bit, and Rachel segued into every detail of her night with Rod. Phrases like "three times" and "so hard," and, of course, "Rod's huge rod" hung in the air like *BAM!* or *POW!* from a superhero comic book. I listened passively and remembered my own evening—how the warm mixture of semen and blood dribbled and chafed like slime against my inner thighs as I walked home in the dark.

MY PHONE HAD died back at the bar, and even if I'd wanted to, I couldn't go home that night. My house keys were in my overnight bag, and my bag was at Rachel's. I'd have had to knock on my door, and Karen would have known right away. She would have taken one whiff of me, placed her bony hands on her bony hips and said, *You had sex, didn't you? You had sex and you smoked marijuana. And you were drunk, weren't you?* So home was out of the question. And Rachel's hadn't been an option either. I considered it, though—shaking Rachel awake while she lay there with Rod on that awful, pleather pullout couch, and telling her what had happened, detail by detail: how Eric lured me into his room, left, and came back for me later, when I'd been asleep—too hazy to realize what he'd been planning. How he'd scrunched my dress up to my neck while I pretended to sleep. How he buried his face into me, even when I tried to kick him away. And how he'd held me down—one hand clamping down on my wrists, the other hand stabbing into me until my body quieted.

I wanted to tell her, but I knew Rachel too well. I knew the way the girl operated, and she wouldn't have seen it the way I saw things. She'd have seen it as betrayal. She'd have seen it as me fucking around with the one guy she had been saving for herself.

So I walked.

It was dark, cold, and everything was damp. The fluorescent lights glowed from inside Pathmark—the grand plaza at the center of town. The automatic doors glided open and a rush of cool air hit me. For the first time that night, I thought I might vomit, and part of me wanted to crouch down behind a Dumpster and pull the trigger in my throat until my guts spilled out on the asphalt.

I stood still in front of the doors, closed my eyes, swallowed the sick back down, and pitched forward into the store. I walked up and down the aisles for an hour or so—the cool, stagnant air and bright lights reminded me of the life that ticked and pulsed inside me, that I existed, even if I didn't exist beyond the stacked cans of peaches and bottles of Chateau Diana. I stalked down every aisle, straightening cereal boxes to proper formation, memorizing the flavors of Ben & Jerry's. Seasonal was packed with wicker baskets, cellophane wrap, Peeps, and Cadbury Cream Eggs, and the thought of all that sugary, pastel Easter propaganda made my throat feel thick. The store was empty except for a new dad buying diapers and formula. He pushed the bum cart toward the register, the front wheel shrieking against the vinyl. I bought a bottle of water, a hair tie, and a small bottle of Listerine.

The cashier eyed me as she rang up my things. I threw a pack of gum down at the last minute. She was older, probably late fifties, and her hair was tied back in this tight graying bun. I caught a glimpse of myself in the soda cooler's door. My hair was matted and frizzed out like a lion's mane, and my mascara had smeared into dark rings around my eyes.

I reached into my bag and pulled out the crumpled wad of damp cash. Seven dollars, and it still smelled like beer from O'Reilly's. The cashier clicked her tongue and tightened her lips. I stared hard while she flattened the bills against the register, and for the first time I wanted to punch a complete stranger.

There were moments when I'd forgotten during those early-morning hours. I'd be walking, or lying flat on my back in Clear Pond Park—not far from the spot where Max died—and suddenly I'd feel normal, calm even. I was still shivering, still cold, still wet and tired, but I'd forgotten why. And then it would hit me, and I would feel it in my throat. It would spread through my chest, and I'd remember.

I'd tried to get to my car earlier, but a cop car idled in the bar parking lot, so each time I walked, heel over toe, toward my Saab, he'd eye me. The second time, he rolled down his window.

"Miss," he said. "Where are you headed?" He was a middle-aged guy with a thick mustache, and he looked like he could be somebody's father. I thought for a second about how to answer, and staggered toward his car. Getting into my own car was not an option at this point. I was sober, at least I felt sober. But it had only been a few hours since my last drink, and there was a zero tolerance law with teens drinking and driving. I could still smell the alcohol on my skin. I didn't want to take any chances.

I started to speak, careful not to slur my words, and careful to stand in a straight line, and wondered what would happen if I told him that maybe I'd possibly been violated. But then I wondered if Eric had even broken any laws. Had I said no? I couldn't remember. Had I even cried? I felt like I had. But maybe I hadn't. Maybe I was frozen into silence.

And then the next sequence of events flashed before me like a premonition: Karen would be called down to the station while I sat on a cold bench with a scratchy, gray wool blanket draped over my shoulders, and Eric would be called, and maybe even Rachel, and then by Monday, the whole school would have gotten word—half of which could vouch for Eric, say they saw me drunk, at a bar, illegally, with my fake ID earlier that night; and that they saw me get into a car with Eric, willingly; saw me enter his house, and sit on his couch, and they vaguely remembered the *cute, but kind of chubby* girl he'd taken to his bedroom, and that was the last they'd heard or seen, except for that body sprawled out on the couch, who would swear he didn't hear me scream.

"I live right over there," I lied, and mumbled something about staying at a friend's house but not feeling well and not wanting to wake my mother. He eyed me for an uncomfortable extra second and asked if I needed a ride and if I was sure I was all right. I remembered that I'd read somewhere that it's a felony to lie during a police report, but I couldn't remember if that was true, or where I'd even heard it, and was it considered a lie if I really didn't know the truth?

"Um," I started to say, and I felt the words tickle my throat, like I might even cry. I didn't have a story, I didn't have anything really, except for the horrible pit in my stomach. But for just a moment I started to say something. But then he cut in.

"Have you been drinking?" I felt myself sink. I shook my head and told him I was just tired and needed to get home. He rolled up his window and went back to reading his paper. I walked away, steady. Heel over toe.

It was more than an hour before the cop finally drove off, and the sky was starting to turn a soft, clamshell purple. I took my third swig of Listerine, swished, and spat it out onto the sidewalk.

"Where are you?" I remember how hard it was to keep my voice flat. I was finally able to charge my phone in my car.

"I'm at Dad's. Sleeping," Eli said. "What's up?" I heard him yawn through the phone. "What time is it?"

"It's like five thirty," I said. "I need you to let me in, but quietly."

He opened the back door, and the screen door creaked as I slipped through. I didn't have a bed there, and I couldn't shower without waking my father, so I borrowed a pair of sweats from Eli and rubbed myself down with a hand towel and a bar of soap in the bathroom.

By the time I hit the couch, the sun was streaming through the skylight overhead. I covered my face with a knit throw, but the light crept through the holes. I flipped over on my stomach and buried my face into the black leather sofa. My neck felt stiff, and my joints ached from exhaustion. I don't think I ever really fell asleep, but I could feel him, his hands fumbling at me. I could still feel his fingers jamming into me. *Phantom pains.*

I woke to my father's voice from the kitchen. I'd forgotten to take out my contacts, and they felt pasty, like somebody filled my eyes with Elmer's Glue, and my sinuses throbbed. I squinted to see the time. Eight o'clock. I'd only gotten in two hours earlier.

"Aubrey," my dad called from the kitchen. "I got bagels." I stood up, groggy, off balance. I couldn't even think of eating. Bagels had been my staple hangover food. Maybe it was a Long Island thing, maybe it was just a human thing, but the only cure and requirement after a night of drinking was an everything bagel, scooped, with veggie cream cheese, and a very large coffee. But that morning, the thought of biting into that starchy, salty sandwich made my guts turn. Water. I needed water. My head felt empty and my mouth felt like it was made of sand. I ground my teeth and walked toward the kitchen, holding onto the walls for balance.

My father sat at an empty table, a cup of coffee and *Newsday* in front of him. His brown, streaked-with-gray hair stuck up in every direction. No sign of bagels anywhere.

"April Fools," he said, loud, too loud. Any other morning, I would have been disappointed. I tore open the case of water on the ground, stretching the bottle through the thick plastic.

"Funny," I said, and walked back toward the couch.

Chapter 21

Wednesday, October 8, 2014.

"CAN I ASK you a question?" I stand outside the Seventh Precinct, my lips stained purple from Pinot, beaming over my ability to walk a perfect line in his direction. I swallow a hiccup and cross my arms over my chest while my entire family and the rest of Seaport pay their respects to the late, ethereal Rachel Burns. The officer is young and has one hand on his car door as if he's about to slip inside.

"Sure," he says, facing me, his free hand lingering near his gun, as if he's trained to always be ready, even in a place like Seaport.

"Well, this is kind of a weird question," I say. He's cute, not much older than I am, maybe late twenties. But he doesn't seem amused. I'm being sort of flirty, but don't think I'm coming off drunk or anything. "What is your protocol for assault?"

"What do you mean?" he says. "Have you been assaulted?"

His tone gets all serious, and I'm starting to regret this whole thing. It was sort of a spontaneous detour after I'd left my house for a cigarette—something I'd played out in my head hundreds of times over the past five years.

I've played that night over and over again, how the cop rolled down his window, how he asked if I was okay, if I needed help. I remember pausing, holding those words in my throat, wondering how everything would change if I just spoke up and actually stood up for myself. But then he'd crushed any courage I'd had with that question: *Have you been drinking?* And I knew I didn't have a shot in hell.

"No, no," I say. "I mean, if a girl comes in here, and says she's been assaulted, sexually," I add, "what are you trained to do? Is she presumed guilty or innocent until proven whatever? Is it a felony if she lies? Even if she's not lying, like if someone just assumes she's lying? Or says she's lying? What's considered a valid report?" He looks at me like I'm a moron and takes his hand away from his holster. I sweep my hair out of my eyes. I'm feeling self-conscious, but I don't want the guy to realize, so I shift my weight on one foot and act relaxed.

"All reports are considered valid and taken seriously until proven otherwise."

"What happens next? Do you call parents? Is it confidential?"

"Well, if the parties involved are minors, then yes, we will have to call parents."

"What if she doesn't want her parents to find out?"

"Well, then there's not much we can do," he says. He eyes

me. "Is there something you're trying to say here?" I shake my head.

"This is all hypothetical," I say. He still looks at me kind of funny. "I'm twenty-three, do you want my license?" He smiles and shakes his head.

"Well, if a female victim reports a crime, we will interview her and suggest that she file an official report and go to a hospital for an examination," he says. "Any more questions?"

"But what if her story is off? Like if she can't remember, because she's nervous or whatever?"

"Why are you asking all of this? Are you trying to report something? I hate to cut this short, but I kind of have someplace to be."

"Research," I cut in. "I'm a writer."

"Okay," he says. "But I'm actually headed to a friend's wake now. If you do need to talk more, I can give you my number." I suck in air and shake my head. Of course he's headed to a wake.

"Rachel?" I deadpan.

"You knew her? It's terrible. We dated a few years back. Briefly," he adds.

"I knew of her," I say. I smile, thank him, and walk a straight line back toward my house.

ON THE WALK back, I spark up another cigarette. Things are different now than they were five years ago. There weren't any Steubenvilles or Maryvilles. There was just silence. Even if I was to open my mouth all those years ago, I have a feeling I would have found out quickly who my real friends were, and maybe it's just a hunch, but I'm pretty sure that number would've been low—if not in the negatives.

The closest thing Seaport had—aside from that fleeting Max Sullivan scandal—was this girl Heather Something, from a town over. She'd been a year or two younger than Eli. Some guys in his grade had gotten her piss drunk at a homecoming party, passed her around with her pants around her ankles, and recorded it all on an iPhone. Apparently the entire county saw the video. I was already in my second or third year of college, so I'd been pretty far removed from the whole ordeal. But I heard the gist of it when I came home for Thanksgiving.

People laughed, because that was the easiest emotion for them to emulate—at least that's what Eli told me. They called the girl a slut, because it was better for everyone to point the finger at the drunk girl who nobody really cared about than to blame a group of *promising young athletes for just having a little fun*. The girl never filed a report. Eventually, she moved. Last I'd heard, she drank some bleach and was hospitalized briefly, before transferring to a town in Suffolk.

She got what she deserved, I'd heard someone say. I'd been home for Thanksgiving and was in line to buy coffee. These two bearded men in puffy vests quipped at each other. They were probably football dads, making excuses for the boys who could have just as easily been their own sons. I knew they were talking about that Heather girl. *That's just what happens when girls get sloppy. That's God's way of punishing them.* Eli stood next to me, and we simultaneously rolled our eyes. I don't think he knew the extent to which those words cut me. I hid it well. I had for years. But as we approached the counter to order, he turned to the men and said, "With all due respect, I think *hangovers* are God's way of giving drunks what they deserve."

Part of me envied that girl—wondered what it would be like to have that video, to have that moment immortalized, to be able to look back and have proof, actual hard evidence, even for myself. Maybe then, I could see if I'd done enough. I'd know if I said *no*. If I fought hard enough. Because each time I play it back in my head, each time I let the events unfold, he gets a little less cruel, and I become more passive, and it all muddles together, like some big misunderstanding.

Chapter 22

April 2009.

IT WAS ALREADY Easter, and I wasn't ready for it. Still, nothing had been resolved. I tried to keep to myself, but Rachel always found ways to trap me into a ride home or catch up with me at my locker.

"Why no talk?" She'd been standing behind me as I fumbled with my car keys in the back school parking lot. We'd always driven together, but that week I'd been taking my own car. She knew something was up, I just didn't know how much information she had.

"Just a busy week. Haven't been feeling great, you know?" I said.

"Yup, I know." She looked at me kind of funny, and I faked a smile, wishing I hadn't given her that opening.

She leaned against the passenger's-side door, dangling her own keys in her hand, and just started lobbing questions at me.

"So what's going on with Adam? If you never met up on his birthday, where did you end up going?"

I felt my face go hot, but I was careful, gave vague answers, and tried to deflect the questions back at her.

"I really don't know. I guess we're over. How about you? What's going on with Rod?"

I placed my books down on the driver's seat, and I noticed for the first time that my hands were shaking. Rachel quirked her eyebrows.

"Caffeine," I said, and turned to her, stuffing my hands in my back pockets.

"So, have you talked to him?"

"Who?"

"Adam. God, Aub, aren't you listening?"

"No, I haven't. I'm pretty sure we're over. I just said that."

"Oh, right. You did," she said. And then she just shrugged and smiled like she was stifling some sort of secret.

MY MOTHER'S FAMILY came for Easter, the Irish side, making small talk, spitting witty banter at each other over half-eaten plates of ham. I feigned amusement at Cousin Peter's back-in-the-day college stories, like they were supposed to get me amped for my own impending journey. We all laughed, pushed around the mashed potatoes with our forks, and smiled politely.

The Cavanaughs never talked about anything serious—I think it's an Irish thing. When my parents announced their divorce six years earlier, my mother's side never mentioned my father again. They never asked my brothers and me how we were doing, how Dad was doing. They just pretended like he never even existed. The Glass side though—the half-Italian, half-Jewish, all-drama side—called at least once a week to make sure we were handling it okay. My uncles would hug me for a lingering uncomfortable extra second, pat me on the back, and say, *How are you doing, huh? How's Mom? Everything okay? Everything good?*

Divorce never bothered me. It was something to be expected. The sort of thing that happened to everyone, and I'd never really gotten too bent over it.

So I was relieved to spend this Easter with the Cavanaughs. Even if they knew something was off with me, even if they could see it, even if it were written all over my face, they would never try to make me talk about it.

It always baffled me as to why Karen became a guidance counselor. She was part of the impermeable Irish, yet spent her days trying to break through to middle school brats who were hung up on their own parents' divorce.

Grandma Kath of Connecticut—that's how she introduced herself: Katherine L. Cavanaugh of Connecticut—sat at the head of the table. She'd always been just as slim and tall as my mother, with reddish hair that fell in a perfect bob just above her shoulders. If anyone could pull off a bob, it was Grandma Kath.

We all sat around the dining room table—the one we used for special occasions, the one we used for my family's first dinner with Adam. I disrupted the mound of peas on my plate, separating them one by one with my fork. I was working with the theory that if I scattered the contents of my dinner, maybe it would look like I ate more, and maybe, *maybe* I could shed the *cute, but kind of chubby* look.

"So, Aubrey," Cousin Peter said. The ice clinked in his glass as he placed it on the table. "Have you heard back from everywhere you applied?" I smiled a tight-lipped grin and nodded. "Good," he said.

"I think we've decided on Brown," my mother said, turning her attention to Peter. "It was her reach school. Nobody thought she'd actually get in. She'll be the first Ivy Leaguer in the family!" My mother cleared her throat. Cousin Peter's ice clinked in his glass. I smiled a tight-lipped grin and nodded.

I pushed the peas around on my plate until they disappeared under the mound of mashed potatoes.

"It's exciting, isn't it?" Peter said. "College? You're going to have the time of your life."

The time of my life. Sure. I took a breath, barely looking up from my plate, smiled a tight-lipped grin, nodded, and pushed up out of my chair.

I'd spent the day before panicked when Karen conveniently announced that she'd made an appointment with a gynecologist the first week of May. I would be eighteen in a few months, and I needed to go before I left for college.

Are you sexually active, Aubrey? I knew he or she or whatever this doctor was would ask.

And what would I say? *Yes, but only once, and no, he didn't use a condom. No, I don't know about his sexual history, I didn't ask because I didn't even know it was happening.*

And then I had another vision of Dr. He-or-She examining me and saying, *Aubrey, you are a virgin. You obviously made this whole thing up. You obviously were too drunk or too crazy. It's obviously all in your head.*

I stood over the kitchen sink and turned the water up as hot as it would go, squeezing orange dish soap into my hands. The potatoes, peas, and gravy made a sort of gray paste and slid off the plate into the metal basin. I picked up a serving bowl, all covered in red crusty sauce, and I started to turn it over in my hands, under the hot faucet, the orange soapsuds filling up the basin. I stared hard as the red goo started to wash away and disappear beneath the sudsy bubbles. Steam rose from the sink, and my hands went kind of numb as I rubbed the bowl with my soapy thumb until it became white, so white that I could see just a glare of my reflection, and I remember thinking that I'd never seen anything so white before.

Karen stood in the doorway.

"Well, that was rude," she said.

"I have a migraine," I said. I didn't turn away from the sink. The steam rose up from the basin, the hot water still poured over me, numbing my hands. There was this sort of stale air between my mother and me—all stale and gray—like we were reading from a script to some black-and-white television show. The air felt thick —maybe it was the steam coming from the sink, but I knew I couldn't stand up anymore. So I just turned, and let my body slide to the granite floor with my back to the oak cabinets.

Karen ran frantically toward me and put her hand over my head, as if I'd spontaneously combusted with a blistering fever.

"I'm fine," I said, pushing her away. "I just want to be alone.

I can't stand listening to that pretentious douche talk about the good old college days for another minute."

Karen's face was all flushed, I noticed as she picked herself up away from me and fumbled around the kitchen, mumbling and slamming cabinet doors.

"What is your problem?" she said. "You've been acting like a little bitch all week." I shrugged, her words just swirling and swinging around me, tangling with all that steam, and my chest felt tight like no air could go through, no matter how hard I sucked in. "Aubrey," she said, "answer me."

She stood over me, her hands on her hips. She was wearing lipstick, I noticed, Jungle Red, I thought it was called, and I just sat on the floor, my knees into my chest, sucking in hot, sink-steamy air, and I wanted to tell her to shut up, that she shouldn't question me, that she should *stop, stop, just stop*, because she didn't want to know the answer and she didn't want to have that burden because it wouldn't be easy, and I wouldn't be easy, and I would never be easy again. I was a mess, a hot fucking mess with a gut-twisting anxiety that bred inside me, and she didn't want to know about it. But instead I just sat quiet, still, numb, sucking in air, trying to fill that hollowed-out space inside of me.

"Aubrey," she said again, and this time I answered. I stood, and smashed the bowl into the granite, the white pieces of ceramic shattering at my mom's feet, but she hardly flinched.

I fell back to the ground, my face to my knees.

"Please," I mumbled. "Just leave me alone." Hot tears stained my jeans.

"Aubrey," she said.

"For five fucking minutes, Mother. Just leave me alone for five fucking minutes."

DUSK WRAPPED ITSELF around the town. I slipped out the back door and onto the street. I couldn't handle another question about where I was going to college in the fall and if I was excited. Because if they wanted my honest answer, I couldn't wait to get the fuck out of this piece-of-shit town.

I scraped my flats against the street. The sky bruised purple and gray. The college kids were still home for break, and I could feel him, clinging to me like cold, hard static. My skin prickled—pins and needles. I always wondered what caused that. But I decided it was when your body tries to distract you with prickly nerves—take your mind off the real pain. It's your body's way of cutting.

I walked past houses adorned with Easter decorations in the windows and I thought of all the families, and what they were hiding and how much they probably actually hated one another.

I took the back road so I wouldn't have to pass his house, and crossed an unnecessary intersection as the cold cut into me like a dull blade.

Cute, but kind of chubby.

I stepped over sidewalk cracks. Excess cars lined the streets.

I needed sleep. I needed to eat. I needed a cigarette.

I approached Adam's house, and the town looked different. For a moment I thought I might actually be dead; I hoped for it, until I brushed up against a streetlamp, and the slightest spark reminded me that I was still alive.

If Adam was still mad at me, I didn't care. Let him be. I had nothing left to lose.

His Jeep wasn't in front of his house. It was only on the walk home that I saw it pulled over to the side on the back road—a road I just happened to take only to avoid passing Eric's house with a front-window view of the Robbins family celebrating the resurrection of Christ.

The engine was running. I pressed my face against the driver's-side window. They didn't see me.

"YOU LOOK LIKE you just saw a ghost," Eli said. I'd been walking, just walking. I had just seen Adam in his Jeep and I needed to walk somewhere, anywhere. Eli approached from behind, coming out of our street. He was alone.

"It's nothing. Just cold," I said. The words felt unreal as they left my lips, like maybe they didn't even really exist. "Did Mom send you out to find me?"

He shrugged, put his hand on my shoulder. "I might have something for you," he said.

We sat, side by side, on the bleachers outside the high school. He lit the joint, spinning it between his lips. He pulled on it, his chest sinking while he inhaled. "Don't let Karen get to you," he said. "I've got her all figured out."

"It's not about Mom," I said, taking the joint from him, sucking it in. He looked so peaceful, still childlike and small.

"Do you ever feel trapped?" I started, already regretting my choice of words.

"You mean physically, like at home?"

"Well, yes and no. Not just in Seaport, but also in my life."
I touched my temple with two fingers and rubbed. "Sometimes
I feel like my life is this perfect little arrangement, in like a
snow globe. And it's displayed up as someone else's decora-
tion. I don't know," I said. "Maybe it's God, maybe it's Karen,
maybe it's just some mean little kid who got it as a gift from a
weird aunt. But whoever's snow globe it is, I feel like I'm just in
it. And whenever they want, they can just pick it up and shake
it, and watch the fake snow—what's that made of?"

"Plastic," he said. "It used to be bone chips and porcelain."

"Right," I said. "Anyway, the plastic just floats around in
the globe, and it's filled with water, which most people forget
about. So, I'm drowning in this snow and water. And nobody
cares."

"That's deep," he said. His eyes are tiny slits, like a kitten. I
twisted my heel into the metal bleacher and took another drag.

"Do you care?" I ask, and it's probably the weed, but I stare
at him while he stares toward the football field. I'd always
gotten along better with Eli, more than with Marc. Marc was
stern and studious, even though he was a big pot head. He had
most people fooled. Eli, though, never took anything seriously.

"Sure, I care," he said. "I mean, I don't know what I'm supposed to be caring about, but if you say you're drowning or
whatever in a snow globe, then I totally get that. It sucks. I care."

"Thanks," I say, rising to my feet.

"No problem," he says, but he doesn't move. "And hey,
whatever it is, you're leaving in like four months. Suck it up.
You're almost home free."

Chapter 23

Thursday, October 9, 2014.

IT'S THE MORNING of Rachel's funeral, and I'm standing at my dresser when I feel someone standing in my doorway.

"So?" Karen says. I know what she's waiting for. She's dressed in black outfit number two, ready to head to the church. Something courses through my veins, something dangerous, and I'm ready, my heart steady. My hands don't shake. I am calm. "It was a beautiful service last night," she says. "Sad." I still don't say anything. "You know who I ran into?"

I shrug into the mirror and rub moisturizer under my eyes.

"Adam," she says. My body stiffens for just a second, but I remember to breathe and close the cap over the lotion.

"And," I say.

"And he asked about you. He seemed worried."

"Worried?" I scoff.

"She was your best friend, Aubrey."

Charlee Fam

"No," I say, with a self-satisfying snort. "She wasn't. She wasn't my best friend." I move around the room, straightening up. The willowy cotton fabric of my gray shirt clings to my damp back.

"Since when?" she says.

"Since when what?" I crumple some papers on my desk and discard an empty bottle of red wine into the garbage pail.

"Since when," she says. "Do you—*did you*," she corrects, "not consider Rachel a friend?" She stiffens her back a bit. "I'm just trying to understand, Aubrey."

"Hmm," I say. I drop my sweatpants—Danny's sweatpants—to my ankles, kicking them off, revealing an old pair of Adam's boxers underneath. He'd given them to me one summer night to wear while we watched a movie. I'd kept them, sort of our equivalent of a letterman jacket. I stand barefoot on the wooden floor; my legs are paler than the rest of my body, except for the tiny white scar from the first time I shaved my legs—barely noticeable beneath my knee.

I pull on a pair of stiff jeans and squat twice, bending at the knees. I don't plan on talking, but I feel so numb, so casual, like the words aren't real anyway.

"Now what were you saying?" It's mostly spite. It's mostly being pushed and doubted and judged by my own mother that I feel the need to prove something to her, to make her feel so incredibly stupid. "Oh, yes. I haven't considered Rachel a friend since—oh, right. Since around that Easter, you remember. When I chucked that dish at you."

Karen stands silent, stoic, in the door. I can feel her breathing in through her nose and out through her mouth.

"You remember I left after that," I said. My voice calm, my body still, numb, but for once I felt it, and something else. Raw enthusiasm. The raw, natural, hard-up rush of enthusiasm. "And the funniest thing happened," I say. I pitch forward and laugh at myself. "I went to see Adam. We'd had this stupid fight, you see, because I wouldn't fuck him. You would have been so proud. I was just a picture of fem power. But he'd made me feel so bad about it, I was just going to suck it up and apologize. Isn't that *crazy?* I was going to apologize for not letting him get in my pants? And then guess what? I was walking on that back road behind Adam's block, just walking, and I saw his car pulled over on the side of the road. So I looked inside. And guess what? Can you guess?"

"Aubrey," my mother says, her voice low. "Please."

"No, wait," I say, the thrill rising in my throat. I can't remember ever feeling this damn giddy. "This is the best part."

Her jaw locks, I can see it in the reflection of the mirror. But I don't look at her. Not yet. This is just too good. I pretend to focus on my own movements. "This is a pretty good exercise," I say, midsquat.

She takes a step closer, and I jolt forward—my fight-or-flight running high. She stops, takes a step back, and steadies herself in my doorway. I bet she never had to deal with anything this fucked up at her middle school, I think, and I want to say it, but I don't think she'll get the joke. We don't seem to be on the same page lately.

"So where was I?" I say. "Oh, right. Adam. Adam was in his car. And guess who else? Spoiler alert," I shout. I spin around to face her. "It was Rachel. And can you guess what they were doing? Well, I can't say for sure, but I think. *I think*"—I hold my hands over my mouth like I'm telling a secret—"they were having sex," I whisper.

Karen's face is gray, still locked in a stoic, wide-eyed gaze.

I suck in my stomach, lifting my shirt slightly.

"So that's when I stopped considering Rachel a friend." I smile, a genuine, raw smile. "Oh, wait," I say. "I forgot the best part." I can feel something bubbling up from my throat. "It wasn't completely their fault, you know. They were actually both pretty pissed at me. And rightfully so." I think about all the things I could say, all the ways I could say it, but nothing feels real. I could be the victim, the liar, the denier, the *desperate slut*. It's all so subjective, and it depends on who's telling the story—on what role I want to play. So I settle for the facts. "I totally let this guy fuck me on Adam's birthday! And guess what? Rachel was *obsessed* with this guy. Like *obsessed*."

"Aubrey," she says. "You need to calm down."

"Ha! I'm trying to tell you a story, Mother," I say. "Don't you want to hear a story?" She takes another breath in through her nose and pushes it out through pursed lips.

"So it was Adam's birthday. And he was mad because I wouldn't give it up to him. But then I totally let this guy do me. On *his birthday?* Isn't that hilarious, Kar? I mean, I didn't really *let* him. But he didn't really take no for an answer. And then I guess Adam found out and Rachel found out and then they decided to really stick it to me. And now Rachel is dead. And I don't care. And Adam is worried. And I also don't care. Do you see now?"

I let out an exaggerated breath and bite my lip. It's all I can do to keep from breaking down into a hysterical fit of laughter. My mother doesn't say much, she just stands back and stares at me. I would think she'd be better equipped to handle something like this. Guess not. She starts to speak. She actually looks concerned, but I cut her off.

"You should go," I say. "You're going to be late, and I've got an appointment for a manicure."

I hold out my hands in front of my face. The cuticles are shredded a bit, bitten short, the dark red polish flaked, but my fingers don't shake.

Chapter 24

April 2009.

HE WAS WATCHING *Family Feud* when I started to let myself into his room—the seventies version with Richard Dawson, and I remember thinking how a guy could get away with kissing all of those young girls right on TV, like right in front of their husbands, fathers, brothers, and no one ever seemed to care that this old guy was just kissing their women right on the lips.

I knocked, even though the door was open. He was on his stomach, the bed was made, and he didn't look up right away. He must have thought it was just his mom bringing up his laundry or something. So he just kept on watching Richard Dawson while I stood in the doorway.

I looked like hell. I knew that, and the mirror on the other side of his room confirmed it. I wore ripped jeans and a baggy sweatshirt that hung off one shoulder. I didn't really say anything, just mumbled something about being sick, and crawled under his blue flannel covers.

"What's up?" That's what he said. *What's up?* I catch him fucking my best friend just the night before, and all he can say is *What's up?* To be fair, he didn't see me.

He stood up off the bed and looked down at me. He was shirtless. His flannel pajama bottoms hung off his hips, and I noticed that his arms and abs looked more defined than I'd remembered. Even though it had only been just over a week since I'd seen him. I closed my eyes and pulled the comforter up to my face, letting his blankets envelop me. I wondered if he'd been working out for Rachel.

"I don't want to talk about it," I said. It was six o'clock on Monday. I had faked another migraine that day.

"Are you drunk?"

I shook my head. "No, just tired."

"Aubrey," he said, his voice cold and hollow. "You should probably leave."

I didn't move, just stayed curled up under his covers, my face pressed against a pillow. "I'm going to take off my pants now," I said, without opening my eyes.

"Aubrey," he said, again, "you don't have to do that."

"Adam," I said, "just shut up."

I needed this. I had loved Adam at one point, enough to want to do it with him. I needed to feel the curves and the familiar weight of his body, his hands, his scent. I needed it. But it had nothing to do with him.

I shimmied out of my jeans under the covers.

"I kissed your dead brother." I didn't even plan to say it, it

just sort of slipped off my tongue. And when I said it, I didn't
feel any less guilty.

He'd lain down on his back beside me.

"I know," he said.

"For how long?" I caught a whiff of myself: coffee and
cigarettes.

"Rachel told me," he said.

"What else did she tell you?"

"Does it matter?" he said, rolling over on top of me. He
pressed his dry lips to my neck, reluctantly at first.

"Are you mad?" I said.

"No," he said, and traced his finger over my pelvic bone.

And then my whole body went stiff and I felt my hand—
deadweight—peel away from my side and swat at him. I didn't
mean to. It just sort of happened, like a reflex. I mumbled an
apology, took his hand, and placed it back at the line of my
underwear.

"Why are you sorry?" he asked. He wanted me to say it.
Maybe it was all in my head. Maybe he didn't even know. But it
felt like he wanted me to say it. Why I didn't love him enough
to have sex with him. Why did I give in to that piece-of-shit
Eric? On Adam's birthday. Why had I been so weak?

He kissed my cheek, and I turned my head to the side.
Hot tears stung my eyes, but I couldn't let him see me cry. I'd
promised myself.

"Relax," he said. *Relax. Relax. Relax.*

"I'm sorry," I said again, and turned my face up toward the
ceiling. "I'm ready now," I said. "I'm just nervous. First-time
jitters, I guess."

First-time jitters.

He grabbed me by the ball of my shoulder, and pressed down, balancing himself over me. I stared up at the ceiling. *One. Two.* I counted the cracks. *Three. Four.* My blood felt like hot cement, filling all the empty spaces before hardening into a cold, gray mold. *Five. Six.* And I swore, one crack and I'd shatter.

I breathed beneath the weight of his hands.

"YOU DIDN'T BLEED," he said, afterward.

"Yeah," I said. "But it still hurt."

HE WAS OFF me in seconds. No cuddles. No nuzzling. I didn't mind, though. I just stayed under his covers, feeling lonely and weak. Numb really. I thought it would help. I swore the familiar curves of his body, his smell, all that Adam stuff, would take the acrid taste of Eric Robbins out of my mouth—take away the weight of his thick chest and masculine scent of cheap drugstore cologne. I was wrong.

I pulled my jeans back on and walked over to his desk, picked up his comb, and started running it through my knotty hair.

"So what did you think?" I asked, eyeing him in the mirror. "Was it worth it?"

"Sure," he said. He slipped back into his flannel pants and sat on the edge of the bed. "I guess."

"You guess?" I pulled the comb through my hair. He watched *Family Feud.*

"Yeah," he said. "I guess."

I picked up the condom wrapper from the floor and tucked it back into the box on his dresser. I never trusted garbage cans. Maybe that's because Karen always checked mine. I peered into the box; it had been opened before today. But I guess he could have taken a few for his car, wallet. I knew for a fact he'd used at least one.

I opened his top drawer and slid the box in the back under a couple of wads of socks, and then I saw it, twinkling up at me. My mockingbird ring.

"Ad, where did you get this?" It was just there, resting against a pair of old boxers.

He stood up, pulled it out of my hand, and slammed the drawer shut.

"Nowhere," he said. "Don't go through my stuff."

"No," I said. "Tell me."

"It's none of your business," his face went red. "Okay? Just drop it."

"It's my ring. Why do you have it?" I couldn't remember the last time I had that ring, but it was before Adam, it had definitely been before Adam.

His face was still. He squinted at me, and then his gray eyes flickered.

"You?" he said, his fists balled up at his sides like a little boy about to have a tantrum. "You're the girl?"

"What girl?" I said. "What are you talking about?" I felt my heart beat from behind my chest, could feel it beating in my head.

I looked back at the ring and back up at his face, and by the time it clicked, he was already pushing me out the door.

The room felt too warm and all of these moments from the past four years swirled and swirled around me in a mass of messy snapshots: Eric, the mattress, Max, Tonya, the ring, Rachel—and then everything went still, before falling into perfect chronological form.

Rachel. Max. Mattress. Ring. Tonya. Adam. Eric. Rachel. Adam. Rachel. Adam. Rachel Adam Rachel Adam Rachel Adam Rachel Adam Rachel Adam.

"Max gave me this ring," he said, his voice slow and sharp. "Before he died. You're the girl he'd been with. You're the girl who was threatening to press charges."

"No," I started, my voice cracking, but he wasn't listening. "No, he didn't get it from me."

"*You* accused him of rape?" He was pushing me hard. "He fucking killed himself," he shouted in my face, spit flinging between us. "You fucking bitch. He fucking killed himself." He was sobbing now, pushing me out the door.

Chapter 25

Thursday, October 9, 2014.

I DRUM MY newly manicured fingers to a frantic beat over the wood counter. The deep red polish reflects the overhead lights of the liquor store. I'd gone with my signature color. *Wicked.*

The cashier rings up two bottles of Jack Daniel's and stuffs them into separate paper bags. He doesn't ask to see ID. I breathe out through my mouth, too loudly, while he swipes my card, and the man looks up at me and apologizes for the delay. I don't mean to rush him and feel almost sorry for the guy, but I've got things to do.

It's just past eleven, and the funeral is in full swing just across town. Right about now, all of Seaport should be gathered around, clad in their best black, as they lower Rachel into the ground. It's the perfect day for a funeral—gray and cold—with a seventy-five percent chance of rain. I hope they brought their umbrellas.

I didn't stick around to see Karen off. I grabbed my car keys and peeled out of the driveway before she could even get a word in this morning. She just stood there, outside my doorway, a dumb look on her face, like I had to explain myself any further. I made myself perfectly clear—a picture of perfect elegance. What's left to say? But all of those things I said keep playing back over and over, pounding like a shot to my throat.

Rachel is dead. And I don't care. And Adam is worried. And I also don't care. Do you see now?

I totally let some guy fuck me on Adam's birthday.

"Here you go," the cashier says, handing me the bag. "Having a party?" he asks, and he's trying to be friendly.

"Nope," I say. "Going to an after-party."

THE RAIN ASSAULTS my car as I sit in the parking lot, and the wipers dance to a furious beat. I smooth the dress over my lap and pass the bottle of Jack back to myself. I'm laughing, I realize, sputtering in my insanity, as I randomly think about this one time in tenth grade when I'd had my tonsils out. It was a cold day in December, and Rachel had taken the day off. She'd been too hysterical to go to school that morning, her mom later told Karen. So instead, she'd spent the entire day leaving voice mails on my phone and calling my mom for updates. When I got home that night, she'd been waiting on my front porch, inconsolable. We'd all laughed about it, my brothers, Adam, and me, and even Karen couldn't help but mock Rachel's flare for the dramatics. It had been a simple procedure. I went into the hospital at 6 A.M. and was back home by dinnertime, but Rachel couldn't stand the thought of losing me, apparently. And I can't see the logic in any of it, looking back.

My phone buzzes from the dashboard, and for a fleeting second I think it might be Rachel. *Surprise! I'm alive! This was all just a test. And by the way, you failed.*

Her voice mail still lies trapped in my phone—a stale and rotting corpse as each day passes. I pick up my phone, the numbers blur and come into focus, and I take another swig of Jack. It's Danny. I ignore it at first, letting the phone fall to the floor, but as the rain strikes up, and the Jack flows through me, I reach down and answer.

"Hello." I almost sing it into the phone. There's silence and heavy breath on the other line, like he's trying to find his tone.

"Where the hell have you been," he says. "I've been trying to get you all day." I stifle a laugh. He'd only called twice and texted less than an hour ago. That's hardly an attempt. Rachel would have been way more persistent than that, I'm sure.

"Did I ever tell you that I had my tonsils out," I start to say, the words slurring off my tongue.

"Aubrey."

"Don't say my name like that. It's condescending." I open my windows, and the rain pounds inside the car.

"I talked to your mom," he says, and I feel my body go slack.

I'd been sort of honest with Danny back in college. Not completely honest, but as close as I could have been.

"It was messed up," I had said the first time he asked me about losing my virginity. "I don't want to talk about it." We were at Brown, squished in his twin dorm bed.

"Who was it?" he'd asked. We were both naked, tangled in a thin jersey-knit sheet. Danny traced his finger over my tattoo.

"It wasn't Adam," I said. He had known about Adam. As much as I was willing to share about him. That was never something I could have hidden from Danny. He was my high school boyfriend, and my mother would forever compare Danny to the first boy I brought home. "It was some guy," I said. "Just some douche bag. I was drunk. I didn't want it to happen. You know how it is."

Danny was quiet. He wasn't appalled, outraged, or ready to vindicate me. I didn't really expect him to be either. Instead, he just pulled himself closer to me and said, "Yeah, it happens."

I can still hear him breathing on the line.

"I talked to your mom," he says again. "She told me everything." I don't say anything, just sit in my driver's seat clutching the bottle in one hand and my phone pressed against my ear. I reach for the radio and crank up the music, Tracy Chapman again, until I feel it reverberate through my shitty old car, and the speakers throb.

So remember when we were driving, driving in your car. Speed so fast it felt like I was drunk.

"Don't call me again," I say, before hanging up the phone and throwing it in the backseat.

I take one last swig, feeling the boozy brown liquid warm my veins, and I hoist myself up out of the car.

I WALK INTO the bar and time stands still. Like a movie, everyone stops and stares toward the door, but it's not a smooth entrance—not the kind where The Girl walks in and she's got this glow around her and everyone just watches, grinning at her in slow motion as she flips her hair back and forth before walking through the crowd. It's not like that at all. It's not glamorous, and no one smiles. They just stare, holding long-neck bottles of light beer to their parted lips. Someone whispers, someone even says my name, but not to me. No one says my name to me.

It smells like Clorox and beer, and the fluorescent lights flicker overhead. There should never be fluorescent lights in a bar; it's unnatural and it illuminates the crowd, who're all still dolled up in their best black. From across the room, I spy the guy from the train—Frank, or Gary or Louis—and he shifts his gaze to the floor. He wears the Rachel T-shirt over his black button-down. The white cotton tee stretches over the bulky material of his dress shirt; he looks lumpy and out of place, and Rachel's face hangs crookedly over his chest; and she watches me, those eyes, and her Cheshire cat grin. Most of the guys have loosened their ties, and I just stand there, in my black cotton dress, and wring the rain out of my hair.

It's nothing like that last night at O'Reilly's—the way the band started up, and everyone danced, and Rachel swung her hips into Rod and I stood back staring at the front door, waiting for Adam. It's not like that night at all. The mood is different—somber, and it's still sort of light out. There's no music, but I see some guy setting up a DJ booth by the back. I remember the college band that played that Pat Benatar song that last night here, and how it sounded hazy and dark, like a bad dream, and I wonder what happened to them, if they ever made it beyond the local bar scene. I think of that night, and I think about Rod, and I wonder if he's here, but I doubt it. He'd been the only guy to notice Rachel that night, and now everybody's here for her and only her. She would have loved this.

I stand near the door, and Chloe's the first to come at me. It takes me a moment to process her face. The last time I saw her, she was twelve, with a mouth full of braces and too much eyeliner. Now she's got a decent set of teeth and her hair hangs in loose curls around her narrow jawline. She looks nothing like Rachel, but sort of moves like her, I notice as she swings her shoulders from side to side and steps in front of me.

"Oh my God, Aubrey," she says. She holds me by the shoulders and looks at me for a second, like she's assessing how much I've grown, but I want to push her off, I want to take her by the face and say, *Little girl, get the hell out of this place.*

She's sixteen, not even old enough to be here. But it's her sister's funeral, and if she's anything like Rachel—if she's anything like me—then she's popped her O'Reilly's cherry way before this.

And then I see him, leaning against the bar, in a button-down shirt and a mint-green tie.

Chloe pulls me closer, rests her chin on my shoulder, and says, "I'm so happy you came. It would have meant so much to Rachel." I mumble something and start to back away toward the door, but she's still got her hands on me, and I can't go anywhere. I feel my phone buzz inside my bag. It's probably just Karen. She's been calling me nonstop since this morning, but all I can think about is that voice mail. Rachel's voice mail, lingering—trapped inside my BlackBerry. If Chloe was the one to find Rachel's body, did she also find her phone? Did she know that I was most likely her final phone call?

I start to feel it in my chest—like a burst of sulfur—and I wonder if she can smell the whiskey on my breath. The dull lights start to spin, slowly, and everything starts to shift sideways. I can still feel them staring.

And then I hear my name again. Chloe's still got her hands around me, and I'm standing stiff, with my arms pinned down at my sides, and then the voice is close—right beside us, but I can still see him, leaning against the bar, laughing, smiling, holding a bottle of Bud.

"Is this Aubrey?" I look up and see this heart-shaped face and wiry blond hair spattered over the shoulders of a charcoal blazer. "I've heard so much about you," she starts, and swipes at her watery brown eyes. I give her this look, like *I have no idea who you are, lady*, and her whole face softens into this weak smile. "I'm Rachel's cousin." Chloe's still got her arms on me, everyone stares, and the bar floor is still slick with Clorox and beer. "Diane," she says, pressing her fingers against my wrist.

I remember the countless times Rachel would casually namedrop Diane into a conversation, like that somehow gave her an edge over the rest of us, like her experiences transferred over to Rachel simply by association. But I'd never actually seen her—not in the flesh—and as she stands before me, blubbering over her poor cousin—I feel like I'm in the presence of a celebrity.

"Diane?" I sputter, pushing Chloe away. I don't mean to laugh, but I do, and I feel giddy, and the cousins exchange a look, and then both put their hands on my shoulders again. "Like 'The Diane'?" I'm talking too loud, I know I am, because both girls lean in close and start to whisper to me. I'm not really sure what they're trying to say, but I don't need to hear it, so I keep on talking. My blood starts to do that buzzing thing again, and I push them away. "I can't believe you're real," I say. "I can't believe you're actually real."

"Honey," Diane says, lowering her voice, "let's get you some water, okay?"

"The Diane," I keep saying. "Un-fucking-believable." I still see him at the bar, laughing, smiling, with his bottle of Bud and mint-green tie.

"Chloe," Diane says, signaling with the flick of her wrist. "Get Aubrey a glass of water." She's got me by my own wrist, leading me to a bar stool. I pull away, too hard.

"Come, sit down, honey," she says. "Sober up." I put my hand up between us.

"Do you realize," I say, I think I may be slurring, just a little bit, "that you directly led to every act of debauchery I ever participated in?" I'm laughing again.

She laughs, too, but it's a nervous laugh, and she looks behind her at Chloe and mouths, *Water. Now.*

"No, listen," I say, backing away. "Like everything we did was because 'Diane did it first.'" I look around the room, but don't take my eyes off of him for more than a few seconds, and everything in me stirs. I see Ally, though, standing nearby, and I wave my arms at her, turning my attention away from him—anything to turn my attention away from him. "Ally," I call across the room. I know she hears me, but she only offers a tight-lipped smile and looks back over at the Girl I Can't Remember. "Ally," I say. "Are you seeing this? It's Diane. It's *the* Diane." She doesn't give any indication that she hears me, and then I remember Monday night at her house, and all those things she said.

We heard you did something bad. You really weren't there for her, were you? She really could have used her best friend in the end.

I look back toward Diane, and I try to smile, but the lights start to spin again, and I'm standing still, but everything else starts to shift.

"Let's not make a scene, honey," Diane says.

"No, listen to me, Diane. I don't think you understand what I'm saying." She feigns a smile and glances toward the exit. I realize I'm stuttering, and I know I need to just shut up. *Just shut up shut up shut up.* But I can't, and I feel the words start to fall out of my mouth again. And I know that Diane is just a temporary distraction, that the moment I stop rambling, I'll have to acknowledge him, in the corner, with his mint-green tie. "She got me to do everything because of you! Because of the glorious Diane!" I say. "Except for coke. Rachel never got me to do coke." I lean in. "You don't have any on you right now, do you?" She drops her hand from my wrist and turns to the crowd of mourners, still in their best black, still here for Rachel.

"I'm sorry," I say. "That was a joke." But Diane is still eyeing the crowd, and Chloe looks like she might cry, or laugh, or both, and everyone else just stares around the room.

"Does someone want to take this girl home?" she says, and

I think almost everyone in the bar takes an awkward sip from their drinks.

Poor Rachel, they're all thinking it. *Poor, fragile Rachel.* The room feels hazy, and I feel the swell of panic bubbling up from my guts, and I think I might vomit if I don't shut my mouth, and bite down on my tongue, and I don't understand what these people are thinking, all standing around, sad and sorry, in their black suits and Rachel T-shirts, as if somehow her death makes her more interesting—a dreamy, romantic image of a young girl, frozen in youth and beauty. But she wasn't beautiful. And the fact that these people now have this image, that she took her own life, so therefore she must have been deep, dark, and complicated—a true tragedy—like somehow her feelings matter more now, the fact that they're all thinking this makes me want to claw my face into ribbons. And I feel cheap. Cheap, like everything I'm feeling, these nerves, these anxieties, they're all just the insecurities of a little girl, a silly, sad little girl.

The room shifts sideways again. And they all continue to celebrate her, sip their well drinks, and say, *It's what she would have wanted. Oh, Rachel, that spark plug!* The center of attention, in life and death. But nobody sees the irony. Nobody sees that she's dead because nobody cared enough to know the real Rachel, the person beneath the party girl. And I want to shout, I want to shout it that she didn't kill herself because she was bored. They didn't know her like I did. They never found the girl sobbing over their bathroom sink because she didn't feel loved by her own mother. They never picked her up from the beach at 3 A.M. after some stocky guy with a buzz cut discarded her like a piece of trash. They never sat across from her at a diner while she pleaded for help.

I start to back out toward the door, my hands at my side, my perfectly manicured hands.

"Get off me," I say, stumbling back. "Who made you Mayor of the After-Party?" My hands flail out, and Diane flinches. I sputter and laugh, and I see him still, calm, casual, spinning his bottle of Bud on the bar. I don't make eye contact; instead I make it a point to get the hell out of here.

I start toward the door, but turn one last time to face the bar. I scan the crowd, and I see Eli and Ashley for the first time that night. They're leaning against the back wall, and she whispers something into his ear, and he shakes his head and stares down at the floor. Marc's near the DJ booth, and he pretends not to know me either. I steady myself, shifting my weight onto my five-inch heels. I realize that I'm still soaking wet, and I can't figure out how they're all so dry. I guess they must have brought those umbrellas after all.

"What are you looking at?" I finally say, loud and sharp, but nobody responds. The room is quiet, except for a couple of muffled whispers near the back end of the bar. "Anybody?" I say. My voice echoes, and still nobody speaks. I feel Diane creeping up from behind.

"Ash?" I say. "What happened? I thought we were besties?" Ashley smiles all nervously, and Eli puts his arm around her and reaches into his pocket for his phone.

"You're not calling Karen, are you?" I blurt, but he ignores me and walks into the bathroom. Ashley trails behind.

"What about you, Melanie?" I say. She catches my eye for

only a moment, and stares down at her drink. It's something dark and pink and mostly ice. She looks heavier than she did at the diner, even though she's dressed in all black and wearing too much lipstick. It makes her look desperate.

"So you're all just going to stand there, then? Like a bunch of fucking losers?"

I step back, and brush against a table near the door that's draped over with a white tablecloth. It's stained with what looks like wing sauce, and whoever's job it was to pick the tablecloth clearly thought nobody would notice. There's a framed photo of Rachel—an eight-by-ten of her high school graduation. It's campy and sad, but at the same time kind of appropriate. Next to Rachel's face there's the row of shot glasses from Ally's, lined up in perfect formation. I walk toward the display and finger the cloth, and everybody watches me. I hear Diane behind me, like she's trying to shuffle me out the door.

"What?" I whip around to face her again.

"You need to leave. You're making a scene," she says. "I know you're upset, Aubrey."

"Don't say my name like that," I say. "It's condescending." I'm raising my voice, and I don't mean to, but she puts her hand on my wrist again, and I snap back, and push her away, and then I feel myself fall, taking down the white, wing-stained cloth, and all the glasses come shattering to the floor.

There are so many sounds, but mostly it's just the buzzing in my own head, and I can vaguely hear Diane's frantic cries as she scoops up the broken pieces off the ground. Somebody calls out for a broom, and Adam comes at me. He reaches down and pulls me to my feet before I can even fight him off.

He's bigger and scruffier than I imagined, but I don't really feel anything when I see him for the first time, and this surprises me. I just feel dull and empty, like I want to nudge him in the shoulder and tell him that we both really fucked things up, didn't we? But I just don't have the energy.

I hear the train rumbling overhead.

And I can't take my eyes off Eric Robbins, in his buttondown and mint-green tie.

OUTSIDE, I STUMBLE across the street to the train-station parking lot. I'm still soaked, but now the rain pounds harder, drenching the black cotton dress, and it molds to my body. I don't care, though. It feels good.

I look up at the brick building and think of jumping. It wouldn't be the worst thing. Maybe some bored sap would even throw me an after-party of my own—my grinning face plastered crookedly over some random guy's chest, my name engraved onto a row of frosted shot glasses.

I see my car ahead, parked up against the station. I walk toward it, steady, heel to toe. The rain saturates my skin and burns my eyes, and I think I might be crying underneath all that water falling from the sky, but I can't be sure; I swore I wouldn't cry, so I can't be sure. I jam the key into the door, fumble until the lock pops, and hoist myself up into the driver's seat. The engine sputters to life, shaking and rumbling beneath me. My hands vibrate against the wheel, and I can't tell where my own body shakes end and the car's shaking begins.

Fuck you, Rachel, I say. *Fuck you Rachel. Fuck you Rachel,* and I keep saying it, I keep saying it until my face crumbles and the tears and rain melt together and I'm full-on sobbing in my Saab, and I laugh, I fucking laugh, because it's somehow hilarious to me that I would be sobbing in a Saab. *Fuck you, Rachel.*

I pull my knees to my chest, and wedge myself against the oversized steering wheel. "Fast Car" plays again. I reach in my center console for a Parliament but I don't smoke it. The thought of putting that thing to my mouth makes my guts twist and my mouth feel like it's made of sand, so I balance it on the ashtray and let the smoke stream off the end.

I dissolve a Xanax on my tongue and reach for the half-empty bottle of Jack Daniel's on the passenger seat. I think of Adam and I think of my life before and my life after Eric and how everything in between stopped mattering and everything after feels like tiny knives carving out my insides and how now I'm sitting in a parking lot with a bottle of Jack and an empty chest. I hold it to my lips and take a deep swig, the hot whiskey burning the back of my throat, burning a hole in my chest where I'm hollowed out like a dead deer.

I picture Eric and his mint-green tie and how he hardly flinched when I walked into the bar and how there'd been no recognition when I walked out, and I'm certain he doesn't even know my name. I take another swig of whiskey and reach in my bag for another Xanax, and I can't stop thinking of summer camp, when I was six, maybe seven, and I built this stupid house out of Popsicle sticks, and I used too much glue.

The car rumbles. I'm running out of gas.

I feel him still, the rough pads of his fingers prodding me, his hand over my mouth, and I swat at my thighs, even though

I know it's only phantom pains, and I take another swig of whiskey, and swish it around in my mouth, and he devours me, piece by piece. I take another swig, and another, and another, until it flows through me like rain, and I'm numb, so wonderfully numb and buzzing and warm, and I pull my sopping dress up over my head and throw it into the backseat, because even though it's been washed and rained on and sat like a stale thing in my closet for five years, even after all of that, I can still smell him: that old drafty bed, his hands fumbling at me.

The sky swirls with rain, and darkness starts to slip over me, I take another swig, the bottle pressed loose over my lips. The hot whiskey dribbles down my chin and onto my bare chest. I lean back, my stomach roils, and I can feel the swill of Jack bubbling up into my throat, and I take one last sip, and I can barely hear the loudspeaker overhead.

The last train to Babylon is operating on time.

Part Two

Chapter 26

Friday, October 10, 2014. 4 A.M.

YOUR MOTHER TOLD me something you said today, Aubrey. Something that concerned her."

I sit up in the bed, the hospital bed, and knead my face with the soft pads of my fingers. It feels like someone scraped out my sinuses and poured Clorox up my nose. Everything is damp and warm, and my temple pounds against the empty, sterile feeling inside my head. The window is open, and I can hear the rain clicking against the metal screen. I can smell it, too—rain, antiseptic, and latex.

"Do you want to talk about that?" Laura says. She'd said we'd had enough for the night, that I could go to sleep and she'd come back in the morning to talk more about what happened after Rachel's funeral. But then she sat back down at the edge of my bed like she'd forgotten to finish the job, and I felt that guilty twist in my stomach, like I might even throw up this time.

"I said a lot of things today," I say. I catch my reflection in the window again, and this time all I can think of is Linda Blair, and my head spinning around on a swivel and spewing pea soup in Laura's hair.

"About sleeping with someone back in high school. About him not taking no for an answer? Did you say that today, Aubrey?" She looks at me, her face set in a perpetual pout. I'd forgotten that I said those things to Karen. It felt like a dream—a hazy, ugly dream—but it only happened this morning. I look down at my newly painted fingernails: *Wicked*. My hands start to shake, slow at first, and my instinct is to reach for a cigarette, and I do, for just a moment, until I realize that not only would it be wildly inappropriate to light up a cigarette in front of a shrink, in a hospital no less, but I don't even have my bag.

"Where is my stuff?" I ask.

"Don't worry about your stuff, Aubrey. It's safe. Now tell me about that conversation with your mother."

"Please stop saying my name," I say.

"I'm sorry," she says. "May I ask why?"

"Because it's condescending, Laura."

"I didn't mean to patronize you, Aubrey." I shoot her a look and she apologizes again. "Tell me about the boy who wouldn't take no for an answer."

"I don't want to talk about this now," I say.

The rain clicks against the metal screen.

"When would you prefer to talk about it?"

"Not tonight," I say. She writes something down on her clipboard. She's close enough now that I lean over to catch a glimpse, but she pulls the papers toward her chest and clicks her pen.

"What about Adam?" she says.

"What about him?" I say.

"Can we talk about him?"

"I don't see what he has to do with any of this," I say.

"He's the one who found you, Aubrey."

Chapter 27

Saturday, October 11, 2014.

I HAVEN'T LEFT my bedroom since Karen drove me home from the hospital yesterday afternoon. They kept me overnight, and I overheard Karen and some doctor whispering out in the hallway about having me committed. Committed to where? I don't know. Probably South Oaks or someplace meant for people much less stable than I am. I sat up in my bed, hearing every word of their seemingly covert conversation. But they forget; I'm crazy, not deaf.

"An extended hospital stay is not necessary," I heard Karen say. She rattled off some facts and mumbled something about being a mental health professional herself and that she can "ensure a suitable healing environment."

On the car ride home, my mother went into the terms of my release. I am required to see Laura at her office, three days a week until the shrink sees fit. My license has also been temporarily revoked. I'm still not sure if that's a legal thing, a hospital thing, or a Karen thing, but I don't question it, because I know I don't deserve to have a car right now.

I sit on the edge of my bed and stare at the hardwood floor. My room is dark, and I can feel the heat blaring from the vent. I've been drifting in and out of sleep all day, barely checking the clock. I hear Karen rustling around the kitchen, so I know it's almost dinnertime, but I haven't eaten since I've been back, and the thought of food makes my throat feel sour, like I could open my mouth and spew out stomach acid all over the walls. I'm about to get back under my covers, when there's a soft knock at my door.

"What?" I say, but my voice cracks and it comes out more of a croak, and I just now realize how thirsty I am. The door creaks open, and I expect to see Karen standing there with a tray full of applesauce or something, but it's not Karen. It's Danny.

"Hi," he says, still partly concealed by the door. I can only see his face. "Can I come in?"

"I guess," I say, and I feel that stomach acid coming up again. I don't have the energy for this. For him.

"I know you said not to call, but you never said not to come." And then I remember our conversation the night of the funeral— as much as I can remember of it—how he'd spoken to Karen about all the things I'd said.

"Danny," I say. "You really shouldn't be here." My lips still feel swollen and cracked, and I haven't showered yet today and I'm not wearing a bra. I know it shouldn't matter with Danny, but for the first time, it does.

"I want you to come home," he says. "You don't need to be here." He stands in my doorway and slips his hands into his pockets.

"You have no idea what I need."

"Yes, I do." He says and turns to close the door. It's just us now, locked away inside my room—my ex-room. "And it's not this. This place is making you crazy. Look at you." He takes a few steps closer to me. I stand up and take a step back behind the bed, using it as a buffer between us.

"Please, go home," I say.

"Why?"

"Don't question me. Just go." He steps toward me and puts his hands on my shoulders. My whole body stiffens and I jerk backward. "Don't," I say, too loudly, and he reaches out again, but I stumble back toward my dresser. I don't need to be taken care of. And even if I did, I don't need Danny to do it.

"I won't leave you," he says.

"You know nothing about me, Dan." I start to speak again, but my voice cracks, and I feel my facial muscles start to contract, and I know I'm about to lose it.

"I know enough," he says. "And look, if you're going to throw everything away because of what some asshole did to you five years ago, then you're right, I don't know you." I feel myself start to shake, and I put my hands up again, maybe to send a warning, but also because I don't know what else to do. I'd mentioned Eric to him only once and never by name—only a vague explanation and we sort of had an understanding. But the fact that he was bringing it up now, throwing it in my face, using it to force some sort of emotion out of me, well, that wasn't fair. But before I have a chance to form a rebuttal, he clasps my wrists in his and pulls me toward him.

"Aubrey," he says. "Listen to me." I don't know what to do, so I scream, shrill and sharp, and pound my fist into his chest.

"Get away from me," I say. My voice must carry through the house, because Karen comes charging through the door like gangbusters. "Go home, Danny," I say. "Just go home. Please. I am begging you."

He lets go, and looks stunned, but before he can catch his footing, he trips back over my bed, catching himself just before he slides to the ground. Karen stands in the doorway.

"Maybe you should go, Danny," she says. "I'm so sorry for this."

"Did you do this?" I ask Karen. There's a stale silence, and they both just look at me. "Was this your doing, Karen? Did you plan this?" I say again when she doesn't answer.

"I'm sorry, Dan," is all she says. "Let me give you a ride to the train."

I'm still seething after Karen takes Danny back to the train, sucking in air through clenched teeth. She had no right to invite him here. He had no right to see me like this. But part of me knows he's right; this place is making me crazy.

Chapter 28

Monday, October 13, 2014.

"WHY DON'T YOU tell me a little about yourself," Laura says. "I don't think I really got a feel for the real you at the hospital."

We're sitting in her office, a small room with blue walls and a window, a mile from my house. I know it's exactly one mile because I ran here today. I'm in my running clothes, my hair is up in a ponytail. I wipe the sweat from my hairline with my T-shirt. It's the first time I've left my house in days. Two to be exact. I want to get back into my bed, bury my face, and numb myself with Xanax.

"I'm not really sure what you want me to say," I start.

"Well, how about telling me what you do?"

"I mean, I guess I'm sort of a journalist," I say.

"Sort of a journalist?"

"I don't really consider myself one. I'm more of a writer, I guess."

"And you live in the city?"

"Yes, with my boyfriend." I stop myself. It feels weird to say the word "boyfriend," wrong, and I realize I haven't spoken to Danny since my meltdown the other day.

I know she's baiting me with her chitchat, and my instinct is to remain vague, give only the information she asks for directly, but as I reel over what to say in my head, I start to think maybe I'm more confused than I thought. "I'm not really sure what we are right now. I sort of left things kind of open," I say, and it feels oddly settling. "And now I'm here." Laura looks at me, like I'm supposed to keep talking, but I don't know what to say. "I had a couple of bad days."

She scribbles something down on her clipboard. The sky starts to turn gray outside the window, and I get that sinking feeling in my chest when I realize I'm going to have to run a mile in the rain.

"Sort of a journalist? And you're not really sure where you are with your boyfriend?" She looks at me, like she's waiting for me to finish her sentence. I don't. "Sounds like you're not really sure who you are right now."

Well, she doesn't waste any time. I don't want to be here. It's mandated. But I'm not sure why. I'm not sure who's mandating it. I haven't done anything illegal—technically. But I don't question Karen, because then she'll start asking questions. And like I said, I'd much rather talk to the shrink.

"I don't know," I say. "I'm not really into the whole journalism thing. And it's a little late to not really know what I want to do with my life. I'm not in college anymore, you know."

"It's never too late to find your passion."

Is she serious? *Find my passion?* It's like she's got a copy of therapist Mad Libs attached to that clipboard of hers.

"I am incapable of passion," I say.

"Nobody is incapable of passion, Aubrey." She crosses her legs and leans forward into her knees. "How about when you're not working. What kinds of things do you like to do?"

This isn't much of a conversation. It seems more like an uncomfortable first date, an uncomfortable, one-sided first date. I look at the clock. Forty minutes left to go.

"I don't know," I say. It's such a simple staple of a question. *What do you like to do? What are your interests?* But I have no idea how to answer it. "I like to drink," I deadpan, "as you already know." It's meant to be more of a joke, but she seems to perk up, in an overly concerned, possible-breakthrough sort of way.

"You like to drink?" Her voice drops a beat, and her face is stricken with a rehearsed delicacy. She writes a quick note.

"That was a joke," I say. I take a slow sip of coffee. "Look," I start. "I know you think I'm completely insane, but you have to understand. I'm basically on suicide watch," I say. "Which is ridiculous, because I'm not suicidal. I just got drunk."

"You drank a bottle of whiskey on the day of your best friend's funeral, Aubrey. You showed up at a memorial, got kicked out, and then removed your clothes and walked onto the train platform, practically in a catatonic state. That's more than just getting drunk."

"My ex-best friend," I correct.

"What were you doing on the train platform, Aubrey?"

"I wasn't going to jump," I scoff.

"So you remember?"

"No. I just know I wouldn't do that. It's stupid."

"Stupid?"

"I'm not suicidal. I didn't try to kill myself."

"Then what were you doing on the train platform?"

"I don't know. Maybe I just wanted to get to Babylon."

"Why Babylon?"

"I don't know. Last stop. End of the line."

"Tell me about that day." She gets all serious, and I cross my arms over my chest. I realize the whole point of this is to talk about that day, *The Incident*, but I don't feel like talking. All I feel is dread.

"I really don't remember much," I say. "I must have blocked it out." I smile and shrug so she knows I'm kidding. I don't believe in repressed memories. I believe in being drunk.

"Maybe you did block it out."

"No," I say. "I did not block it out. I remember the beginning of the day. I got my nails done. I got in a fight with my mother before the funeral. I was never going to go. But I went home at some point to change into the black dress. I don't really know what happened after that. But it's not because I blocked it out. It's because I got drunk."

"Tell me about Adam," she asks, and my throat gets thick.

"I just hadn't eaten all day."

"Tell me about Adam," she says again.

"He was my high school boyfriend," I say. The air is too warm. I watch the rain start, fat drops hit the window behind Laura's head. I try to swallow. "We broke up five years ago."

"When you left Seaport."

"Yup."

"That's about the time you stopped being friends with Rachel."

"That is correct," I say, leaning back against the leather couch. Karen must have briefed her, because she knows more about my life than I've let on.

"What happened five years ago, Aubrey?" I close my eyes involuntarily and catch myself just before she can read my face.

"Look," I say. "I don't want to talk about Adam. I don't want to talk about Rachel. I know what you're doing. You're trying to force some sort of emotion out of me, but it's not going to work. I am cold and incapable of feeling." I take a deep breath, take a sip of coffee, and try and keep my hands from shaking.

Laura looks at me with a subtle smile. She doesn't say anything for a moment, and I fidget in my seat, flipping the tab on the top of my coffee.

"I see an emotion coming through very clearly," she says.

"And what's that?" The rain stops and the October afternoon sun creeps through the window shade behind her head.

"Anger," she says.

Laura's observation of my anger just makes me feel angrier, so I start to let up, just a little bit. I don't want her to think she's outsmarting me here. I'm impermeable to this psycho bullshit. I am half Irish, after all.

"Look. I'm anxious. I know that. I have anxiety. That's nothing new. And I know why, it's not a mystery or some repressed memory. It has nothing to do with Rachel's death but everything to do with Rachel."

"Oh." She perks up again, and lifts her pen, ready to go.

"But," I cut in, "I'm just not ready to talk about it yet."

"Okay," she says. "That's fine. "But can you do me a favor, Aubrey? And this is more for you than me." I shrug, and she leans back in her chair. "You said you're a writer. So do you think it would help if you started writing about what's going on? Just jot down your thoughts and feelings in a notebook. Sort of like a diary. You don't have to show me or anything. This is just for you."

"I can try it, I guess," I say. She smiles, looking pleased as ever with herself.

Chapter 29

April 2009.

I ALWAYS HATED the way teen turmoil was portrayed in books, TV, and those horrid Lifetime Original Movies—especially when it came to sex, specifically the unwanted kind. God, it was all so dramatic and unrealistic. The same shit over and over again: Good girl sneaks out to a party for the first time in her pathetic little life, and BAM! All of a sudden she's a walking ball of gloom and Goth, and her parents don't understand, and her friends disappear, and her teachers think she's underperforming. And then at the end, she has this inspiring epiphany and somehow finds the courage buried inside her to speak out and say those words, and declare that she was a victim. And then everything goes back to normal, and her parents are relieved, and her friends are so sorry they didn't understand, and her teachers exempt her from finals.

That doesn't happen in real life. Especially the part about the friends.

I stood outside Rachel's doorway, my fist pressed against the wooden door, but I didn't actually knock. I could hear her inside, the radio playing some forgettable song.

Jeff had let me in. He chewed on an apple and smacked his lips together and clicked his tongue against the roof of his mouth, and I felt so sick, like I could upchuck all over their beige carpeting.

"Rach's upstairs," he said, and smacked his lips again. I stood in the doorway too long, and a part of me was convinced that he could tell just by looking at me that I'd lost it in a drunken stupor while his stepdaughter got pounded right downstairs. I crossed my arms over my chest and darted up the stairs, away from his glazed stare.

My fist pressed against the door, and I thought about knocking, but waited, frozen, empty, until the door swung open and Rachel stood there in a pair of neon-green shorts and a wifebeater.

"Oh," she said, like she'd been waiting for me. "Coming in or just gonna stand there?" I stepped inside. Her room hadn't changed much since we were kids: baby-blue-painted walls, a day bed with a white floral comforter, her collection of American Girl dolls and stuffed bears. She went back to her dresser, leaned into the mirror, and picked up a brush and a palette of purple eye shadow.

It had only been two days since Easter—since I saw her in the car with Adam. I thought she'd be nervous, jittery even, to see me, but she just eyed herself in the mirror, calm and casual, and colored her lids with shades of violet.

I watched her and put off what I came there to do, what I came there to say. I concealed my shaking hands behind my back and bit my lip until I tasted blood. I felt the words in my throat, like I was about to be caught in a lie. Only it wasn't a lie. For once, what I was about to say wasn't a lie.

"Rachel," I said.

"Mm?" She didn't look up as she applied charcoal liner to her eyes.

"Can I tell you something?"

"Mm-hmm," she said again. Her tone felt cold, like she'd been waiting for me to say it. I steadied myself on her bed frame.

"Promise you won't freak out. Because I'm freaking out. And I sort of need you to not be pissed at me right now." She put the eyeliner back down on her dresser and turned to me. Her face stoic and her lips set into a thin line.

"I already know what you're going to say, Aubrey," she said. She stepped closer, lifted her hand, and brushed the hair out of my face. I felt myself twitch. She smiled. "I just want to hear you say it."

"Say what?" I asked. A part of me thought she might say it for me, that she'd finish my sentence, take me into her arms, and tell me she was sorry, she was sorry for ditching me, sorry that I had to go through that, she was so sorry, and she'd always be there for me. That we were Rachel and Aubrey, best friends, forever branded by the *heartigram* etched into our left hipbones.

But like I said, that doesn't happen in real life.

"You know what, Aubrey?" She was still smiling, but it wasn't the *I'm sorry, I'm understanding, I'm here for you* smile that I'd been hoping for. "I know you fucked Eric," she said. "And Adam knows you did, too."

I looked at the floor and tried to swallow but my throat was dry and I needed to get the hell out of that room.

"Rachel," I said. I felt my face go numb. "It wasn't like that. I swear. He made me. I didn't know what was going on," I started.

"Yeah, sure. *You didn't know* what was going on. You were *drunk*. You were *bored*. He *made* you," she mocked. "But really, I don't care. I think we both know what happened."

"He held me down," I said. My face stung now, like coming inside after being out in the snow too long. "I told him to stop."

"For once, you didn't have the guy, so you had to take him from me. Adam deserves better than that, Aub, and so do I."

I felt her breath on my face; she smelled like Red Hots. All I could see were the photographs lined up on Rachel's dresser. They were mostly of herself—Rachel riding a horse; Rachel at Junior Prom; Rachel at the beach; at the Jumps; on my front porch. The sharp words rolled off her tongue. "Don't pretend like you didn't know what you were doing," she said. I finally looked up. Tears streamed down her pale face, her brown eyes bloodshot, and it almost felt staged, like she'd dowsed her eyes in Visine while I wasn't looking. "You're just a desperate slut," she said.

I stared back, shook my head, and almost smiled, before turning around and backhanding all of the frames off of her desk with one swift motion.

Glass shattered onto her hardwood floor. Rachel stood there, her mouth hung open in a limp, gaping hole, and before she could even react, I raised my hand again and slapped her dead across her face—the sound like a rubber band snapping.

A sound escaped from the space between Rachel's teeth— shrill and animalistic, and she stepped back like she might charge at me like a deranged orangutan, tear out my hair, shred my skin to pieces with her fingernails. But I didn't wait around for that. I turned—cool, casual, calm—and sauntered out of her room, and didn't cry until I got back to my car.

Chapter 30

Wednesday, October 15, 2014.

Aren't we only as good as what other people tell us? Since birth we're called a smart baby, then a great reader, an excellent student because some random teacher says so and gives a report card to prove it. You're a good writer—but only because this one time in this one class this one professor told you so, and your mom agreed. And maybe it's true, but also, maybe it's not. You're a good friend, because someone tells you. And if no one tells you that, then chances are you're probably not a good friend. You're probably a really shitty friend.

Laura thinks I seek validation.

I don't think there's such a thing as validation. I think it's just what we know. The way we feel about ourselves is always based on feedback from others. We are trained to accept that. It doesn't mean I'm insecure, or unsure, or insane. It just means I'm human, and I have, above all else, self-awareness.

So when she asks me to describe myself, I start with the qualities others have given me.

"People say I'm cold."

"Who says?"

"My mother," I say.

"What does she know?"

"Well, she's the reason I'm here, isn't she?"

"No, Aubrey. You're the reason you're here."

I scoff, hating how she has to make everything so serious.

Rachel would have called me many things, depending on the year and her own level of happiness.

Best friend, desperate slut, bitch, traitor, only friend. I couldn't keep track, and God knows what she thought of me when she died. Maybe that voice mail would have the answer. I reach for my phone, just to make sure it's still there. Not that I plan on listening to it. Ever.

"How are you feeling? How's the anxiety?" Laura asks through an overly warm smile. I shrug.

"It's okay, I guess," I say. "Thank God for Xanax." I grin, awkwardly, and I can tell she still doesn't get my offbeat sense of humor. She writes something down. Probably about cutting down my prescription—not that she really has a say anyway. She's not even a real doctor.

"What about the panic attacks? Have you had any since our last session? Since the incident?"

"Nope," I say. "No panic attacks." I'm not even sure I would call what happened that night a "panic attack." Laura says it was cathartic. I call it a meltdown.

"Great," she says. I unscrew the cap off my water bottle

and take a long sip while I wait for her to lure me into some sappy confession. The water has been sort of a buffer for me. It buys me time—allows me to choose my words carefully when she tries to catch me off guard. "Let's talk more about Rachel today," she finally says.

"What do you want to know?"

"Well," she says. "You harbor a lot of resentment toward her. But surely there must have been something good about her. She was your best friend for ten years."

I knew this was coming, and I'm prepared. I practiced the answer in my head on my run over here.

"Honestly," I say, "I don't know why I was friends with her. Maybe I was just a lot like her, you know, shallow in some ways. So she made me feel better about myself. I guess she made me feel like less of a villain." I take another sip of water, and hold it in my mouth for three seconds before swallowing.

I tried to come up with something a little more genuine. I really did. But the harder I thought about it, the more I realized there was nothing good about Rachel, except that I really had no one else. Except for Adam.

"Everyone we grew up with was pretty much exactly the same," I say. "We all had the same agenda." I try not to smile, but I think I'm really nailing this therapy thing.

"What was that?" she asks, scribbling something in her notebook, I'm sure about my low self-esteem.

"Get paid and get laid." I think she almost smiles, but she leans forward in her seat.

"What about Adam? Did he just want to 'get paid and get laid'?" When she says it back to me, it sounds sort of ridiculous.

"In some ways," I say. "He was a decent guy. He had his moments. But he was a good a guy. It was Rachel who ruined him for me."

"What do you mean, ruined him?" I bite down on my lip and immediately regret my choice of words.

"That's not really what I meant," I say, and I'm trying to backtrack, but my mind feels blank.

"Well, what did you mean?" I take a sip of water, and stare at the wall. I'm trying to look pensive, but really I'm just buying time. "Aubrey?" I pull in a sharp breath. She's not letting this go.

"Things just didn't end well with us. And I guess I've always blamed Rachel for that."

"But you said 'ruined him.' How was he ruined for you Aubrey?"

"Maybe I meant that she ruined me for him."

Chapter 31

April 2009.

I TURNED INTO my driveway and allowed myself five minutes of cold, hard tears before wiping the snot off my nose with the back of my sweater and pulling it together.

Pull it together. Pull it together.

I said it out loud, over and over, until that pinch in my lungs dissipated and I could breathe again.

Pull it together.

I had three fears: one, Rachel would show up at my house and cause a scene, which led to fear number two: I'd have to relive the words and face the fact that maybe I was a desperate slut.

Desperate slut. Desperate slut. Desperate slut.

And this all led to fear number three: Karen finding out. Karen finding out about Eric. Karen finding out about Adam. And even Karen finding out that that I slapped my best friend across the face. Ex-best friend. I was pretty sure this was the end for Rachel and me.

But Karen wasn't home when I slipped through the front door. Cheerleading practice, I remembered. She had cheerleading practice on Tuesdays.

I went to my room, climbed into my bed, and started up my laptop.

A picture of Adam and me glared from my desktop background. It had been from the First Friday of our senior year, right before we snuck away and saw each other naked for the first time. My stomach buzzed, and I opened Internet Explorer to cover up our grinning faces.

And then I Googled his name. *Eric Robbins.* His college lacrosse photo popped up along with a couple of stats. The glow of the screen illuminated his gap-toothed grin, and it suddenly felt like bugs were crawling all over my body.

I stared until my eyes ached. The laptop warmed the top of my thighs. I opened the Google search box again and typed *Rape.* I stared at the results but I didn't feel them. They were just words, just hollowed words, jumbled up and meaningless on my computer screen. *What is rape?* I typed. It seemed like a stupid question; of course I knew what rape was. *Was I raped?* I typed, and the results thinned, but I didn't click. Even if the Web held the answers to these burning questions, I didn't want to know. Ignorance is bliss, right? I thought about what Rachel had said, how she'd mocked me with my own words, and as my computer screen blazed up at me, the Internet never felt more intimidating—an all-knowing wizard with a crystal ball. I don't know what I thought I'd find.

Chapter 32

Friday, October 17, 2014.

"You seem uncomfortable today," Laura notes.

"Well," I start, immediately regretting my defensive tone. "I told you I wasn't ready to talk about Adam."

"That was Wednesday, Aubrey," she says. "You just seem to be doing a lot better; I thought maybe we could delve into your relationship with him a bit today. But we can stop if it's too much for you."

"It's fine," I say. "Adam and I had a complicated history."

I wait for her to ask a question, but she just nods and motions for me to continue. The sun blares through the window behind her head. She's wearing the same yellow sweater she wore that night at the hospital.

"Adam's brother, Max, was my first kiss. He would have been a senior when I was a freshman. But he killed himself." It's the first time I've said the words out loud, at least in this context. "I mean some people think it was an accident. But most people think it was suicide."

"Wow," Laura says.

"I met Adam at Max's wake. It was really awkward, a complete accident. I was looking for Rachel, and I ran into him outside. I felt bad, so I said hi and that pretty much opened the lines of communication." I take a sip of water and uncross my legs. "We just started walking to school together. That's how we started."

"That's a lot," she says. "To lose a brother to suicide. Was he seeing a therapist?"

"Ha," I scoff, "Adam, ask for help? He once told me he was 'unshrinkable.'"

Laura laughs, for once.

"I like that term," she says. "Well, what about you? Didn't he confide in you?"

I think about this for a moment, scanning the years we have known each other. "Maybe," I say. I notice that Laura is smiling, all creepy, like she's waiting for me to have a big epiphany. Laura looks wired today. Her eyes bug out of her head, like she just can't wait to get to the bottom of me. I approach with caution.

"So, Adam never saw anyone about his brother's death?" Laura asks. She's still stuck on this. It's like a therapist's wet dream. Two suicides, a messy four-year affair. Just wait until she finds out the rest.

"Nope," I say. "But I don't see how Adam is important right now."

"You know why he's important, Aubrey," she says. "He's

the one who brought you to the hospital. The night of the funeral." She says it as if she needs to clarify, as if I frequent hospitals and have alcohol-induced breakdowns.

I take a sip from my water, even though there's hardly any left. I know Laura can tell I'm starting to get uneasy. She just smiles and nods and waits for it all to sink in.

"I know that," I say. "You don't need to remind me." I start to twist the plastic bottle in my hands.

"That must have put a lot of pressure on you, being so young, if he wasn't talking to anyone about his brother's death. Did you ever feel like he was leaning on you, pressuring you?" I don't like the amount of eye contact she's using today and I let my own gaze fall to the window behind her head.

"Sure," I say. "I definitely felt pressure from time to time."

"Emotional pressure? Sexual pressure?"

"Both, I guess," I say. "I mean there was this one fight we had. Senior year of high school. It was sort of the beginning of the end for us."

"What do you mean?"

"I was kind of a prude," I say. "We'd been together for almost four years, and he was starting to get impatient. You know. He wanted to have sex. I wasn't really ready. I was getting annoyed that he kept asking. So I kind of shut down with him."

"What happened?"

"We were on the floor in my bedroom. The door was open, and we were just play wrestling, you know? Just fooling around, kissing, tickling, laughing. Nothing too scandalous."

"Right," she says.

"And then he just snapped. Like completely went off on me how I was fucking with him. I was a cocktease. I needed to make up mind. I owed it to him. You know, typical teenage boy." I started to unscrew my water bottle again. "But I was going to do it. I knew I wanted to before college. It was just that now he was pressuring me. And I was just being stubborn."

"And then what?"

"I just ignored him. It was only supposed to be two days. I sort of planned it out. You know, until I calmed down. I wanted to make him sweat a little. It was the longest we'd ever gone without talking. I didn't respond to his texts. And then it turned into this sick twisted game. Like I would text, and he wouldn't. And then we both just stopped." I took the last little gulp of my water. "But I loved him. I really did. I think I was just afraid to lose him."

"But you did lose him," she says, and the authority of her voice sets me back into defensive mode.

"Not yet," I say, and I'm not sure if I'm warning her against cutting me off, or I'm simply telling her that the loss came much later.

Chapter 33

Monday, October 20, 2014.

I STARE DOWN at the blank page in front of me, tapping my pen against the bed frame. I've actually been heeding Laura's advice, writing out my *feelings*, but today, nothing's really coming out. I've been using the back of the *As If* notebook and have been filling up the pages pretty quickly up until now. I'd forgotten what it was like to write—not just write—but to write for myself, without deadlines and guidelines and Jonathan's passive-aggressive periods. Somewhere between all the crime reports and five-alarm fires, I'd lost the desire.

The morning sun streams through my open window, illuminating the pages. I flip back to last night's entry, and the words glare up at me—igniting beneath my hovering hand. I'm afraid to touch them, like they'd spark and singe the pads of my fingers right off. I've been good with the booze lately, lying low while I'm dealing with all my shit, but I'd given in to a glass or

three of wine last night, and I'd let the words flow through me
into my tattered old marble notebook, and part of me wants to
tear the page out and put it through Karen's shredder. I don't
know what made me do it, aside from the wine; write a letter to
Rachel using my good handwriting—the kind used for birthday cards, job applications, and suicide notes.

Dear Rachel, I'd started.

*It's, me, Aubrey. Your "best friend." Is that what you
really thought? Or did you just use that label to keep a
hold on me, to control me, to guilt me into playing the
sidekick in your warped little production of a life? I took
a psych class in college, and we learned about Stockholm
syndrome. I couldn't help but think of you and me, and
how I'd been caught up in your lies and charm for so long.
Did you think it would last forever? Did you think I was
that stupid, that vapid and needy, that I'd let you take
everything from me, and I'd be waiting with open arms
when you decided you needed your "best friend" back?*

I stop reading. I'm dizzy, too warm, and slightly hung over.
I lean back against my pillow and pull my knees up, balancing
the book in front of me. It's funny, I don't remember writing
most of this, and I'm not really sure what to make of it.

*What did you think you'd accomplish with your little
call? Did you think I would have talked you out of it? Tell*

you that I'm sorry, that I love you, that I need you, too? That I forgive you? Ha! Did you intend for me to revel in guilt for the rest of my life, harboring the secret that I could have done something? That I could have stopped you? Then what? We'd go on as best friends for the rest of our lives, grow old together, attend each other's wedding? You'd be my Maid of Honor and give a heartwarming speech on how'd I'd always been there, how I saved your life? I don't blame you for what happened with Eric. I've learned a long time ago that you can't control the actions of others. But I do hate you for all the rest of it. For those things you said. For Adam. Five years, Rachel. You let five years go by before you even pretended to give a shit. That's on you. You've always been delusional, Rach. And you've always been selfish. And even in your dying moment, you felt the need to put me in this position, and for that, I will never forgive you.

I stare down at the page, and remember to breathe, but I'm having trouble, and I can't be sure if I meant what I said, about never forgiving her. My phone alarm goes off; it's almost time for my appointment with Laura. I slam the notebook shut, stuff it under my mattress, and decide that it's time to talk.

I'M CALMER THAN I thought I'd be when I walked in. I'm wearing a gray cotton T-shirt, a cardigan, and a pair of black yoga pants. I even blew out my hair today and put on mascara. The first time I've made an effort since I've been home.

Laura notices right away. "You look great. What's different about you?"

"Nothing," I say, but the question calms me.

"I guess you just look relaxed, then," she says.

I take a deep breath, lean back into the leather couch, and take a slow sip from my water bottle.

"I've been thinking a lot about the writing. How it feels," I say. "And I've been sorting through some stuff. I think I'm ready to tell you why I am the way I am right now. Why I was so angry with Rachel."

Laura smiles, leans back in her chair, and tosses me a box of tissues. She knows I won't use them, but I appreciate her attempt at humor.

I LEAVE FEELING oddly winded, like I'd just run a marathon hung over. Winded but revitalized in a way. I pull the cardigan closed over my chest, as I walk out onto the street. There's a chill in the air, a quiet breeze. Laura tells me I'm suffering from PTSD. So the things I'm feeling are either (A) Normal or (B) Totally in my head. It still doesn't make sense to me, even if I've finally found some sort of validation—even if she's my shrink and she's paid to validate me.

I'm still in the denial stages, she says, even though it's been five years. It's supposed to be like grieving, but I haven't lost anyone I really cared about, so I'm not too sure what that entails. She says I'm grieving Rachel, even if I don't realize it yet.

I may be crazy but I'm not grieving Rachel. That much I do know.

Rachel is the reason for this. She's the reason for everything.

Laura also tells me that it's not Rachel's fault. And it's most certainly, without a doubt, not my fault. It's no one's fault, she pounds into my head, over and over and over again. It's no one's fault but my rapist's.

My rapist.

The word doesn't sit well with me. In a way it feels like I'm relinquishing all responsibility for what happened, and Laura says that's the whole point. But even so, how can a boy who I've known almost my entire life become *my rapist?* How does he suddenly belong to me? At what point did I claim possession of him, and at what point did he become my responsibility? *My rapist.* Laura says it with such casual grace, as if she's talking about *my brother* or *my sweatshirt.*

"If he's my rapist, does that make you *the rapist?*" I said. She forced a smile and let out a long sigh, resting her hands on her knees.

When I say it—*my rapist*—it feels forced and cheap.

I know I made a big deal about telling her what happened, but part of me regrets it. Yes, Laura, I feel like saying, I'm anxious. I have anxiety. I get it. But I'm high functioning and I don't need to be here. I didn't realize she'd make this out to be such a life-shattering confession. Maybe if I knew, I would have kept my mouth shut.

I told her a vague version of that night, and said, *See this is why I hated Rachel. Do you understand? No big deal. Shit happens.*

And then something shifted.

Laura called it rape, and says the sooner I accept that, the sooner I can start "the healing process."

It's a process. It's a process.

If I have to hear that "it's a process" one more time, I swear I will jump. But I don't say that out loud, because I'm still home, and home is better than the hospital.

I'm having a hard time using the R-word. I've never really been too comfortable with it, and I never said it out loud. Except once. And even then, the first time I let the word slip away from me was unintentional.

It was May—the weekend Danny's two-year-old nephew came to stay with us in the city. The kid was into everything—wiping his grubby little paws all over the TV, climbing into the liquor cabinet. He refused to nap, and when he did finally sleep, we had to be silent, which meant no getting up to pee, no talking, and absolutely no sex. I had casually made a joke, comparing watching a toddler to being raped: "I can't sleep; we can't have sex; and all I keep saying is 'Stop,' 'Don't,' and 'No.'"

Danny didn't laugh—he promptly changed the subject.

Laura kept calling it "The Rape," like it was some big event—like *The Wedding* or *The Hurricane*. There were times during the session when I thought she just said it to gauge my reaction.

Sometimes there was no reason for it at all. We'd been talking about a random fight I once had with Danny, and she said, "Well, you know, control is very important to you. You know, with *The Rape* and all." And every time she said it, I felt my body tense up, my left eye twitch, and she smiled. It was real subtle. But she smiled, and I know it. Like she knows that it gets to me, even when I won't use the word—unless it's in the context of an off-color joke.

"Do you feel like you're a victim?" she'd asked.

"No," I said. "I don't feel like a victim."

"Do you feel like a survivor?"

"No, I don't feel like a survivor either."

"How about taking legal action? Have you considered this?"

"It's been five years. Statutes of limitations, and all that. I don't think it's something I'd be able to go through with anyway."

"Why's that?"

"I'm not interested in justice. He'll get what's coming to him eventually. Life has a way of making sure of that." She sits, silent. "And I know you say I'm in denial, but I don't think that's true."

"Okay," she said, and signaled for me to keep going.

"I know what triggers me. I sort of seek out triggers, if that makes sense."

She shook her head, and I began to get frustrated.

"You know, triggers, like listening to Tori Amos, Googling Eric's name—really cliché shit like that; reading *The Bell Jar*. I like making myself anxious."

"Okay," she said. "I think I get it."

"I don't know," I said. "It's like when I get into a funk, and I start to really think about things and get really anxious, I don't try and make myself feel better. It's like I challenge it. I trigger myself into a panic attack. You know. Triggers. Isn't that like a big shrink term?"

Laura smiled and nodded, and I knew she wanted me to keep talking before I lost the thought. It was a tactic she overused—not speaking—so I'll feel awkward and fill the silence with all of my deep, dark emotions.

"I'm trigger-happy."

I let my body relax onto the leather couch and unscrewed the cap of my water bottle.

When I told her this, I thought she'd be impressed. She'd think it was wonderful that I was facing things head-on, but instead she said, "This is the equivalent of self-mutilation, Aubrey."

I rolled my eyes. I can't win with her.

"Do you ever think about cutting yourself?"

"No," I said.

But that wasn't entirely true.

I was with Danny. We were at one of his frat parties in college. I was drunk, like really smashed, and Danny was talking to some awkward freshman girl. I'm not really the jealous type, but God, she wasn't even pretty.

I was sitting on the attic stairs with my roommates. "She's not even pretty," I kept mumbling. "She's not even pretty."

"Here, just drink more, babe," they said, tilting the beer cup to my lips. "She's not even pretty. You are so much prettier."

The four of us just sat there, slurring until I hoisted myself up on the broken railing and made my way to the bathroom.

"She's not even pretty," I said again.

I was alone in the bathroom and I stared at myself in the mirror. I had sweated most of my makeup off and reeked of beer. The mirror was already cracked. I remember it was cracked, so I put my fist through the glass.

My reflection shattered, and I screamed through my teeth. Someone banged on the door, and I said, "Shut the fuck up. I'll be out in a minute."

As I pulled bits of glass out of my knuckles, I just remember feeling. Like really fucking *feeling*. Not good or pain or bad. Just feeling. So I grabbed a shard out of the sink, lifted my shirt, and pressed down until I drew a shallow red line across my stomach. I started at the hipbone, cutting into my *hearti-gram*. My *heart-on. R A.* I didn't press too hard, didn't go too deep, but just enough to bleed.

When Danny saw me, he dropped his beer. "What the hell happened?" he asked, ready to fight someone. I smiled at his young freshman friend, my hands covered in blood.

"Someone broke the bathroom mirror. I fell," I said. He grabbed my hand.

"Does it hurt? Do you need to go to the hospital?" His breath was sour and yeasty.

"No, I just want to go to bed," I said.

At home, he wrapped my hand in gauze, gave me a Xanax, and turned off the light. We were lying side by side. He traced circles over my wrist, something he always did to help me fall asleep.

I leaned in and kissed him on his forehead, his nose, and finally parted my lips over his mouth.

"Are you sure you're all right?" he asked. It was dark, but I could feel him propped up on his elbows, assessing my situation.

"Uh-huh," I said, taking off my shirt. He hadn't seen what I'd done to my stomach, but I needed him pressed against me.

"No," I said again to Laura, "I've never thought about cutting myself."

Chapter 34

Wednesday, October 22, 2014.

IT COMES IN waves. It flows through me, but I remember just a moment, a sound, a smell. Mostly I remember Adam. I remember Adam, even though I never actually saw him that night.

Laura's been having me work on memory. I try to explain that I do remember. It's not something I've ever really stopped remembering, but she insists there are still things that I haven't let myself think about yet—that I haven't allowed myself to feel.

Part of me thinks it's bullshit. Part of me is just telling her what she wants to hear. But part of me wants the help.

Maybe she just wants to hear me talk about the details. But that's not really something I think I'll ever be able to do. I told her that he'd been inside me, even though I said no. I told her that he sat on top of me so I couldn't leave, and I demonstrated what he did with my hands and rammed three fingers into the air, like a mute, broken child.

But I didn't tell her how he scrunched up my dress, and when I told him to stop, he said, *You can keep it on.* How he locked his elbows around my knees. I didn't tell her how I'd stopped fighting and had just lain still, like a dead fish, because I thought he'd eventually get bored. I didn't tell her how I'd been so oblivious, so numb, that I hadn't realized what was going on.

And maybe that would have been okay if he had stopped there. If when I reached down to push his hand away from me, I hadn't instead grabbed a handful of *heart-on.*

"I have a condom," he'd said.

"I'm not having sex with you," I said.

And maybe it would have been okay if he'd stopped there. Because maybe, just maybe, it could have been passed off as an honest mistake between two drunk kids.

Laura was a real bitch today. I'm sick of talking about it. I'm sick of her assuming that every little insignificant action is a direct effect of Eric Robbins. That I have no control over my emotions, but it's okay, because *I'm A Victim.*

It's just after four, and the sun is blazing over Sunrise Highway. It's rush hour, and traffic is stopped from Wantagh Avenue all the way down to Massapequa. I jog along the train tracks so I don't risk anybody seeing me. I'm in my workout clothes, and I've got sweat under my tits, but I see O'Reilly's: the door wide open and the bar empty.

I think about what Laura would say—if she knew I walked

out of the session and took a brisk jog right through the open
door of the bar that started it all. She'd probably look at me
with her fake empathy face and ask if I felt I needed to regain
control, because of *The Rape*. She'd say it was symbolic and
moving.

And I'd say no, I was just fucking thirsty.

All bars smell the same in the afternoon—warm beer,
Clorox, and just a hint of vomit. There are a few middle-
aged, mustachioed men in fishing hats at the other side of the
bar when I walk in. It's quiet and dank, and I order a shot of
Cuervo. It sits in front of me, next to a limp lime, wetting a
bar napkin.

The bartender is a short guy with a faux hawk and an Irish
accent. I'm not sure where he came from or what he's doing in
Wantagh, but he offers me two for one on a Wednesday afternoon. I don't hate it.

A television drones low from behind the bar—the news,
talking about some storm coming next week—maybe even a
big hurricane.

"Saying we might be an evacuation zone," Irish says, spilling tequila over two shot glasses.

"Said the same thing last year," I mumble. I take the shot
and let it burn the back of my throat, brassy and boozy—just
like I remember. I feel a body come down on the stool next
to me.

"Don't I know you?" That voice.

My back stiffens, and I know not to turn around. *Don't turn
around.* But I do, and I'm right; it's him.

I hold the shot below my lips, eye him up and down, and
I laugh. I think it's a laugh. Maybe a grunt. I'm not sure. But
everything else seems hazy.

"No," I say. "You don't know me." He squints at me
and smirks, this crooked smirk that almost, *almost* seems
charming.

He signals to the bartender. "I'll have what she's having."

"I'll take another, too." Irish eyes me, pours two shots, and
slides the saltshaker between our glasses.

"Shot for shot?" Eric asks. I don't say anything and lick
the salt off my hand before throwing back the glass—barely
flinching this time. He does the same, but his face puckers up.
He tries to smile through it. "I do know you," he says, flicking
the liquor off his tongue. "You're that chick who flipped out at
Rachel's party."

"You mean Rachel's funeral?"

He grins again, shrugs, and signals for two more shots. The
Cuervo starts to make my blood buzz, and for the first time
I'm looking at him—really looking at him. Not at a mug shot
or some college lacrosse photo. Not in my fucked-up memories, but in real, cold, hard, fucked-up life.

Did you know that memories are not like movies, despite
what some people might think? They're not snapshots either.
It's actually more like theater—a really shitty stage play in the
basement of some dingy East Village coffee shop. No perfor-
mance is the same. It all depends on the mood of the actors—
the lighting, the season, whether or not the star has her period,
or the guy got laid the night before. No scene is the same either.

And memories, well, they aren't real. They're just a replication of the last time you remembered, not the actual event. And I wonder how much has actually changed since that night.

I can't tell if he remembers. I can't tell if it's some sick form of denial, playing dumb, or if he genuinely can't place me—the *cute but kind of chubby* girl he held down and shoved his dick into.

Eric takes another shot. He starts to get that glazed look. He's thinner than I remember, maybe not as strong as I'd thought either. And then it hits me. Where I am. Who I'm with. I reach for the glass and realize that my hands are shaking. But I'm not afraid. I'm not afraid of him. I'm not his victim.

My entire body hums. I can hear my breathing in my ears, and I remember what Laura says: *Stay grounded. Stay in the moment. You're safe.*

I'm safe.

He puts two fingers up, and Irish brings two more shots, but gives me a look, like he's about to cut me off. I flash him a sweet smile—maybe it will buy me one more.

A song plays dreamily from the jukebox, and I feel my body sway like a feather on the stool.

Eric raises his glass to me. We clink and throw back. The lines on his face begin to blur, like he could be any guy, but somewhere beneath the haze of my buzz, I can feel him still, his fingers jabbing into me, his hand over my mouth.

And then I'm not sure how it happens, but I have him by the hand, and I'm guiding him to the bathroom.

I push him up against the sink and stare through him into

the mirror. I notice the dark circles under my eyes, but can't decide whether it's just the awful lighting or the tequila.

Eric leans in and kisses me. Softly. Gently. And everything inside me aches. I bite into his lip. He flinches and pulls away for a second before coming back in harder, his tongue darts into my mouth, and he grips my waist. I have to swallow hard to keep from gagging. I bite him again, harder than before and feel the pressure on his bottom lip, like I could split his lip in two if I really wanted to.

He spins me around and tries to perch me on top of the sink. I reach up and backhand him in the jaw. He's stunned, and I smile, and kiss him again, and he's still confused and pushes me up against the mirror, harder, and then I punch him again, and bust his lip open. Blood seeps through his bleached teeth.

He starts to say something, and I kiss him again, his blood mixing with my saliva. It tastes metallic, and I bite down again, and he pulls away.

"Easy," he whispers, but it's almost a threat—*Easy*. So I shrug, and say something along the lines of *Sorry, baby. I like it rough*. And then I start to undo his belt.

"Wait," he says, his eyes shifting toward the door, and he pulls his jeans back up.

"Come on," I say. "You can keep it on." I'm on my knees, looking up at him, his face still a perfect blur. I tug at his jeans again, until he gives in. "Get on the floor."

"Why?"

"Just do it." He quirks his eyes at me, the blood still dribbling down his chin, and he lets his body fall onto the sticky, damp floor. I have him by the shirt collar, hard. The room spins with a dull grace. My tongue is bitter and thick with the taste of straight Cuervo and lime—and the metallic taste of blood and salt.

My brain is telling me to stop. But everything is spinning. And everything feels right.

"Easy," he says again, and then I'm pounding the soft side of my fist into his face. He jolts up and slams his palms into my chest. I feel my head crack against the white tile wall. I hear it crack, but I don't feel anything. I pounce back on him and I'm punching him again.

"What the fuck is wrong with you?"

He has me pinned up against the wall now, his pants around his ankles. And I start to scream, a high-pitched, bloodcurdling scream. Eric stands up and bolts for the door, his pants still dragging past his knees.

"Crazy, bitch," he mutters before swinging the door open. Nobody comes. A girl screams in a bar bathroom, and nobody comes. I start to laugh, and the longer I sit on that bathroom floor, my back to the white tile wall, the more time passes, and I just laugh.

Chapter 35

Wednesday, October 22, 2014.

I'M STILL CRACKING up when I step out of the bar and into the street, like really laughing. It's guttural, and I'm cackling like a maniac, head thrown back, shoulders shaking. That kind of laugh. A minivan rolls past me and pulls into the train-station parking lot, and I can't wipe the shit-eating grin off my face. I reach in my bag for a cigarette, balance it between my lips, and strike a match—my hands steady.

The sun is low, big and gelled, and glowing orange. Purple clouds bruise the sky, and every time I try to compose myself, every time I try to keep a straight face, I lose it again, laughing and smoking and grinning and I can't stop. Because all I can see is the beautiful blood seeping through Eric Robbins's teeth, and I feel all airy inside, like a Vicodin dream. I take a deep drag, letting the purple smoke ribbon through the fibers of my shirt, and I hold on to the hope that he feels violated,

humiliated, devalued—that he will never know what it's like to
relax again.

Welcome to my hell, Eric.

I walk, my fists balled up at my sides and my knuckles starting to bruise. I flex my hand. I think it may be sprained, but it
was totally worth it. I walk east, cross over Sunrise Highway,
it's still rush hour and bumper to bumper. A driver holds down
a horn, and I don't even startle. I know what I have to do next.

The sun glows down onto the pile of shriveled and dead
leaves on Adam's front lawn. For the first time I notice that
it's almost Halloween. A single, sad pumpkin sits on his stoop.
I walk over to the side of his house, reach down, and pick
up a smooth rock. I toss it at his bedroom window. Nothing happens. So I throw another, and another, and I'm just
about to turn around and go home when I see him standing on the sidewalk. He's wearing a blue-and-gray plaid shirt,
and I know he's probably just come from work at Jason's dad's
marina grill.

"Isn't that my move?" he asks. His hands are in his pockets.
His face is scruffy. He's put on some weight, the way men do
when they hit their twenties and fill out around the jaw, all
beer bloat. But when I look at him, all I can see is the shy boy
with his blue hoodie and backpack, ready to walk me to school.

"Hey," I say.

"Hi," Adam says. He looks down at his sneakers.

We stand like this for a while.

"I've been meaning to stop by," he says. "To make sure
you're okay. I just figured you didn't want to see me." I feel
myself quirk an eyebrow at him. It's involuntary.

"Yeah, well, you didn't have to," I say.

"I mean after that night at Ally's. I meant to call."

"Oh," I say. "Right. I forgot about that," I lie. Well, it's only half a lie. I didn't forget, I was just never sure if it even happened. A part of me thought I'd dreamed up the whole thing, that I'd slipped into some alcohol-induced black hole, driven myself home, and placed a mason jar full of water on my night table.

"What even happened that night?" I ask. "I mean, I was pretty fucked up. It's sort of a blur."

"Um," he starts. He's nervous. I can tell. And it's weirdly empowering. "I was driving home from work, late shift, and you were just there, puking your guts out in the middle of the street. So I brought you home, put you to bed. You don't remember." I shrug. That's not how I remembered it. He runs his hand through his hair and shifts his gaze toward the street.

"Well, thanks," I say. "I guess."

"Twice in one week." His mouth falls into that crooked grin, and my stomach drops.

It's surreal, standing here with Adam, but his words just flow through me, and I know they're meaningless. But I don't say this. I just stand there, my tongue swelling up in my mouth, as all the things I never had gotten a chance to say come bubbling up in my throat.

"I have something to say to you," I finally blurt out. I suck in a sharp burst of air and rub my sore knuckles with my other hand.

He stands there, and even though it's been five years since I've seen him—not counting the after-party—he's still got that signature Adam face, that sulking, brooding, stupid face, and everything I've ever felt for him comes rushing over me, and the words split my tongue.

"I hated you," I say. "I fucking hated you." I stand on his lawn, my arms stiff at my sides, and the afternoon sun starts to spin. Everything starts to spin, but there's nothing to grab on to. I dig my heels into the grass to steady myself, but all I can see is Adam, and all I can feel is Eric and his bloody mouth, pushing me up against the bathroom sink, and all that tequila swirls in my stomach and up into my chest.

"I hated you, too," he says. His dark hair is shorter than I remember, but it still falls to his forehead. I take a step closer to him and stare into his cold, gray eyes. He clenches his jaw. Something inside of me shifts, and I see him in his car—hovering over Rachel's body—how easy it was for them both to move on. How I've spent the past five years at war with myself—and how he has the balls to say that *he* hated *me*.

"No," I say. "Don't do that. You don't get to do that." I take a step closer. My eyes sting, threatening a salty rush of tears, but I don't cry. I swore I wouldn't cry. "You have no idea what it was like for me, Adam." The skin around my eyes starts to tighten, and I bite down on my lip.

Pull it together. Pull it together.

"You have no idea," I say.

He just looks at me, his jaw clenched, this sad look on his face, and then it happens. I lose it. I fucking lose it and the tears flow like rain, and I feel my cheeks going all red and blotchy, and I can't catch my breath. I suck in the air, and I'm gasping, and sucking and gasping, and it's like knives in my chest, and Adam comes at me, his hands out like he's approaching a rabid dog.

"No," I say, and I fall back, and I'm gasping, and sobbing, and gasping, and I all I can see is Adam, and all I can feel is Eric, and all I want to do is collapse onto the grass and dissolve, just dissolve and disappear forever.

"Aubrey," he says. "Please calm down."

"No," I say again. "You're going to fucking listen to me." A car door slams across the street, and two kids round the corner on bicycles, but I don't waver. "Do you know what it's like to feel completely abandoned and there's no one there to fall back on?" I'm still gasping for air, and the tears are coming out hard. Laura would call it catharsis. I call it a meltdown.

"Everything changed for me after that night. Nothing seemed important anymore. Nothing mattered. But you could have," I say. "I still wanted you to matter." I wrap my arms around my chest and rock forward. He doesn't look at me. "I don't know what Rachel told you, and I don't know what you heard, but I didn't cheat on you, Adam. I swear. It wasn't like that. I didn't want to." The words tangle with spit and tears and everything flings from my mouth and floats like dust.

"I know," he says. "And I'm sorry. I never meant to hurt you, Aubrey." His words don't feel genuine, but they don't feel like bullshit either, and I know it's time to set things straight—to set everything straight.

"And Max didn't get that ring from me. But I know where it came from." I let my body fall back onto the grass. It feels good to just lie, let the damp ground saturate my T-shirt.

"Where did it come from, then?"

"I'm not going to tell you."

"Why not?" He's disappointed, but not surprised.

The tears stop. My breathing calms. "Maybe your brother didn't hurt anybody, but maybe he did," I say. "Either way, it's not my story to tell."

His face scrunches up and his jaw clenches again like he's about to fight me on this, about to tell me what a horrible person I am, always was, but he remains still and nods his head.

"That's fair, I guess," he says.

"Anyway. That's all I have to say. I just needed this closure. We never did have any closure."

"What did you expect? You showed up at my house, you threw yourself at me, and then just fell off the face of the earth. You just left for college. You didn't even say good-bye."

"What else was I supposed to do? I had no one in my corner. My best friend fucked my boyfriend. My boyfriend fucked my best friend. Any which way you say it, just sounds fucked, doesn't it?"

"I'm sorry," he says. "I didn't know about Eric." He looks right at me as he says it, for the first time since I've been here, and I can feel my eye twitch when he says his name. "I just thought—you know—I just heard what I heard. I was stupid. I'm sorry."

I hate that it's all he can say and I think I deserve more than that. I think I deserve his anger, his vindication, but all he can say is *Sorry. I didn't know.* But I guess I can't expect much from him.

"I'm not crazy, you know," I say. "I know that everyone here thinks I am. But I'm not crazy." My voice sounds childlike and small all of a sudden. I look down at my own bruised hand.

"So I guess I fucked things up pretty bad for you by calling an ambulance? I'm sorry. I was scared," he says.

I scoff, and then feel sorry, so I take a breath and say, "I guess I deserved it. But I wasn't going to jump."

"I believe you," he says.

"But, hey, you got to play Batman twice in one week." He smiles, that lopsided grin, and sits down on the grass next to me. I sit up and pull my knees into my chest.

"So you're really not going to tell me about that ring?"

I shake my head and think back to that first night I saw him—that mute, broken boy in a suit that didn't fit quite right. And I think back to that afternoon on the mattress with Max. My mockingbird ring twinkling from my bloated finger. *Tequila Mockingbird.*

"Max was good to me," I say. "That one time I met him. We kissed. And that was it. But you knew that already. He saw my ring. He said he liked it, but I still had it on when I left."

"He was your first kiss."

"Yup."

"I knew about you and him, you know."

"Yeah, Rachel told you. I know," I say.

"No. I already knew before that. Max told me." I squint at him, and feel the tequila sweating out of my pores.

"Max told you?"

"He came home that night and said he kissed a girl. That she was in my grade, and I'd probably really like her. I don't know how, but I knew it was you when I saw you at his wake."

"So you knew the whole time?"

"Yup," he says.

"So I was just your sloppy seconds." I smile and fall back onto the grass. He flashes his perfect, white teeth, but he just seems so sad.

WHEN I GET home, I walk next door to Tonya Szalinski's house. I knock twice. No answer. I don't expect her to be home, and I have no clue what I would say if she answered. Maybe I would tell her about Eric—tell her about my sessions with Laura. Maybe I could listen to her story, to whatever happened with Max and Jason. Maybe it was something. Maybe it was nothing. But either way, I'd listen. Something nobody ever did for me. I feel the guilty twist in my stomach as I walk back down the path to my house.

ADAM TOLD ME what happened that Easter five years ago. I admitted that I had seen him and Rachel. He asked if I really wanted to know as we both sat on his lawn right out in the open, and I said I was sure, that I wanted all the gritty details. That I needed to know. For closure.

Rachel had texted him, said she had something important to tell him. He picked her up after dinner, and they'd driven down to the beach.

"Adam," she'd said. "You know Aub's my best friend, and I wouldn't tell you this if I didn't think it was completely fucked up."

She took a casual breath, and began to tell him how she'd gone back to Eric's with Rod that night. How she'd left me at O'Reilly's. How I'd been waiting for him to get there. How I must have gotten bored.

"I was at Eric's, you know," Rachel had said, her voice raspy and matter-of-fact. "She knew that I liked him, too, Adam."

Adam drove down the parkway. He just waited, his hands still gripping that wheel—or that's how he told it.

"I don't know exactly what happened," she'd said. "But she went up to his room and then snuck out a few hours later, before it even really got light out. But I saw her leave. Her hair was all fucked up, so you know . . ." She trailed off, sucked in a breath, and said, "They obviously hooked up."

Adam said that his truck had rattled over the drawbridge, and Rachel kept on talking, but he couldn't really hear the words anymore—just phrases like *Rod said* and *someone else in the room, too*, and *definitely had sex.*

"I'm only telling you this because I'm fucking pissed," Rachel said. "And it was on your birthday, which is like double fucked up, you know?"

Adam slammed on the brakes and made a U-turn over the grass divider. Rachel gasped and grabbed the handle over her head.

He said he'd pushed his foot down on the gas and headed back toward Seaport, but he wanted nothing more than to slip off the road and sink his truck into the bay.

He said he'd pulled onto his street and realized that he'd forgotten to take Rachel home. The car was still running when he pressed his forehead into the steering wheel and started to sob. Like really sob. He said he couldn't ever remember making sounds like that—not even when Max died. And this was all over me and our stupid fight.

He pounded his fists against the horn, shook the wheel, and

just screamed through gritted teeth. Rachel sat there, silent, for the first time since he'd known her, and rubbed his back.

The sounds got stuck in his throat, he told me, and it felt like bile was pushing its way through, like if he didn't remember to breathe, he'd just upchuck pure acid all over his dashboard.

"Relax, Adam," Rachel had said. "Just breathe, Adam. You're too good for her." Her voice got real soft, and she pressed her lips against his ear. "Shhh," she said. "You're too good for her."

And then it happened. In between his boyish sobs, his hysteria, she kissed him—again, that's just the way he told it. First it was his neck, then she took his face in her hands and turned him toward her.

He said he'd never noticed the color of her eyes before. They were just brown, nothing spectacular, not like mine. He said he'd been close enough to Rachel's face to see the freckles concealed by makeup that didn't quite match the color of her skin. He never realized that she had freckles either. Freckles like Max.

"I can't," he said. "I need to talk to Aubrey. Maybe you're wrong. I fucked up."

"Adam," she'd said, her voice calm and motherly. Nothing like the Rachel he had known, nothing like the inconsiderate, self-obsessed Rachel that I always bitched about. "I'm not wrong. And there's something else." He'd looked up at her, willing her to bring it on. "She hooked up with your brother, too. Right before he died. That's why we were at the wake."

And then he kissed her. He pushed her up against the glass window.

She didn't fight it. She reached down, unbuttoned his jeans, and wrapped her dry hand around his dick. He leaned back into the seat and took long, deep breaths.

He said he'd tried to push any image of me out of his mind.

An eye for an eye.

Rachel climbed into the backseat, keeping eye contact all the while as she propped her legs up over each front headrest. And then he'd buried himself into her.

"I don't have a condom," he'd started to say, but it was only a few seconds before he pulled out and came onto the gray upholstery.

Chapter 36

Friday, October 24, 2014.

"So what are we talking about today?" Laura says, pulling her sweater off of her shoulders. I know that she does these things to make me feel at ease—takes off her sweater, puts her feet up, checks her phone for text messages. We are in her office now. Our sixth session. I walked over, even though it had started to rain.

"I don't know. I guess we can pick up from last time. Whatever you want," I say. I decide not to tell her about Eric and the bar and how I pummeled his face. One step backward.

She sits there, not saying anything for a moment, and pushes her hair out of her face.

"Aubrey. I get that this is hard for you," she says. "And it's important that you don't pressure yourself."

I unscrew the cap of my water and screw it back on without drinking.

"Well, what about my progress?" I cut in. "I mean, how am I doing with all this? Am I getting any better? I sort of need to tell my boss when I'm coming back. This mental health hiatus can only go on for so long."

She glances down at her clipboard and shakes her head, and I'm self-conscious that she thinks this is all one big competition to me, that I need her to tell me that my progress is the best she's ever seen, or I'm her number one patient.

"Your anxiety was definitely a lot higher. You're a lot more at ease. I can tell when you're nervous, or feeling awkward or uncomfortable. I'm not seeing that so much anymore," she says.

"Okay," I say. "I guess I can see that."

"Do you see yourself as a victim, Aubrey?"

"No," I say in a whiny voice that I wish I could take back. "No, I really don't. I already told you that." I realize that I wanted to add her name at the end of that sentence. Like she had done to me. *No, I really don't, Laura.* But I cut it short, and my chest feels like magnets pulling, pulling. Like using her name, just saying her name makes this conversation more intimate. It felt strange when she said my name. And every time she added "Aubrey" at the end of the sentence, my chest went heavy again. It's personal.

"I think that's the problem," I say.

"Why is that a problem? If you don't, you don't."

"I don't know," I say. "I guess it feels cheap. We weren't that innocent—Rachel and me—it makes sense why it happened."

"So you're blaming yourself?"

"Yes, I am obviously blaming myself," I say, taking a swig of water. "We were shooting tequila and making out with boys on mattresses at fourteen. What did I expect?"

"It's not uncommon to blame yourself," she says. "But guess what, that makes you a victim."

"I don't know. I still don't see it that way. It seems so cliché." I squeeze the plastic bottle in my hand.

"I don't know if I'd call it cliché. I'd call it a rationalization. It's a defense mechanism, to justify," she says. "You need to come up with some sort of rationalization so you can deal. You need to have control. You need to know why it happened."

"What if I had just gone along with it? What if I just went with it, and then it would have been just another night. A bad hookup."

"What about Adam?" she asks.

"What if I just wanted to get back at him?" The room starts to get hot. I unwrap my scarf from around my neck.

"Did you?"

"No."

There is a long pause, and I chug my water bottle.

"Tell me about Adam," she says.

"What about him?" I ask. "I thought we covered him." My breath feels heavy and tangled in a nervous laugh.

"I think we both know you're not telling me everything."

"Yeah," I say. "I guess."

"What happened with Adam?" I shrug, swallow, and choke on my own breath. "Don't rush yourself if you're not ready."

The wind rattles the plastic windowpane behind Laura's head, and the muscles in my shoulders start to spasm.

"Adam wasn't so innocent either," I say, sucking in air through my nose until I feel it spread beneath my breastbone. "He," I start. "Um." The words split my tongue. "He cheated on me," I say for the first time ever.

"Adam," Laura says, in that all-knowing way of hers.

"Right," I say. "With Rachel."

"Oh." I can tell she's shocked, and something about this makes me smile.

"I never told anyone this before. I mean except Karen, but I'm not really sure if that counts."

"Do you want to talk about it now?" she asks.

"Do I have a choice?"

"You always have a choice."

I let out an obnoxious laugh and take a sip of my water bottle. I should have known she'd say that.

"It was actually shocking. I didn't see it coming at all. It was right after the—you know."

"The Rape." The word hits me again like a sucker punch to the gut, and I have to close my eyes, take a breath, and gather my thoughts before I continue. I hate how effortlessly she can unravel me with that word.

"Right, whatever," I say. "It was Easter right after that. I went over to Adam's because I was going to tell him what happened. I thought maybe I could trust him, and he'd tell me it was all right, and then we'd take it slow. And when I felt comfortable, we could do it the right way. And I wouldn't have to pretend I was a virgin anymore."

"Rape does not equate to your virginity. You do know that, right?"

"Of course I know that," I lie. "But I didn't know that then. So, as I was saying."

"Okay," she says, and picks the clipboard back up.

"I went to go talk to him. I had this whole speech planned, but I saw his car parked on the side of the road. It was running, so I was about to knock on the driver's side, but saw him."

"What did you see?"

"He was hovering over the center console, with his pants around his knees. And Rachel was fumbling around the backseat. I guess trying to get her clothes back on."

Laura looks at me with her famous empathy face, and I realize I'm smiling.

"Sorry," I say. "Just feels good to finally say."

"That's actually extremely traumatic," she says.

"Yup," I say. "That one I can agree on."

I E-MAIL JONATHAN from my phone on my walk home. I don't have a set return date yet. I've been on "medical leave" for the past two weeks. I'm still waiting on Laura's approval, but I decide to plant the seed with Jonathan. It's the least I can do.

> Jonathan,
> Let's talk about opportunities for advancement when
> I get back. I would like to grow with the UESP but
> need to know there's room for advancement.
>   Thanks.
>   Aubrey Glass

Chapter 37

Monday, October 27, 2014.

I DIDN'T SLEEP well last night. It wasn't a nightmare or anything. I don't have nightmares. I don't have nightmares and
I don't have flashbacks. Laura continues to ask every session,
but I honestly can't imagine ever losing that much control over
my mind. But I'd been lying in bed, and it sort of felt like the
air around me was stale and pressing down onto my chest. It
wasn't a panic attack either.

I tell Laura about it. It's nothing new. But I'm trying to be
more open with her.

"What happens when you get anxious?" she asks.

"I don't know," I say. "Either I have a cigarette, pop a Xanax,
have a glass of wine. Sometimes, I'll take out my laptop, like
I told you, and Google Eric Robbins or Google what happens
after, you know—"

"Rape," she says.

"Right."

"So you can type it. You just can't say it."

I shrug. "Anyway. But if I don't do any of that, then I just have to sit back and take it." I can feel my hands start to shake, so I stick them under my thighs.

Laura puts her clipboard down at her side and her hands on her knees.

"How is that different from everything that's happened to you? You had to take it." Her voice gets soft, like she's waiting for me to cry or something. She should know by now that will never happen.

"But I didn't," I say, and I can feel my voice straining. "I could have gotten up. I could have walked away. I did not just have to sit back and take it. I could have fought Eric harder. I could have stood up to Rachel. I could have confronted Adam. I didn't *have* to take any of it."

"In other words, you're blaming yourself for not doing enough to stop him?" She's trying to hold eye contact, but I'm having a hard time. I hate how she repeats the same revelations over and over, like it's something new. I get it. I blame myself. We've covered this.

"I don't know," I say. "I guess I almost wish he would have just punched me in the face from the start. That way I'd have a right to be angry. Like really angry. I wouldn't have had to feel out the situation, worry about whether or not I was being polite." I've never said any of this out loud before. It doesn't feel good. It doesn't feel bad either. It just *feels.*

"No one's here to judge you. But what we need to work on is you forgiving yourself. You just really need to sit with it. To feel it. You've been running away from this for so long. Aren't you tired?"

"I'm exhausted," I say. Laura stays quiet. I shift in my seat. The silence is a two-ton elephant, but I know she wants me to *sit with it*, as she says, *to feel it.* I let the words replay in my head. *I'm Exhausted.* And I am. I'm so exhausted, and saying it out loud feels significant for some reason, and all I want to do is go home and nap.

I look at the clock. We only have thirty minutes left, and there's so much I need to say, so much that's swirling around in my brain, that I can't even single out one thought to start with. "I don't know," I say to fill the silence. "This all still feels kind of silly."

"Silly?"

"Well, I feel like I don't even have the right to be sitting on a shrink's couch talking about it. I feel like it shouldn't be a big deal. I know that sounds fucked up. But to me, I just can't acknowledge that he did anything wrong. I mean, I know it was wrong. I know what it was. I just can't bring myself to say it. I just keep seeing it from Adam's point of view and Rachel's point of view and how I didn't stop it, and I hurt so many people." I realize that I haven't taken a breath. "Does that make any sense?"

"What you're saying to me is that you don't feel justified in what you went through. But you were a victim, and I know you know that."

We both sit there for a moment. Silent. Processing.

It's a process.

"You're mourning something," she begins—and I want to

stop her, we've already talked about this, but I let her go on. "You're going through the stages. And there's denial in there. And that's your lack of acceptance right now. But you'll eventually get there. And you'll go through periods where you're really angry. A little bit of depression. It's just going to snowball a little bit. And just remember, this is a healing process. Just try not to run from it and don't put the Band-Aid on it with alcohol and cigarettes and Xanax."

It's a process.

I nod. It's all I can do. I'm spent. Every fiber of my body aches. It takes everything in me to not curl up in the fetal position and go to sleep.

"Do you remember what you were thinking about that night? While it was happening?"

"It was five years ago," I say.

"So?" she says. I exhale, too loud, close my eyes, and rub the bridge of my nose with my thumb and forefinger. I know how dramatic I must look, but I need to start choosing my words more carefully.

"I was thinking about how to talk my way out of it. I was thinking about what I would tell Adam. And, I remember thinking about summer camp."

"Summer camp?"

"Yeah. It's so random because I don't even remember anything about camp. I couldn't tell you one person I met there. I think I was like five or six at the time. I just remember that we did one of those arts-and-craft projects. You know, with Popsicle sticks. And I remember making this huge mess, with glitter and glue."

"Do you think it has any significance?" she asks.

"I honestly don't know," I say. Laura smiles and bites down on the top of her pen.

I STIR UP the blackness in my coffee and signal for Melanie. She hobbles over with a stack of menus under her armpit.

"What do you need, Aubrey?" Her voice is shaky and cold, like she's trying to assert herself but is seriously falling short. I decide I feel bad for the girl. Rachel must have done a real number on her with that "Melons" bit if she's this bad at being a bitch.

"Do you have cinnamon?"

"Sure," she says hastily, and sidesteps behind the counter. I pretend to read yesterday's *Sunday Times* in front of me, but eye her over the paper. When she comes back, she slides the cinnamon across the table to me. She waits for me to pick it up.

"It's the only one we have, so I'm gonna need it back," she says. So I lift it and shake it over my lukewarm coffee. Too much comes out. I swear I hear her snort. I hand her back the plastic shaker and stir my coffee again.

"Look," I say, before she slinks away. She turns and faces me, her cheeks pink and slick. "I'm sorry for the whole Rachel thing. I shouldn't have said that to you," I say. I wait for her to respond. She looks all twisted, and stutters, and finally gets the words out.

"It's fine," she says. "Don't sweat it."

"How was the rest of the party?" I ask. She shrugs and mumbles that it was okay, and simpers away back behind the counter. I see her whisper to another waitress, and they both shift their eyes toward my table, but I just grin and stare down at the *Sunday Book Review.*

I order a muffin when she comes to refill my coffee, and scribble some stuff about Adam down in my notebook. It's nothing significant, just some random details about our first kiss that I'd forgotten about until now. I'm getting to a good part, when the front door jingles and a group of women file in. Their voices carry over to where I'm sitting, and I'm midsip when I realize it's Ally.

We make eye contact, and her mouth gapes into a sick smile, and she makes sure the rest of her posse knows that there's been an Aubrey Glass sighting right here in the Seaport Diner. I act unfazed, as much as I can, and pick up the pace with my pen.

I hear Melanie's high-pitched laugh while she takes their order, and they all sort of glance my way. It should bother me that I actually bothered to apologize to the girl, and then, the first chance she gets, she's standing over Ally's table, giggling like a hyena, undoubtedly about my recent public meltdown. But it doesn't. It all just seems so petty and childish when I really think about it. And besides, I get to go back to my life. They're all stuck here.

I shut my notebook and stuff it into my tote, but leave the *Times* on the table. I have no use for it. I'm feeling jittery, but I think it's only the caffeine, so I walk right by Ally's table— cool, casual, calm Aubrey. I wonder if they've heard about Eric, if he told everyone that the crazy girl from the after-party beat the crap out of him in the O'Reilly's bathroom. I seriously doubt it, though.

My plan is to slip out the front door, without a scene, to be the bigger person for once, but I hear Ally call out before I can make my escape.

"Well, well," she says. "Looks like they let you out of the asylum." They all laugh—Sasha, Ellie, and the Girl I Can't Remember. I stop, my breath catches, and I spin around to face them. It's almost like they don't expect me to react, and Ally looks nervous now that she sees me. I'm calm, stoic even, but I feel all these words burning up inside of me, and my face gets hot.

"Yeah," I say. "They did." I can feel Melanie and another waitress frozen behind me, staring, waiting. "And you know what? I made some serious breakthroughs." Ally glances around the table, and I take a step closer. I'm hovering now, and they all flinch and scoot into their seats, like I'm going to deck one of them, but I just press my hands into the table and get real close to Ally's face.

"I know what you think about me: 'Oh, Aubrey! She's so crazy and selfish and slutty, and oh, what a horrible friend she turned out to be!'" I take a sip of Sasha's water and slam it down on the table. "But you know what? I don't give a fuck. You all suck. You're dull and generic and there's literally nothing going on in that empty space up there." I reach up and poke my finger right into Ally's forehead. "And maybe Rachel was a bitch, and yeah, we had our issues, but at least she was real. She didn't hide behind a posse of vapid airheads. Rachel may have done some shitty things to me, but at least she was honest, and she didn't pretend to be something she wasn't. I have zero use for any of you." I take another gulp of Sasha's water.

They all look unaffected by my words, and they scoff, like it's supposed to break me into believing that I'm this irrational beast of a human. I turn to each one and offer one last zinger: "Ally, you're just pathetic. You're a carbon copy of Rachel, but less interesting. And, Sasha, obviously misery loves company. All of a sudden you're skinny and not afraid to be a bitch? Ellie, I don't even have anything bad to say about you, because you literally have no personality. And you," I say, turning to the Girl I Can't Remember. "I don't even know who you are." I take a breath and squint at the girl. "Seriously, who are you? What *is* your name?"

They're too busy staring at each other, eyes wide, mouths hung open, trying to absolve themselves of everything I just said. But I don't have time to wait around for a reaction, so I swing my bag over my shoulder and head for the door. I'm halfway down the street when I reach for my phone. I stare down at the voice mail, and for the first time since I've been home, I actually wish I could call Rachel. She's the only person who'd have appreciated that scene. *You should have seen their faces*, I'd say. *It was perfect. I've never seen Ally keep her mouth shut for so long!* I catch myself laughing and instead call Danny.

"I'm really sorry," I say, when he picks up on the first ring. He doesn't say anything, but I can hear him on the line. "I was really shitty to you. You don't deserve that." It feels staged saying it, but I guess most apologies do. It's the best he's going to get out of me.

"This must be killing you," he says. "I've never heard you apologize for anything in your life."

"It's pretty rough," I say. "But I mean it."

"I know," he says. We're both quiet, and then he sighs. "Is everything okay with you?"

"I'm better now," I say.

"Are you coming home?"

"Soon," I say.

"You're not going to hit me again, are you?" I smile and shake my head, even though I know he can't see me.

Chapter 38

Wednesday, October 29, 2014.

"I HAVE GOOD news," Laura says. I'm sitting in her office. The window is cracked, and it smells like burning leaves. "I think this will be our last session." I look back at her, sort of confused, but she cuts in before I can ask any questions. "This was always meant to be temporary, Aubrey."

"So, I'm cured? Just like that?"

"No," she says. "Not even close. You obviously still have a lot of work to do. But you have a life you need to get back to, and I don't think it's necessarily benefiting you anymore to stick around here." I can't tell if I'm relieved or terrified, but I feel pretty dense for not expecting this.

"Wow," I say. "Okay. So are you like breaking up with me?" She smiles, a dry sort of smile, and I'll take it. I guess she'll never appreciate my humor.

"I'm referring you to a therapist in Manhattan." She crosses her legs. "Look. It's going to be a long road. And it might even get worse before it gets better. But I don't think it's anything you can't handle."

I nod, and start to really think about what it will be like to go back to my life. Back to my job. Back to Danny.

But I still have one last secret.

"I have a confession to make," I say, and I can feel the words burning up inside me. I pick up my BlackBerry; the tiny envelope flashes at me.

"I lied about Rachel," I say. "I spoke to her. I saw her."

"When?" Laura asks. She doesn't seem surprised.

"Two weeks before she died," I say.

Chapter 39

September 2014.

IT WASN'T MY scene. The strobe flashed and swirled around us, beating against the paint-spattered walls. The DJ spun some techno, fist-pumping beat, and I clutched my drink in my sweaty palm—vodka-soda-splash-of-cran.

"You getting another?" I called out to Ariel, who raised her glass of pink ice toward the ceiling. I think we were in a warehouse, or a church, or a meat freezer—somewhere downtown, between SoHo and the Meatpacking District. It really, really wasn't my scene.

Ariel didn't hear me, she just spun around as this guy in a wifebeater thrust his junk up against her, so I walked up to the bar myself. I raised my empty glass and a twenty-dollar bill, and mouthed "another" to the shirtless bartender. He nodded, threw down a drink in a small plastic clear cup with too much ice, and took my money.

I took a sip of my watered-down vodka, turned back to the bartender and asked for a shot of tequila.

"You got it," he shouted over the pounding music. He put down a thimble-sized medicine cup.

"Yeah," I said. "Make that a double." He threw down another.

"Thirty," he said. I threw my card at him.

"It's a hundred-dollar minimum," he said, his voice raspy, and I wondered how he could do it night after night.

"Whatever," I said, throwing back the shots. I winced as the rusty-key-flavored booze flowed down my throat.

Tequila Mockingbird.

This was girls' night out. Or at least it was supposed to be—but I hadn't seen Casey in hours and Ariel was about to have dry sex on the dance floor with a guy who couldn't be more than nineteen.

My phone buzzed from inside my clutch. I hoped it was Danny with some pseudo emergency so I'd have a reason to slip out of this place. But when I looked at the phone, I had three text messages—all from Rachel.

1. Thinking about you today.
2. Would really like to talk.
3. Please, will you just give me a minute to talk?

I'd deleted her name out of my phone, but I'd had her number memorized since we were thirteen, and just seeing those numbers splayed out over my screen made me want to crush my phone with my sweaty, vodka-soda-splash-of-cran-holding hand.

. I read over the texts one more time. This wasn't the first string of messages she'd left me. It had started about a month earlier, with a bizarre request: *Let's go to Montauk tomorrow.*

And the texts kept coming, rapid-fire, like we were still thick as thieves, like nothing had changed between us five years ago. I never answered—not one of them. Just deleted them, piece by piece. But there was something about the buzz that I was feeling that night, in that old warehouse/church/meat freezer, that almost, *almost* made me want to answer.

I stuffed my phone back into my bag and shouldered my way through the crowd toward the bathroom. A knot twisted in my stomach, like a tightly wound noose, and I knew that if I didn't get myself a toilet bowl or some air very soon, I'd end up losing it again. I could see the line for the bathroom snaking against the back wall, so I opted for the exit instead.

There were too many people, and as I squeezed through limbs and writhing bodies, I tried to remember whose idea the night had been.

I felt hands fumble at me. I was so close to the exit. When I thought I was almost to the door, the hands fumbled again, and he pulled me up against his groin, his hairy arm squeezing around my waste. My whole body stiffened, and he whispered something breathy and inaudible into my ear. I squirmed out of his grip, but he didn't let up, so I did the only thing I could think of and thrust my elbow into his gut. He fell back and mumbled something.

"What did you just say?" I whipped around, and saw the

guy doubled over. He had a goatee and looked like he might
have been balding.

"I said"—he stood up and got in my face—"that you're a
dumb, fucking slut."

I didn't think. I didn't breathe. I just wound up, and with
one swift motion, brought my open palm into his face.

I was dizzy. The lights flashed, the strobe pulsed, and my
chest felt tight. The last time I'd slapped someone across the
face, it had been Rachel.

When I got outside, the air hit me. I fell against the brick
wall of the building, pulled my knees into my chest, and sucked
in air. It stopped before reaching that point in my chest, and
the streetlights started to spin, so I reached into my bag for a
cigarette. Panic attacks weren't unusual for me those days, but
I pushed through. I breathed and I smoked and I went off by
myself, like a cat going off to die. I felt my phone buzz in my
pocket, and without thinking, I answered it.

"Hello," I managed between shallow, panicky breaths. I
held the cigarette between my lips and lit it.

"Aubrey." Silence. "I didn't think you'd answer." It took
me at least five seconds to realize that it was Rachel. The air
punched out of my stomach. I wanted to hang up, I needed to
hang up, but I saw the bouncer coming at me, so I clutched the
phone in my jittery, sweaty palm and listened.

I took a deep drag of the Parliament and let the smoke
ribbon into my lungs, filling that hollowed space.

"What do you want?" I said. My throat felt dry and made
of sand, and I wondered for a moment if she could hear the
panic in my voice, but quickly decided that she couldn't. She

couldn't five years ago, and she didn't now. Some things never changed. I was about to hang up, but it was like magnets pulled my BlackBerry toward my ear.

"I just wanted to talk to you," she said. And then I sensed the panic in *her* voice. It was shaky and sad, nothing like the Rachel I remembered. "Things aren't so good," she said.

"Mm," I said, taking another deep drag. There were too many people on the sidewalk, and my hands were still shaking, so I closed my eyes.

"I'm having suicidal thoughts," she said; her voice was calm and plain, like she was telling me about a new job. "I'm depressed. I really want to see you. It would mean a lot."

"You're depressed?" I scoffed.

Her voice broke on the other line. "I don't get what I did to you," she said. "Could you just meet me? For coffee? Just give me that much?"

THE NEXT MORNING, we sat in the dim diner, next to the coffee grinder, and I could already smell the deep fishy aroma of slick espresso beans settling into my T-shirt, and I made a mental note to shower before dinner.

Rachel sat across the booth, her back stiff against the blue vinyl cushions. I sat with my legs crossed, slouching, and held a paper cup to my lips. I blew soft ripples into the black coffee and sipped. When I'd asked for a cup to go, the waiter looked at me funny, but I planned on making a swift exit and didn't feel like wasting a perfectly good cup of coffee.

I agreed to meet her against my better judgment. But only

if she came to the city and only if she promised to keep the meeting between us.

I eyed Rachel over the top of my cup. She fidgeted with a napkin, and I waited for her to talk first.

"Thanks," she said, twisting the napkin in her hands. "For meeting me here, I mean."

"What else would you mean?" I asked, a dry, bored sound to my voice. I almost, almost felt bad for her.

"Look," she said. "I know you hate me." She paused, and when I didn't correct her, she started up again. "But I really need my best friend back."

"Rachel," I said.

"Please." She wouldn't look at me. She just stared down at the table, tearing off pieces of napkin and rolling them into tiny balls.

She looked different. Thinner. Her hair looked like a shiny layer of plastic. Maybe just greasy. She wore a baggy gray sweatshirt that hung off one shoulder.

"What did you expect?" I said. I could feel my throat dry and that swell of panic just beneath my breastbone. "We've grown apart. We just aren't friends anymore. We have completely different lives. I've moved on." As I said the words, they sounded rehearsed. But they weren't. I was just trying not to let myself feel the words. Because if I felt them, then she'd know. "Why can't you just get that through your head?"

"Why?" she said. "Why aren't we friends? I don't get it, Aubrey. You left for college, and that was it."

"You know why."

"No, I don't. You just stopped caring about everyone here. Me, Adam."

"You? Adam? Are you fucking kidding me right now?" I started to get that dizzy feeling behind my eyes, and I tried to focus on the words in my head. I tried so hard to keep my eyes fixed on Rachel, but everything started to spin. "You and Adam were just fine," I said.

"You don't understand," she started. "I need you. I am depressed. You are my best friend. I don't know who else to talk to." She was crying now, and it just fueled my rage. I could feel the eyes of everyone in the diner on us, on the poor sobbing girl, and that cold bitch who made her cry. *Cold Bitch.*

"Get a fucking shrink," I said. I started to grab my coat, but she said something that made me stop.

"I only did it because of what you did with Eric."

Chapter 40

Wednesday, October 29, 2014.

LAURA JUST PINCHES her lips and nods along when I tell her about my last meeting with Rachel. I have a feeling she knew that I'd seen her, but if so, she hadn't let on. I still don't tell her about that voice mail; that's between me and Rachel, and I think it always will be.

"So how do you feel about the way you left things off with Rachel?" she finally asks. I think about it for a second and place my hands down at my sides.

"I don't know how I feel," I say, and I mean it. I don't know. I should feel guilty, and maybe I do on some level, but for now, I can't say. "Do you think I should feel guilty?" I ask.

"I think you should feel any way you feel."

"What if I don't know how I feel?"

"You will," she says. "Give it some time."

"Can I ask you something?" I say. I can feel my hands start to shake.

"Of course."

"Do you think it was my fault?" I breathe in, and I'm not sure if I'm ready for the answer. "Rachel, I mean."

"Aubrey," she starts, her voice low. "I know this is our last session, so if you take anything away from our meetings, I want it to be this." She looks at me with an uncomfortable intensity until I nod. "You are not responsible for anybody's actions but your own. You cannot control the way other people feel."

"I guess that's true," I say, and I'm not sure if I completely buy it, but I feel better hearing her say it.

KAREN'S IN THE kitchen when I get home. I head straight for my room, but turn into the kitchen instead, removing my scarf and jacket.

"Hey," I say. She turns, startled.

"How was your session?"

I stand in the doorway for a second.

"Pretty good, actually," I say, and instead of turning, I slide onto the chair and slump over the kitchen island. She's got this look of pleasant surprise, and it sort of makes me feel guilty for the way I've been with her—even though Laura says I shouldn't take responsibility for how other people feel.

"Coffee?" She holds her hand over the cabinet door and waits for a response.

"Sure." I catch a glimpse of the mason jars, but she shuts the door and pours me a mug. She pulls an unopened container of nondairy creamer out of the fridge and slides it across the island.

"I went shopping," she says. "Figured you were getting tired of drinking it black."

"Thanks," I mumble, and bring the mug to my lips. "So," I start, and there's a moment of awkward silence, but Karen perks up at the tone of my voice. "The shrink says I can go back to the city."

"Oh," she says. Her voice rises to a high pitch, and I detect a hint of disappointment there, but can't be sure. Maybe she's just surprised. "Are you sure you're ready for that? What about Danny?"

"I think so," I say, and I shrug. I'm not really sure, but I don't feel unready, and I think that's a start. I don't say that, though. "We'll be fine," I say. "I'm not worried about me and Danny."

"Okay," she says. "When were you planning on leaving?" She acts busy, opening and closing drawers, emptying the contents of the dishwasher.

"I was thinking a six o'clock train," I say. "Is that okay?" I don't know why I'm asking for permission.

"Oh," she says. "I guess that's okay. I just didn't realize you meant so soon." There's a moment of cold silence, and I don't know what to say. I want to get up and walk away, but something keeps me still in my seat, sipping my coffee, waiting for my mother to collect her thoughts. "Well, I'm glad you're feeling better," she says, and takes a breath. She pours herself a cup of coffee and leans on the island in front of me. "And, Aubrey, I'm sorry."

"Sorry for what?" My insides start to turn, and I stare down at the counter. Despite these past two weeks of therapy, and everything that's happened, I am still not up for a mother-daughter bonding session.

"For putting Rachel on a pedestal, when it should have been you." I wasn't expecting that response, but I'll take it. "And everything else," she says.

"Don't sweat it," I deadpan and take a sip of coffee. I try to keep a straight face.

"I'll miss having you around," she says. "Really, though. You're a handful. But I'll miss you." I roll my eyes, and stretch my arms out over the island. "Can I make you something to eat?" she asks, walking toward the refrigerator. The photo is gone—the one of Rachel and me at the Halloween parade in our matching hippie costumes. "I bought you one of those dairy-free pizzas," Karen says. I'm about to ask what she did with the photo, if this was her idea of a peace offering, but instead, I remember the Montauk photo that I let fall behind my desk that first day.

"Sure," I say. "Pizza sounds good."

I GO BACK for it behind my desk. It's right where I left it.

Rachel's eyes burn into me from the glossy print—the Montauk sun glares. We're still sprawled out over that purple sheet, half of my face cut off by Rachel's horrible photo-taking abilities. I hold the picture up toward the light. It's dusty, and slightly faded, but still glossy in that CVS print sort of way. Photos are like shards of glass—a snapshot, a sound, a smell—broken pieces, but nothing I can really hold on to.

Chapter 41

MY TRAIN IS at six, but there's one more thing I have to do before I go back and leave this twisted town once again.

It's early afternoon—the temperature hovering just around fifty-five. I pull a cardigan closed over my chest and walk. When I get to his house, he's under the hood of his truck. I scoff under my breath. Adam was never the car-fixing type.

"Hey again," I say.

"Hi there," he says.

"Any chance you could do me a favor? For old times?"

"It depends," he says. "I got you put in a hospital." I smile, and for the first time in weeks, it's natural; the skin stretches a normal amount around my eyes.

"I need you to take me to the beach. There's something I need to do." He sighs, like he might say no, but shrugs and opens the car door for me.

I roll the window down as we ride in silence down Wantagh Parkway. The air tangles my hair. I turn up the radio, and

Coldplay plays through the speakers. Everything blurs past us—the trees, the dunes, the bay. Everything is moving as we're bounding toward the edge of the Island. We're just two kids with a dead friend. Just a boy and a girl who tried to have boundaries in a place that doesn't believe in that sort of thing. I stare out into the bay as we speed down the parkway and then I look at Adam. He's tense, but he'd always been tense, and he still smells the way I remember—like coffee and cinnamon— with just a hint of french fries and sea salt.

"You're still working at the marina?" I ask. Small talk.

"Yup. Still working with Jason. I'm a manager now."

"I can smell it on you," I say. He laughs and pulls his thermal up over his nose.

"Man," he says. "Didn't think anyone else would notice."

"That's your smell." I smile and he smiles and for a second, just a second, I forget about our own twisted history—how even from the start, he was never meant to be my first, and after everything else, he was never meant to be my last. Call it fate. Call it circumstance. I just call it shit luck.

Adam pulls into the Field 4 parking lot.

I reach into my pocket and pull out the photograph. It's bent now, but it doesn't matter.

I step out into the empty parking lot. Adam waits in the car.

When I get to the water's edge, I plop down and kick off my flip-flops.

I pull two Parliaments out of my bag—my last, I promise. I light them both, balancing one between my lips while I hold the other one out toward the ocean. I let it drop and sizzle out in the salty rush of the Atlantic. I place the photograph down in the undertow and watch it float away with the limp, wet cigarette.

I remember. Or at least I think I do. The rain, my car, the whiskey spilling over my bare chest, the music fading as I slipped into that gray hole. I remember thinking about Eric, and what he did, and what I didn't do, and I wondered which held more weight. And then there was Rachel and Adam, and what they did and didn't do—and what it really comes down to—all it ever really comes down to—is the people you love or think you love and what they do to you or don't do and what you do to them and don't do—and if you really stop to think about—like *really* stop and *really* think—it's maddening. Absolutely fucking maddening.

I still don't remember getting onto that train platform, and I still don't think I wanted to die. Like I've said, it would have just been tacky and melodramatic. Maybe I just really wanted to get to Babylon.

I lean back, letting the frigid tide rush over my feet. I look down at my toes and notice that the dark red polish has started to chip.

Chapter 42

I JUST MAKE the six o'clock train and slip into a double seat away from the bathroom. It's one of the new trains with the blue and green seats and too much air-conditioning.

I take off my headphones and stare down at my BlackBerry. The tiny envelope still blinks up at me. I can hear the guy punching tickets behind me. *Click. Click. Click.* The sound gets closer, and I pull out my own ticket and stick it in the metal clip on the seat in front of me.

I haven't heard back from Jonathan yet, but plan to give him an ultimatum if he gives me a hard time about a promotion. I need the job, but I've been into writing for myself lately—branching out from my literary collection of suicide notes and breakup letters. And I think that's where my real talent is—real writing. I don't see much of a future in weekly crime reports.

I ran out of space in the *As If* notebook, so I've moved on to typing everything up. So far, it's just bits and pieces of my childhood with Rachel, memories, stuff about Adam. I guess I'm sort of rewriting our history, but on my terms. I've started embellishing even, going into the what-ifs of everything. Laura says writing about Rachel and Adam gives me a new-found sense of control. I think for once she might be right. And who knows, maybe it will make a good book someday.

The sun is low in the sky, big and gelled, and it shines against the window next to my head. I press my face against the cool glass and hold my phone up to the light. Through the glare, I can still see the envelope. Blinking. Waiting to be heard. I think about Rachel's voice—wrapped up like a neat little thing—her last words, her last cry for help, maybe even a reason.

Click. Click. Click. The ticket punching gets closer. I stare down at the unopened voice mail one more time. I brush my thumb over the enter key, and let it hover before pressing down. *Click. Click. Click.* I hold the phone up to my ear and listen.

And then a voice comes over the speaker.

This is the train to Penn Station. The Next Stop is Rockville Centre.

Acknowledgments

FIRST, I'D LIKE to thank KG and Megan. Thank you for showing me what true friendship is. SN for life.

I obviously have to give a big shout-out to my agent, Jenn Mishler, for taking a chance on a bathroom pitch and making this book possible. I'm still amazed by how quickly you made this all happen.

Thank you to my editor, Chelsey Emmelhainz, for your unwavering enthusiasm and feedback. You took this book to a whole new level.

Of course I need to thank my family—all of you—especially for your collective dark senses of humor and for always encouraging me to write: Mom, Dad, Sean, Maria, Rocky, Thomas, Taylor, Grandmas—and the list goes on.

Where would I be without my Hawley family and our late-night wine readings? You were always the first to read and critique my stories. Without you guys, this book would have been about "gravy boats."

I can't forget to acknowledge Marv. You make every day an adventure.

And finally, Matt. Thank you for all of your love and support over the past seven years. You read the very first draft and you immediately encouraged me to go out and find an agent. Without that nudge, I may have never written the rest of this book. I'm one lucky lady.

About the author

About the book

Read on

Insights,
Interviews
& More . . .

Meet Charlee Fam

Matthew Ring

CHARLEE FAM is a twentysomething novelist living in New York City. A native of Long Island, she graduated from Binghamton University in 2010 with a degree in creative writing and several awards to her name. *Last Train to Babylon* is her first novel. ∽

Why I Wrote
Last Train to Babylon

On Location:

I grew up on the south shore of Long Island in a town so much like Seaport that I actually only changed half the name in a futile attempt to mask its identity. I'm not really sure why I felt compelled to change the name. I may feel a sense of responsibility to protect the image of my hometown. While it was a wonderful place to grow up, I painted a very dismal scene of "Seaport" in *Last Train*. But regardless of how it's portrayed, I always felt a strong connection to my community— to Long Island. It's home and it will always be home—even when I'm living a train ride away.

On Friendship:

I'd be lying if I said Rachel wasn't a composite of people I have known in my life, though she's not based on any one person. She and Aubrey embody the toxic relationships that so many girls experience. And while sometimes these friendships are based on genuine affection for one another, other times they're mostly selfish—saturated with emotional manipulation, insecurity, and codependency. They're the kind of relationships you're meant to outgrow.

I always knew I wanted to write a novel set in Long Island about the complicated relationships between girls and how they grow up and apart. ▶

Why I Wrote *Last Train to Babylon*
(continued)

When I started shaping the relationship between Rachel and Aubrey, I wanted to explore what happens when you don't allow yourself to grow: when you hold onto a friendship until it implodes and how you hold yourself responsible for everything that follows. I'm fascinated by those dynamics—which is probably why *Now and Then* has always been one of my favorite movies.

But at its core, this story isn't about a friendship. It's about a young woman's relationship with herself in the midst of a premature quarter-life crisis. Regardless of class, race, or sense of entitlement, I think this sort of experience speaks to millennial American culture— certainly not to the extreme of Aubrey's meltdown, but to the experience of at least a fleeting moment of uncertainty most of my peers have had during their twenties.

On Rape Culture:

Of course, I'll have to address the rape culture aspect. I'm not speaking from personal experience, and I'm certainly not an expert, but I will say that Aubrey's story is far too common. To Aubrey, there really is a gray area about what happened to her. She never actually calls it rape. And depending on which character you ask, each offers a different take on the events of that night. Unfortunately, it's all about perspective, and this is typical in reality. People base their beliefs on their own values and personal experiences. There seems to be a missing empathy chip when it comes to sexual violence: those who can't relate, often refuse to relate. In turn, society constantly devalues the experience by creating excuses: she was drunk, she dressed like a slut, she was into it. This mentality is beyond frustrating.

It's not about making bad choices. It's about basic human respect and the right to drink as much as you want, dress however you want, act however you want, and not get raped. It's that simple. In a way, it's a positive thing that the news is saturated with stories like the Steubenville and Maryville rape cases, and even that ridiculous term "legitimate rape." Not positive that it happened, but positive that people are willing to talk about it, get angry about it, and keep an open dialogue about it. It's a step in the right direction.

When I first wrote the story in college about Aubrey and Eric Robbins, mainstream media wasn't talking about rape culture. I had never even heard the term. There was no political motivation behind my writing, and there still isn't. I never wanted this to be an issue book. It has always simply been a story about a girl who was dealing with her past in an unhealthy but realistic way. ⌒

What's on Charlee Fam's Bookshelf?

The Girl in the Flammable Skirt—
   Aimee Bender
Holidays on Ice—David Sedaris
The Bell Jar—Sylvia Plath
The Perks of Being a Wallflower—
   Stephen Chbosky
The Rules of Attraction—
   Bret Easton Ellis
The Brief Wondrous Life of Oscar Wao
   and *Drown*—Junot Diaz
The Virgin Suicides—Jeffrey Eugenides
Franny and Zooey—J. D. Salinger
In Cold Blood—Truman Capote
The Things They Carried—Tim O'Brien
The Lovely Bones—Alice Sebold
Gone Girl—Gillian Flynn
Summer Sisters—Judy Blume

Don't miss the next
book by your favorite
author. Sign up now for
AuthorTracker by visiting
www.AuthorTracker.com.